THE QUAKE CITIES

THE QUAKE CITIES

Mark Wheaton

This first world edition published 2020
in Great Britain and 2021 in the USA by
SEVERN HOUSE PUBLISHERS LTD of
Eardley House, 4 Uxbridge Street, London W8 7SY.
Trade paperback edition first published
in Great Britain and the USA 2021 by
SEVERN HOUSE PUBLISHERS LTD.

British Library Cataloguing in Publication Data
A CIP catalogue record for this title is available from the British Library.

ISBN-13: 978-0-7278-9052-8 (cased)
ISBN-13: 978-1-78029-717-0 (trade paper)
ISBN-13: 978-1-4483-0438-7 (e-book)

All Severn House titles are printed on acid-free paper.

Severn House Publishers support the Forest Stewardship Council™ [FSC™],
the leading international forest certification organisation.
All our titles that are printed on FSC certified paper carry the FSC logo.

| MIX |
| Paper from |
| responsible sources |
| FSC C013056 |

Typeset by Palimpsest Book Production Ltd.,
Falkirk, Stirlingshire, Scotland.
Printed and bound in Great Britain by
TJ Books Limited, Padstow, Cornwall.

To Laura, for believing

BOOK 1

ONE

She shivered as she opened her eyes. Wherever she was, it was dark. Her skin was wet, clammy. As her hand brushed her body, she realized she was naked.

Wa . . . wha?

She tried to speak. Nothing. Not just no sound – words struggled to form in her mind. As if she'd forgotten the basics of language.

Wh . . . where?

She felt around. The floor was cold, hard, flat. Her hands found a wall. It had a dappled texture, thousands of tiny raised bumps, like textured paint. As they ascended, her fingertips reached a raised placard. Her fingers traced over ridges. Letters? Numbers? There wasn't enough light to read it. She traced the first letter. What was it? The letter D? B?

Is this . . . is that me? she wondered. *Does my name begin with D or B?*

Terrified, she realized she had no idea.

She was kneeling, her legs so numb they felt detached. She tried to stand but fell forward, body slamming into the wall before she slumped to the floor. When her head struck the ground, she grunted.

'*Gnh!*'

'That's her!' a voice cried out.

A light flashed, reflecting off walls. She was in a hallway, not a room.

She tried again to get to her feet, but the lower half of her body refused.

Am I paralyzed?

She struck her foot against the floor. There was a distant, tingling pain. Good. Not paralyzed. She wanted to call out, signal to those she heard, but a hand suddenly clamped over her mouth. Turning, she came face to face with a dark-haired young woman. Her face, glistening with sweat, was barely visible in a wash of dark green light.

'Quiet,' the woman warned. 'I'm Este. I'm not going to hurt you.

But I can't speak for them.' She nodded down the hallway. 'Can you walk?'

She shook her head.

'Are you injured?' Este whispered.

She shook her head again, but she wasn't sure.

Este grasped the woman's wrist in her right hand, checking over her body with the left. The mute woman flinched and twitched under her touch. The flashing lights drew closer, accompanied by clattering footsteps.

'Nothing's broken,' Este said quickly, flashing the green light down the dark corridor. 'I'm going to lead them away. When you're up for it, there's a way out that way. Lotta stairs but go as fast as you can. Got it?'

The woman nodded. The green light blinked off. Este vanished down the hall.

Alone again, she fought against rising panic. She had no idea where she was. Was she in danger? Who was that woman? She didn't even know her own na—

Alice. That was it. Alice Helena Rhodes. Alix to some. Allie to none.

OK, that's a start.

The feeling was coming back to her aching legs now. She couldn't get to her feet of her own volition, but she could crawl.

'There!' someone yelled.

Alice whipped her head around, terrified by the anger in the voice. Before she could flatten herself against the floor, gunfire roared down the corridor. She tried to scream, but all that emerged was a squeak. She threw herself down as muzzle flash lit up the far end of the hall like a strobe light.

The only good news was that they weren't shooting at her.

She took a quick breath. Then a second one. Then struggled to her feet. Her ankles gave way, and she staggered but managed to stay upright. Fighting the pain, she took a step, then another. She tripped again, sprawling to the floor and skinning her bare knee on the wall. But she jumped back up.

This time, when she tried running, she kept her feet.

The farther she got from the gunfire, the darker the hallway became, until she could see nothing. She slowed, not wanting to trip or step on anything sharp, given her bare feet. She finally reached a dead end.

There's a way out that way, Este had said. *Lotta stairs.*

Turning, she followed the wall, tracing it with her hand until she reached a corner, then felt around for anything that might signify a way out. *Nothing.* She moved back and tried the opposite direction. This time she found the metal crash bar of a fire exit. She pushed it down, praying that whatever was keeping the lights off in the corridor would prevent an alarm from sounding, and shoved it open.

She stepped cautiously through the gap, her hand finding a railing. Feeling with her feet, she found stairs going both up and down.

Oh, God, which way?

She refused to be ruled by panic. She closed her eyes and concentrated. If she could only remember where she was.

Nothing came. Not what building she was in, not what city, not even the day of the week. She couldn't even remember where she was from.

Then, from out of nowhere, she felt the memory of a touch. A hand wrapped around her own, a feeling so potent she could almost believe there was someone there in the dark with her. Rather than a threatening presence, it was one of warmth, of love even.

His name was Rahsaan. He was her husband.

It wasn't much. But it had the heartening quality of feeling true in a moment when everything else around her felt pulled from a nightmare. She waited a second longer, growing cold in the stairwell, thinking this might be the moment she woke up. When morning came, she'd tell Rahsaan about this insane dream she'd had and they'd laugh, wondering what it meant.

But the chill remained.

As if making the decision for her, Alice's foot rose, and she placed it on the ascending staircase. Driven now, she hurried up the short flight and found that it wound around, like a stairwell in an office building. She felt around for doors that might lead out into further hallways, but there were none. She imagined she was climbing into a silo rather than a skyscraper.

The air grew warmer, and Alice's body grew slick with sweat. At least she wasn't shivering anymore. Above her, the darkness lessened, the black changing to charcoal. At first, she thought her eyes were just adjusting to the dark, but a few more flights and the space above her was almost tinted blue. She could even see the outline of the handrails above.

The stairs ended abruptly on a landing. On the facing wall was a door, framed in dull light. Alice opened it, and sunlight streamed in. As she shied away from the blinding glare, she saw that the walls of the stairwell below her were cracked, broken, like a crumbling mausoleum.

She hurried out into the light, fearing she'd find herself on a rooftop. It was another corridor. Like the stairwell, the floor, walls, and ceiling were riven with cracks. She could see her own body now, her bare legs and arms. They bore a few scratches from where she'd run into the walls but no serious damage. In the back of her mind, she feared she'd been attacked, maybe hit on the head. That would explain her missing clothes. And her missing memory. But this didn't seem to be the case.

The nearer she got to the light, however, the more damaged her surroundings became. The hallway opened into a small lobby containing a security desk, a bank of elevators, and a glass-enclosed waiting room. Only, the glass was shattered. The ceiling inside the waiting room slumped onto the furniture, which was covered in dust and debris. The elevator doors were bent out of their frames.

What in God's name? Had there been a fire? Had the building crumbled on its own?

She reached the exit – double doors now lying in a shattered mess of glass pebbles – and carefully picked her way across it. The light outside was so bright she had to cover her eyes again. As she did, she was struck by the silence. No people, no traffic. Nothing.

Which made it an even greater surprise when she finally opened her eyes and found herself on the sidewalk of a wide boulevard in some major metropolis. Only, there were no buildings here. No cars. No telephone or electrical poles.

At least, none that were upright.

Instead, as far as her eyes could see were piles of shattered concrete, twisted metal, broken glass. Utility poles were cracked in half as if leveled by the strike of a great axe. Wires trailed in every direction like snakes sunning themselves in the warmth. Trash was strewn everywhere, veritable forests' worth of paper dropped haphazardly through the streets. A handful of vehicles dotted the street, but they were few and far between, all covered in a fine gray dust like pulverized cement.

It reminded her of a demolition site, a building dynamited to make way for new construction. Only in this case, an entire city appeared to have been leveled.

She stepped into the street, believing if she peered far enough, she might see the end of the destruction, some demarcation line between the obliteration and something whole, something that had survived.

The devastation reached the horizon.

TWO

Este leaned against the cracked sewer wall to catch her breath. She hadn't run that far or that fast since . . . what? High-school gym class? From the bus stop to her front door to make curfew before her mom called out the National Guard? (Not just a figure of speech, given that her mom was a retired Army captain.)

'And for a 'steader!' Este exclaimed quietly, incredulously, to herself. 'You almost got yourself killed over a 'steader?'

Of course, this wasn't true. Este almost got killed because she'd led what she'd *thought* was a fairly benign, fairly low-key tourist group into the heart of the LAQZ only for them to whip out guns and go claim-jumper on a group of even more heavily armed operators already excavating an underground site in mid-Wilshire.

A group, by the way, that outnumbered them three to one.

No more last-minute jobs. No more waiving background checks. No more day-of alterations to the schedule. Particularly if they involved items targeted for salvage and retrieval that kept changing in size and description every time you spoke to the increasingly sketchy client.

Lesson. Learned.

Este sighed. It had been a while since she'd felt this ridiculous. She knew she was an amateur in a world that called for professionals. But every so often, she managed to convince herself otherwise. Not today. No, today was a painful reminder that despite almost two years of pathfinding for pay, she was still little more than a twenty-six-year-old former nurse – a well-trained RN – playing dress-up in the big, bad LAQZ.

And she'd not only endangered her own life, she'd also put Wilfredo and Casey's lives on the line. On the other hand, she may have saved some scrawny naked woman. What had she been doing in the bowels of the building, anyway?

Wilfredo, well, he knew the dangers. He'd been with her since the beginning. Worse, he'd warned Este off from working with these bozos. She was going to get a healthy helping of *I told you so*.

But Casey? Casey had loved these guys since the day they'd met. They'd brought him stuff from the Land of Plenty, stuff he'd never come across in the Quake Zone, so he'd decided they were his new best buds. Part of his enthusiasm was because he was only five years old. Another part was that he was an Alsatian. And bacon-flavored puppy chews, available in any grocery store back in the world, were a thing of the past in the ruins of Southern California.

Of course, the minute the clients dropped their façade and proved to be *utter assholes*, all memory of puppy chews exited Casey's brain. Este had never seen him get his hackles up so fast. If Wilfredo hadn't reined him in, she knew they wouldn't have hesitated to shoot him.

So . . . who were *those guys?*

They didn't have insignia. They weren't in uniform. But their heavy weapons, high-tech equipment, and no-nonsense, no-negotiation response to threats from a bunch of low-rent interlopers told Este they were either government contractors or at least operating with tacit government permission. They fired their weapons like folks who knew they were above the law.

She didn't know how the firefight went down. The minute her clients pulled guns, she began to back away, keeping an eye on the exits. She wanted her body language to be as specific as possible – *I don't know these morons*. She'd signaled to Wilfredo to cut right and exit through the excavation tunnel with Casey. Then she'd take the broken sewers under Wilshire. A precarious route, sure, but one that LA first responders used to save many lives in the days following LA-1, the first of the three major quakes that had destroyed the city.

Este had done paramedic duty attached to a search-and-rescue outfit during those three days of nearly constant aftershocks. It had given her a real sense of the new post-quake geography of the city, which led to her career as a pathfinder-slash-tour-guide. The trouble was, when LA-2 was followed so quickly by LA-3 – coupled with the outbreak of quakes suddenly decimating cities up and down the West Coasts of North and South America – all search-and-rescue ops were halted. Despite the catastrophic damage, Este and her team were never sent back in from their staging area at Edwards Air Force Base in Lancaster.

A few weeks after the third quake, when she finally made it back in, using the LA River culvert to bypass National Guard checkpoints and cross into the newly established QZ illegally, the city was unrecognizable. There was almost nothing left standing.

But if you had a grasp of the old layout, the courage (or stupidity) to sneak in, and connections with survivors, salvage teams, or disaster tourists, there was money to be made. There were other reasons Este couldn't leave the LAQZ – not yet, anyway – but these she kept to herself.

Where the hell is that service hatch? Este asked the darkness.

She craned her neck, looking for the exit by the thin shafts of light streaming in through the endless cracks. The light came in mostly at haphazard angles, like the lighting design of an avant-garde – read: *pretentious* – art installation, the kind Este's sister Inés used to drag her to. She was looking for four beams of light, descending like perfectly rounded columns from machine-tooled apertures in the manhole cover at Wilshire and Little Santa Monica, that marked her and Wilfredo's fallback rendezvous location.

She idly wondered if the 'steader had gotten out. 'Steader, short for homesteader, was the name everyone used for the survivalist/prepping-for-the-apocalypse types who had moved to the wholly unlivable-in and extremely dangerous QZs to 'live off the grid'. Este figured the 'steader had gone into the sublevel offices looking for food or shelter. But all that was down there was the empty canister it seemed Este's own clients had come to the LAQZ to find. That said, their description had always been hazy – at one point, they'd said it was a pressurized metal box about twenty inches by twelve. At another, that it was a series of three syringe-type devices kept together in a pack.

On the day they arrived, however, they'd had a new story.

'It's like a large metal test tube,' the group's spokesman told her. 'But heavy, with a cap. The only identifiers on it are a barcode and an eighteen-character alphanumeric string. Cool?'

When they'd arrived in the subterranean complex, finding room after room in utter disarray, she didn't think they'd find anything like that. Most metal objects not nailed down – and many that were – had been hauled off by previous salvage teams.

Casey discovered the canister. It must have been ejected from some nearby machine, perhaps during an aftershock, and had rolled under a crushed shelving unit. Este had grabbed it, thinking she could earn a bonus by 'discovering it' once the clients had all but given up hope.

Then, of course, the guns flew out and it all went to hell, so there was no way to know.

But given how much money her clients had likely coughed up to hunt for the thing, Este figured there might be others looking to pay for the canister as well. She flipped it around in her hand again, noticed nothing new, and dropped it back in her pocket with a smile.

Maybe the day won't be a total bust after all.

A waving hand appeared on the ceiling like a gopher popping from its burrow.

'Este!' Wilfredo yelled. 'That you?'

'No, it's Shrek,' Este shot back. 'Got the ladder?'

Wilfredo laughed. Their flimsy emergency ladder unrolled from the ceiling, the bottom rung barely a foot off the ground. Este stared at it, wondering if she was too exhausted to climb it. But then Casey's face appeared at the top, tongue already raining slobber over her.

'Hey, Casey – you gonna help me climb, boy?'

The Alsatian leaned closer to the top rung, an encouraging look on his face. Este sighed. She could refuse this dog nothing.

'All right,' she said, as much to herself as to the darkness, and began to climb.

When she reached the top, Wilfredo grabbed her hand and helped her to solid ground.

'You good?' he asked.

'Yeah,' Este said, though she felt anything but. 'You get followed?'

'Nah. When I circled back to get the bikes, I saw our clients, wrists and ankles zip-tied, being loaded into trucks by whoever the hazmat-suit Army guys were.'

'Anyone injured?'

'Couldn't tell. But one of our guys was *crying.*'

'Jeez,' Este said, dropping to her knees to pet Casey. 'If it'd been up to you, you woulda bit all of them, huh? They'd *all* be crying.'

Casey licked her face in apparent agreement.

They were a motley crew. Wilfredo had been living with his parents out in Santa Clarita, navigating undergrad at Pepperdine in hopes of pursuing a law degree, when LA-1 hit. Casey was a trained search-and-rescue dog out of New Mexico that had been attached to Este's paramedic unit at Edwards. Following the abrupt halt of all recovery efforts after LA-2 and -3, Este and Casey met Wilfredo in a refugee facility in Twentynine Palms. Rather than sit with the tens of thousands of others waiting to be assigned government-assisted relocation housing in the country's interior, the trio cut out for the nearby California desert to eke out a living close to what still felt like home.

Este had known then what she still knew now. She wasn't ready to leave yet, to feel like a pitied outsider in her own country.

The quakes brought down LA, San Diego, Tijuana, San Francisco, and Seattle – to say nothing of the ones in Vancouver, Havana, Edmonton, and Winnipeg – and mass migration followed. When the refugee housing issue became an international crisis, they knew they'd made the right call. It was Wilfredo who'd first heard of salvage ops, making money on items recovered from the QZs, and suggested they try it out.

As they headed to their motorbikes – an old Kawasaki KX 450 dirt bike for Este, an ancient US Army Harley-Davidson with an all-terrain sidecar for Wilfredo and Casey – Este pulled the canister from her pocket.

'Can you check the boards later, maybe see if this is worth anything?'

Wilfredo looked it over skeptically. 'You think it's anthrax or something? Our clients kept changing their story, as if they had no idea what they were really looking for. But the operators on site were suited up like they expected chemical warfare.'

'Nah,' Este said. 'They probably just know how much toxic crap got trapped underground out here. Besides, if it was anthrax, that 'steader would've been a corpse.'

'True,' Wilfredo said. 'Think we've got enough light to make Victorville?'

Este eyed the sky. 'Let's do the Blue House in case anyone's keeping an eye on the exit points.'

Wilfredo nodded and handed the canister back. 'Come on, boy,' he told Casey, leading the Alsatian to the sidecar.

But Casey stood stock still, nose angled to the northwest, eyes on the horizon.

'Este!' Wilfredo said.

Este tensed, knowing what was coming next.

THREE

Alice closed her eyes. Opened them. Closed them and opened them a second time. The obliterated cityscape was still there. She thought that as her eyes adjusted to the bright sunlight, she'd finally see signs of life – or at least, signs of something intact – in the distance. Instead, it remained the same, horrible, endless ruination.

She took a deep breath and remembered her pursuers below. Still naked, she felt utterly exposed on the empty city streets. She had to find clothes and shelter. Her lack of memory meant she had no idea which way the gunmen would expect her to go – left? Right? Straight ahead? Maybe head north then double back and pick a new direction?

For that, though, she'd have to know which way was north. There were no familiar landmarks, only a ring of distant hills wrapping around the basin like a wide half-crescent.

She went left. The rubble was even higher down that way, so in case of trouble, she could duck low and hide. Just when she was thinking herself clever, she looked back and saw a trail of blood – drops interspersed with near-perfect outlines of her feet.

Bloody footprints. Good one, Alice!

Knowing she wasn't going to like what she found, she checked the soles of her feet – bits of rock and tiny pieces of glass. She'd been in pain but had convinced herself it was just minor cuts and abrasions from the torn-up road. She walked more carefully now, planting her left foot on its side, but it did little to limit the damage. She looked around for something to wrap her feet in, preferably something soft, but found nothing.

To make matters worse, she could already feel her bare skin burning. Fair-skinned since birth, she had always considered the sun something of an enemy. She could usually handle it with some sunscreen and a hat. Being naked added a brutal new dimension.

She kept moving. As the adrenaline rush of her escape receded, her thoughts focused on two questions – what had happened to her? And what had happened to this city? She feared the answer to the first one. The most obvious reason one might awake naked and disoriented would be that she'd been attacked. But though she was injured, she didn't feel as if she'd been violated in any way. Still, this was something she would revisit once she was in a safer location.

As for what had happened to the city, she had no idea. A few faded pages of newspaper along the curb and a sign in a half-shattered store window were in English, making her believe she was still somewhere in America, at least – she *was* American, right? A license plate on a burned-out shell of a pickup read *California*, but she didn't take that as confirmation she was on the West Coast. As far as she could remember, she'd never been to California . . .

Colorado. She was from Colorado. Boulder originally, but now living in Denver. The memory practically burst out of her. Born there, raised there. Birthday? September 17, 1975. Went to Fairview High School and University of Colorado for college. Mom's name was Marguerite, Dad's name was Patrick, siblings . . .

She drew a blank. She returned to her mother, trying to imagine her face. It wouldn't come. She did the same with her dad but only scrolled through flashes of male faces, none of which seemed familiar. She tried to conjure a picture of her childhood home, but couldn't.

Rather than panic, she surprised herself by considering it objectively. Ten minutes ago, she could barely remember her own name. The rest would come.

She scanned the hills again. Too short to be the Rocky Mountains, so that ruled out Colorado. No snow caps, either. Did California have mountains? Near the big cities? She had no clue.

Then she remembered one of the only things she did know about California. It had earthquakes. *Could this be from a quake?* she wondered.

Though the wreckage far exceeded anything she thought a quake capable of, it was the only solution that made sense. She'd briefly considered a nuclear attack, but it seemed too far-fetched. An earthquake also explained how she might have been injured, though the place she'd emerged from hardly seemed like a hospital.

Rahsaan. Had he been with her during the quake? She prayed that wherever he was, he was safe.

She had to find him.

Coming to a half-destroyed row of shops, she hurried across the burning pavement. The first was a restaurant, possibly Korean. She wasn't hungry but knew she wouldn't last long in the heat without water. She searched the restaurant's mostly intact dining room but found nothing. The kitchen was completely demolished – she couldn't even enter it.

The next store over seemed to have sold electronics. No water there. The third, however, was some sort of athletic supply shop. Alice exhaled in relief. The shop's floor was covered in broken glass. She hauled a table over from the Korean restaurant, placed it face down, and shoved it into the athletic store. It crunched down onto the glass, providing her with a tiny island from which to work.

The store owners had kept their inventory in an attic over the sales floor. Helpfully, the ceiling had collapsed, so hundreds of boxes of shoes had come down in a great pile. Though many boxes were empty and several more were waterlogged, the result of rain or a broken pipe, Alice managed to find a few pairs intact.

Sitting cross-legged on the table, she carefully picked the slivers of glass and stone from her feet. She couldn't remember her shoe size, so had to try on a few pairs until she decided on an eight and a half. When she searched her memory to see if that matched, nothing came back.

Feet now protected, she picked her way to the back of the shop, where she'd spied bags of socks and racks of clothes. Instead of the sweatpants and T-shirts she'd expected, she found rack after rack of outfits made from the stretchy synthetic material that she associated with bicycle shorts. A package containing a sports bra stated it was made from a 'revolutionary synthetic, moisture-wicking fabric'.

When in California, she mused, slipping it and the other clothes on.

The store's checkout counter was beside her, now crushed to the ground. The register and display case were in pieces, but several stickers – LA Bike Club, Southern California Road Racers, *Club de bicicletas de Los Ángeles* – were still visible on the broken glass.

Los Angeles, Alice realized. *I'm in Los Angeles.*

Movement caught her eye. She ducked down only to see a couple of telephone lines outside over the street slowly swaying back and forth, a lazy jump-rope ready for someone to jump in.

Then came a low, thunderous rumble, roaring up the broken street like an invisible train. Beneath her feet, the ground began to shake.

Earthquake.

FOUR

Probably because she grew up in the extremely urban environments, first of Houston's Third Ward and then Angelino Heights, Los Angeles, Este and her sister had always loved hearing about how animals had a greater inherent understanding of the natural world than humans did. Like how Irish villagers could predict the severity of incoming weather based on how high up the nearby hills their sheep were grazing. Or how residents of Victoria, British Columbia, knew what the day's temperature would be based on the number of turtles basking on a specific log in a particular lake near the center of town. Or how rural Chinese rice growers would wait until the exact moment the region's swallows returned after winter to plant, as it was a better yardstick of the season's coming rainfall than any other metric.

So, it wasn't so much a surprise as a delight to Este to learn that dogs picked up the so-called P-waves – primary waves – given off by an earthquake in advance of the S- or secondary waves that contained the devastating energy capable of laying a city low. Though a few paramedics told her that was an urban legend, when an earthquake was in the offing, Casey *knew*. Sometimes it was a few seconds in advance, sometimes a few minutes. Each time, his alarmed response was so specific, Este could tell it apart from any of his other barks.

What he couldn't predict was the severity of the coming jolt. So, whenever Casey went off, she and Wilfredo prepared for the worst.

Luckily, they were in a wide-open section of the city. Este grabbed Casey's collar and hauled him to the other side of the block.

'Lie down,' she ordered.

Wilfredo took a seat next to them as the roar of the coming quake – really, the sound of already near-pulverized buildings jostling around like boulders on a concrete billiard table – reached their ears. Este felt Wilfredo's hand grip hers, not with urgency or some misplaced sense of romantic fatalism. More a reminder that they were in this together. She liked that.

Great plumes of concrete dust rose from the surrounding

wasteland, towering up to block the sky. Este managed to get a bandanna around Casey's nose and mouth before the cloud reached the dog, but it swept over her tongue and into her own lungs. It tasted of iron shavings, stone, and the sickly-sweet residue of long-dormant chemicals and plastics.

'*Gnh*,' she grunted, reaching for her satchel to extract a dust mask and goggles only for Wilfredo to hand ones over to her from his own pack.

Casey tried to shake the bandanna off, but Este held it in place, keeping the toxic airborne brew from his lungs.

It's not gonna be a short one, she figured.

Her eyes burned from the chemicals and when she pulled her mask down, the fetid air seemed to be trapped even closer to her eyes. She grabbed for a bottle of water, took off the mask, sprinkled some onto the lenses, shook the mask out, then pulled it back over her face, all while violent tremors bucked her off-balance. She'd grown so accustomed to this feeling, the need to constantly bend, twist, and redistribute her weight in response to a quake, that she thought she'd do OK on the rodeo circuit at this point.

In a few moments, the quake was over. They waited a few more seconds, then Wilfredo leaned in close, voice muffled by his mask.

'What was that? A Mag 5.5? A 6.0?'

'A 5.3,' Este said, stroking Casey's back like someone else might do with prayer beads.

Wilfredo nodded. Este was never off by more than 0.1 or so these days.

There was a new rumbling, this time from the east. Casey's ears pricked up, but he didn't bark.

'Here we go again,' Wilfredo said.

But as Este stared at the Alsatian, she saw something different in his eyes.

'Gotta find cover,' Este said, tapping Wilfredo's shoulder.

There wasn't enough time to descend back into the sewer, so Este led them to the mouth of a collapsed parking garage a hundred feet up a side street. Though the garage had fallen in on itself, the recessed entrance still stood. Even better, anyone just inside would be obscured by shadows but would still have a clear view of Wilshire.

They'd only just reached it when the first of three helicopters – Sikorsky King Stallions with the rear ramps down – soared past overhead, bearing west. On the main road, a convoy of all-terrain cargo trucks, massive tires taller than any person, rolled over the debris-strewn streets like it was a bed of silk. Like the helicopters, the trucks were standard five-ton, six-by-six military vehicles downgraded for civilian use. In the back of one of them, Este saw – to her amusement – the clients, now prisoners, looking glum.

In the last two trucks, she could make out racks and racks of canisters, the same as the one she'd found. Confirmation that this team was after the same thing that the clients were.

She took the canister out of her pocket again, turning it over to see if there was anything she'd missed. A private operation like that – complete with air support – was easily in the ten-million-dollar range.

She divided that by a rough estimate of the number of canisters and came back with a cost per item in the high five figures. *Very high.* When they realized they were missing one, she wondered if she could barter them up to double if she guaranteed delivery.

Nah, she thought. *Let's say triple.*

FIVE

A lice was nauseous. Though she'd never been in one, at least to her own recollection, she had an idea that quakes lasted a few seconds at most. A jolt or two and it was over. This one had already lasted a full minute, maybe two. Her dizziness came not only from the ground shifting beneath her as she sat but also from watching the telephone wires swaying in front of her. She remembered what someone had told her once about avoiding seasickness: pick a point on the horizon and fix your gaze on it.

But what if the horizon was shifting, too?

She finally gave up and closed her eyes. Both of her hands were flat on the ground to keep her upright, but she barely managed to keep from being thrown onto her back. When the broken city was still and quiet again, she opened her eyes.

'Jesus,' she said aloud, more to cut the daunting silence than anything.

She stood up, as if daring the city to begin shaking again. Instead, the telephone wires slowed and everything was motionless. She re-examined her surroundings. Nothing seemed to have changed *that* much. Some shoe boxes had shifted, and a few pebbles atop a pile of rubble had skittered to the ground, but that was it. What had happened to Los Angeles must've happened some time ago, she realized. This aftershock, powerful as it was, seemed to have had little effect. The damage had long been done.

Things I've survived today:
- *Near-total memory loss*
- *Subterranean labyrinth*
- *Gun-toting maniacs*
- *Broken glass on bare feet*
- *Running naked through the streets under a blazing sun*
- *Earthquake in an already destroyed city*

All she needed now were snakes, locusts, and a hurricane, and she'd feel owed a prize.

Alice heard the helicopters before she saw them, but instinctively ducked back into the shop. When they came into view – big, hulking, military-type transports – she knew she'd made the right decision. She couldn't be positive that these were the men who'd fired on her, but she figured it was better to err on the side of caution. After they disappeared from view, she did a slow count to sixty, five times over, before emerging back onto the street.

It took her a second to realize she was shaking. She had no idea what would happen next, and worse, she had no control. She needed to get back to her life. The one that made sense. She had to find her family.

It was so overwhelming. She pushed back tears, fearing she wouldn't be able to stop crying once she started. She returned to the feeling of Rahsaan's hand enveloping hers, hoping to find calm. To her amazement, it worked, at least a little. She pictured his face again, letting the emotions roll through her. She wanted the memory to lead elsewhere – where she was when she last saw him, what they had talked about. But nothing came.

Alice began to walk. She didn't have a destination but spied what looked like a trail going up one of the hills. If she could reach it, she could get a bird's-eye view of the city as well as what was on the other side. Did Los Angeles end at the hills? Or keep going? She couldn't remember but wasn't sure she'd ever known anyway.

As she walked through the rubble-strewn street, she considered her pursuers. Sure, they were shooting, but how did she know they were after her? She'd taken the word of a stranger that she had to get away from them. What if they were the ones who could help her? To her best knowledge, she'd never been arrested, maybe gotten a single parking ticket in her life, and always renewed her license, registration and passport well before their expiration dates. The idea that she was some kind of wanted fugitive was absurd, so why was she acting like one?

Another memory returned to her, this one of putting her registration sticker on her car. Her *first* car. It had been a used blue Honda Accord that her father had bought off a neighbor. This led to a memory of her first new car, a silver 1998 Volkswagen Jetta. She saw it parked in front of an apartment complex. Her home. *Their* home, the place she and Rahsaan had moved into after graduation. The street name? Timber-something. Timberline? Timber Pines? Timber Oaks?

That was almost it. Oh, wait – Timber Oaks *Place*.

The elation of more memories made her so dizzy she almost tripped over a curb. She had a destination now. An address in Colorado. She could find her way home.

Broken houses and apartment buildings rather than office towers now lined either side of the road. There was something else different about them. They were marked with some kind of cryptic code in bright orange spray paint, an 'X' with numbers in the top and bottom sections and letters on either side. Written in the top pie piece was '5.9.24', 'No Ans' on the right, '2D' on the bottom, and '79 Inf' on the left. She had no idea what any of it stood for, but saw variations of it painted on building after building, some repeating the '79 Inf' or 'No Ans', others with '40 Inf' or '7D'. The only thing she could work out was 'No Answer.'

A few more blocks and the streets, sidewalks and crumbled buildings were scorched black as if from a great fire. This made sense. If there were no emergency services, any fire that took hold would burn out of control. The hills had burned, too. A few bushes and tufts of grass had returned, but the only other sign of life was the handful of blackened, skeletal tree trunks poking up from the dark soil.

Alice reached a trailhead at the top of a steep road. The trail was paved, easing her ascent. She was halfway up before realizing again she had no water or food. Not that she was hungry, but she hadn't been diligent about looking for anything along the way. If she'd been trekking through a desert or on some island, her survival instincts might've kicked in. Because she was in a city, however decimated, her mind probably took it for granted that she could pop into the nearest convenience store.

She looked back over the city. Stretching out from the hills to the ocean, every corner of Los Angeles had been destroyed. Every building and every bridge. LA more resembled a rocky beach than a major metropolis, an endless sea of stones that had once stood to serve a populace no longer there.

The number of victims must've been incalculably high.

The trail finally ended at a road, a street sign dangling from a nearby post marking it as Mulholland Drive. She crossed and looked over the other side.

To her horror, it was just as bad. More shattered buildings, broken highways, and long fingers of black extending across the landscape, outlining the paths of great fires.

There were no signs of life.

Alice fought down panic. The whole world couldn't have been devoured by earthquakes, right? She'd seen people. The helicopters were going somewhere. There was an ocean, which could mean ships.

She walked back to the other side and peered out over the water. She saw no ships, but that didn't mean there were none. Driving or walking out of LA didn't seem possible. But if she could find even the smallest boat, she could follow the coast. It wasn't much of a plan, but it was better than nothing.

Her thoughts were interrupted by four wisps of black smoke rising from an area of the city where the great piles of rubble were so high they looked like hills in their own right. Downtown skyscrapers, maybe? She waited for the smoke to dissipate, spread, or vanish as a wildfire might. Instead, it steadily rose higher from a single location.

As if it was manmade.

SIX

The Blue House was a one-time mansion in Bel-Air that Este and Wilfredo had discovered on a recovery job, amazed to find it mostly intact. Far enough off the beaten path to go unmolested by 'steaders in the LAQZ, they used it as a stash house

when they didn't have the time or inclination to go all the way back
to the Mojave after a job.

Este stared at the ceiling of what had once been the dining room.
She waved her bare foot at the somehow still hanging chandelier,
luxuriating on the mattress they'd found two doors down and dragged
over a few months back to serve as a bed.

Is there anything better than crisis sex? she wondered idly,
reflecting on the events of the last hour or so. *Well, maybe a hot
shower. Or even a working shower.*

The chandelier could've paid for a shower. Could've probably
paid for a whole house somewhere beyond the QZs in the Land of
Plenty. She'd looked it up online once. It was eighteenth-century
French, a bronze, crystal and gold-leaf creation of a French sculptor
named Pierre-Philippe Thomire. Very valuable. The only problem
would be transporting the delicate fixture out of the house, away
from the LAQZ, and safely to a buyer.

It was *so* above her and Wilfredo's skill level that, even if they
did get it out of the ceiling in one piece, she knew they'd get robbed
by one of the more unscrupulous salvage gangs operating in the
area – the Russian *bops* (which was how their rivals mis-transliterated
the Cyrillic lettering actually pronounced as 'vor'), the siphs (named
for the start they got siphoning fuel from abandoned cars and gas
stations in the QZ), or even one of the cartel-run operations that
occasionally preyed on independent operators in the QZ.

So instead of dragging the chandelier down to one of the still-
operational ports in Mexico, where it'd get auctioned off to the
highest bidder, packed on a container ship, and sent off to Asia or
India, it remained in the Blue House, a rare item of opulence.

She tried to remember what Indian or Asian cities were left.
Guangzhou, Jakarta and Chengdu were gone, as was Bangkok,
which was hit twenty-four hours after Manila. She thought Delhi
was gone but realized she was thinking of Dhaka. For a time, the
American media covered the countries not by name but by what
they represented as trade partners to get folks ready for shortages.

'You all right?' Wilfredo asked, coming in from the backyard,
still shirtless.

'Can't complain,' Este replied.

He settled onto the mattress next to her. 'Your hound out there
was trying to dig under the fence. If I hadn't yanked him back, he'd
be halfway to the Palisades by now.'

Este scoffed. She knew Casey wouldn't range far. Maybe a little farther than Wilfredo, but he'd come back. Wilfredo put his arms around her, bringing her in close. She liked how he smelled, like something that was hers alone. Their relationship, if one could call it that, was more about trust than romantic love. Someone to share a little intimacy with after surviving something that could easily have gone the other way.

'You left this last time,' Wilfredo said, handing over a laminated postcard. 'Found it in the kitchen.'

Este kissed him full on the lips. The postcard, really a postcard-sized photograph painted over by her sister, Inés, was the only image she had left of her family. It had been taken at the end of the Santa Monica Pier by her stepfather, Ruben, and showed Este, Inés, and their mother in a rare moment where all three were smiling at the same time. Inés had given it to their mother for some birthday or other when she'd been too broke to buy something. Este thought it was a pretty lame gift, but her mother had kept it on her dresser ever since.

Este had found it there two months after LA-3 when she'd returned to the LAQZ to recover Ruben's and her mother's bodies from their ruin of a house in Encino. As her sister's name hadn't appeared in the records of any of the refugee camps, nor among the six million who were claiming survivor benefits, Este thought she might find Inés's body in her mother's house, too, despite having been estranged from the family in the preceding months.

That the rubble only surrendered two bodies and that Inés still hadn't turned up was one of the main reasons Este found it impossible to put the LAQZ behind her. She couldn't leave without knowing she'd done everything she could to find her sister.

'Thanks for this,' Este said, indicating the postcard. 'Can't believe I left it here.'

'Yeah, me neither,' Wilfredo admitted, already rolling over to pull up his laptop.

The computer was one he'd modified himself to connect to the (admittedly spotty) satellite broadband. Twin battery packs gave it almost twelve hours of power. He logged onto the encrypted message boards they used to bid on recovery projects and began typing. These were technically part of the dark web and required a dedicated browser. Surprisingly, the traffic on the darknets seemed largely unaffected by the global disaster.

'What're you doing?' Este asked.

'Making sure other teams steer way clear of our claim-jumping clients,' he said. 'Don't want anybody else getting shot up.'

'Good thinking,' she said, scanning the newest listed job postings. 'Wait, what's that?'

The listing that jumped out at her was labeled time sensitive and password protected, requiring any contractors to direct-message the poster before being allowed to read the listing. Este reached past Wilfredo, typed in a request, and waited.

'Probably somebody's stamp collection,' Wilfredo said. 'Maybe another batch of hard drives from some company in Culver City.'

A chat window opened with a password.

'Nice to know we're on the approved list,' Wilfredo said as Este typed in the password. 'But if it's time sensitive, you really want to head right back out into the field after the day we just had?'

'We gave up a lot of jobs for this one,' Este said. 'We could use the commission.'

'That's what's up,' Wilfredo acknowledged.

The post had all kind of warnings, disclaimers and legalese. Este had seen stuff like this before, generally when a client wanted to insulate themselves from a potentially dangerous job. But the more Este read, the more the post seemed to indicate the item to be recovered was hazardous, toxic even, and should be approached with care.

'Holy cow!' Wilfredo exclaimed, indicating a sidebar. 'Look at the bounty!'

Este did. Then she looked at it a second time to be sure her eyes weren't lying. The contract was for a one-time payout of $1,000,000.

'That's insane,' Wilfredo said. 'They looking for someone to liberate a nuclear warhead or something?'

Este's mind raced. She glanced to her clothes still piled in the corner of the room. A million dollars? Hazardous materials? Take precautions? All kinds of secrecy?

Could this be for the canister?

She quickly scrolled to the bottom of the page. A graphic of the recovery item appeared next to yet another warning. Este's eyes went wide.

'Whoa,' said Wilfredo. 'What's *that* about?'

The image on screen wasn't of the canister but of the woman Este had seen in the underground labyrinth. A person was the million-dollar target.

SEVEN

Alice spied water as she descended the trail. In the center of a ruined apartment complex at the bottom of the hill was a swimming pool with at least six or seven inches of standing water, possibly left over from a rain shower. What had caught her attention wasn't the water itself but the steady stream of birds gathering around it.

Once she was off the trail, climbing over the wreckage to reach the pool proved treacherous. Alice tested each step before putting her weight on it. It reminded her of balancing on a schoolyard teeter-totter as a child (another memory!), only this time, one wrong step could send her crashing through glass or impale her on rebar. Without so much as a first-aid kit in sight, this could spell disaster.

The birds eyed her strangely, some taking flight as she neared but others regarding her as an interloper on their turf. The water itself, shades of copper and green, didn't look particularly appetizing – probably even had its own bacterial ecosystem going on – but she didn't have a choice.

If the birds aren't dead, how bad could it be?

Crouching on the lowest step of the pool, she dipped her hand in, scooped out a palmful of warm liquid, and drank. It tasted of rust and something less formless than water, a slime of some sort. She spat it out.

She tried again, clearing the surface before plunging her hand lower into the water, but still she came back with a handful of sediment. It wasn't drinkable. Giving up, she turned to leave when she saw a human face staring back at her from under the crushed building. Or, well, what was left of it.

The body was a skeleton. Frayed bits of rotten cloth clinging to it was all that remained of a person likely killed in the initial collapse. Alice closed her eyes, willing herself away from here.

She resumed her hike to the highway that led downtown, checking in on the occasional shattered building for food or water, but everything was picked clean. She had just checked a gym when another quake hit. There was no preamble this time. No shimmying power lines, no thunder. Just a sudden shuddering of the ground beneath her feet, followed by a second and a third.

Though the quake was a surprise, what shocked her more was how unafraid she was – as if she'd already become acclimated to this new world. When all was still again, she walked on.

The highway was as big a mess as the city. Its overpasses, bridges, entrance and exit ramps had crumbled, in many cases with vehicles trapped beneath. The same bright orange Xs as on the fallen buildings were spray-painted on various cars. Though she still couldn't decipher most of the code, she had a bad feeling she knew what the 1D, 2D or 3D in the bottom section of the X represented.

It was late afternoon by the time Alice made her way to the remains of downtown. She'd worried that the fires would be out or that she'd discover they were caused by some natural phenomenon. Instead, when she was still maybe a quarter-mile away, she spotted a group of young people in shabby clothes, apparently just hanging out, smoking and chatting. Behind them, tents and other makeshift shelters wound their way into the ruins of downtown.

As she drew nearer, she saw even more people, a village's worth, maybe two or three hundred, most dressed similarly in jeans, T-shirts, dirty shoes, and ever-present wide-brimmed hats. The majority were young, although she saw a few older folks as well. A few pushed carts or wheelbarrows, others held tools or carried boxes.

Alice scanned the area for any sign that these people might be aid workers or search-and-rescue types. They looked like stoners or hippies camping out before a festival, not survivors of a cataclysm. The encampment, which she'd initially thought small, spread over several blocks. Some of the shelters had multiple rooms stretching down a block along the downed skyscrapers, while others appeared to have been constructed from several different tents and tarps all skillfully woven together. Their colorful patchwork gave them the appearance of brightly colored mushrooms nestled beside the stumps of long-felled trees.

'Hey.' A young man in a tank top and filthy canvas pants sidled up to Alice.

'Hey,' she replied.

'Want a beet chip? They're . . . more tasteless than terrible,' he said, holding out a cloth bag.

'Thanks,' Alice said, grabbing a couple.

The chips tasted like beet-flavored bark. She could've eaten the whole bag. She turned to thank the man, but he was already gone.

As she stepped into the tent metropolis, she thought she'd be stopped or questioned. But no one seemed to notice her. There were several hundred tents, some smaller and lightweight, as if used by individuals, others more like open canopies protecting workspaces. They were spread down a sloping, centralized mall that bisected the downtown area like a public park. In the center was a large, thin wooden sculpture that looked like a postmodern, propeller-shaped maypole rising two or three stories into the sky. There were markings on it, but Alice couldn't read them.

Alice tracked the source of the smoke down to a pair of kilns, a furnace and a forge being used to craft a variety of objects. Freshly fired ceramic pitchers sat on a makeshift table just down from someone else blowing glass. By the forge, a third person pounded smooth what looked like a newly minted shovel head. In the back of one of the tents, a young woman worked away converting the bed of a salvaged pickup truck to a wagon.

It gave the area the feel of some sort of Renaissance fair, oddly surrounded by mountains of industrial rubble.

The collision of smells coming from the various tents was almost overpowering, but one managed to break through the rest – the scent of freshly baked bread. Alice followed it to its source, a deeply tanned middle-aged woman pulling a pan of rolls from a wood-fired oven.

'New arrival?' the woman asked, catching Alice's gaze.

'Yes,' Alice said, sounding more tentative than she meant to.

'I'm Old Lucy,' the woman said. 'Not to be confused with Young Lucy, who – rather ageistly – is simply called Lucy.'

Old Lucy offered a roll to Alice. 'Take one. Newcomer discount.'

'Thank you!'

The roll burned her fingertips, but she didn't care. She tore it apart, steam puffing out, and waited a full three seconds before tossing a piece in her mouth. It was almost without taste, hard to chew, and poorly baked. Hard on the outside, still gooey on the inside. Alice devoured the whole thing.

'Here, take a couple more,' Old Lucy said, grabbing two more.

'I couldn't,' Alice said.

'Oh, it ain't charity. When you get something to trade, you'll be back.'

Alice wasn't so sure.

'Are you planning to stay?' Old Lucy asked. 'Or just passing through?'

Alice considered this. She'd meant to keep going to the ocean but didn't think she would make it by nightfall. She needed a place to stay.

'Hoping to stay the night, at least,' she agreed.

'There's space to bunk down near the old City Hall,' Old Lucy said, pointing down the mall. 'It's the longest walk to the latrines but they're digging new ones down that way. Should be ready by the end of the month. Are you skilled or unskilled labor?'

'No idea,' Alice said, the answer not in her memory.

'That's OK,' Old Lucy said reassuringly. 'A lot of us washed up here having no idea either. But we're of the mind that everyone has value; everyone is just waiting to be woven into our communal tapestry here. You'll find your contribution.'

'Thank you,' Alice said.

'Now, I don't know if you've visited the other homesteads around the LAQZ, but here in D-Town, you owe your 'stead seventy-two hours of work a week,' Old Lucy explained. 'I know it sounds like a lot, but that's the only way things can work around here, particularly with all the new builds. If you need hours this week, you can work with me in the kitchen until you find something else.'

Alice eyed the wood-fired stove dubiously. Old Lucy laughed.

'Not here,' she said. 'There's a mess hall and a work tent behind it for cooking in bulk. We start early – three o'clock in the a.m. – to get breakfast going for those heading to the farm. The unwelcome news is, you're over blazing hot cooking fires. The good news is, the night is cool.'

'Sounds good,' Alice replied, happy to know there might be a place to stay while she mentally regrouped should her ocean-going plan prove too ambitious. 'But I need to make a phone call. Is that even possible here?'

'Not really,' Old Lucy said. 'Got a couple of satellite phones floating around with the medical workers; there are occasionally WiFi drone flyovers, but those are for emergency extracts. No phone lines, no cell towers. You didn't know that coming in?'

'Um, I guess I did,' Alice said quickly. 'Was just hoping to reach someone back home to say I made it.'

'Where's home?' Old Lucy asked, convivial again. 'I trekked in from York Harbor, Maine, myself.'

'Denver,' Alice replied.

Old Lucy whistled. 'Were you in the camps? Or did you just book it out of there?'

'What do you mean?' Alice asked.

'After the quake. Was just a few months back, right?'

Alice paled. 'I don't know what you're talking about.'

Old Lucy held Alice's gaze for a second then shook her head and got to her feet. 'Hey, I've been wrong before. Thought it was Denver.'

She stepped out of the little tent and moved to the propeller-like sculpture in the center of the park. Alice followed, seeing for the first time that there were words carved into the piece.

City names. Followed by numbers.

Near the base was Los Angeles followed by 5.3.24 and San Francisco followed by 5.6.24. Above that was Guangzhou, 4.18.24, then Jakarta, 7.1.24, followed by Medellin, 1.29.25, and Vancouver, 3.13.25, above that. Alice's gaze traveled to the top. There were at least forty cities listed on the blade with room for more.

'There,' Old Lucy said, pointing toward the top. 'Denver.'

Alice spied the name of her hometown followed by three numbers, 2.14.25.

'What are the numbers?' she asked.

Old Lucy eyed her with suspicion. 'Dates?' she said, her voice lilting up questioningly at the end as if to prod Alice's memory.

'Of . . . what?'

Old Lucy took a step back, as if wondering what was wrong with this young woman.

'We don't like to dwell on death here, but we do mark the transition of a location. We had to add Kuching, Malaysia, down here at the bottom, 3.2.2024, as it was only really understood later to be the first.'

The year 2024? And 2025? What was this person talking about? It was 2003. Her memory felt certain about this.

'What're you talking about?' Alice asked. 'You're saying these cities are what . . . all gone?'

'Well, yeah . . .' The older woman sounded incredulous. 'How'd you think this happened? And I don't mind you telling stories. Everyone here has a past they're looking to put behind them. But maybe don't tell folks you're from Denver then not know it ain't there no more!'

Alice turned the dates over in her head, trying to convince herself that these homesteaders must mark time by another calendar. That her brain was scrambled from the day's trauma, or even from trauma before that. But it didn't matter. Nothing changed what her memory was telling her.

It was 2003.

The president of the United States was George W. Bush.

There was a war in Iraq, though President Bush announced it was over with a big 'Mission Accomplished' banner on some aircraft carrier a few months back.

The space shuttle *Columbia* had been destroyed upon re-entry to Earth's atmosphere, flashing Alice back to when she saw the *Challenger* blow up on TV as a little kid.

The third *Lord of the Rings* movie was about to come out.

Mr Rogers had just died and everybody Alice knew was broken up about it.

The worst wildfire Colorado had ever seen happened the summer before. Alice remembered seeing the smoke for weeks.

More and more memories returned to Alice, building out the entire world of 2003 around her – from the increasing ubiquity of e-mail to her hatred of the cell phone she suddenly felt compelled to carry everywhere.

What was this person even talking about? Is it 2025? If it was 2025, she'd be fifty-one years old.

'Excuse me,' Alice said absently to Old Lucy. 'I need a second.'

Alice moved away, looking for a reflective surface. She found it in a jagged wedge of glass sticking out of the nearby rubble. The face staring back at her she recognized immediately as herself. Her twenty-eight-year-old self, skin taut and unwrinkled.

She couldn't catch her breath. Her vision didn't so much go blurry as it did shades of gray, like white noise on a TV screen. Either the entire world had gone insane, plunging her into a nightmare she couldn't escape . . .

Or she had descended into madness herself.

EIGHT

Though much of the Hills had burned, there were little pockets here and there that had survived. Some of this was just a quirk of geography. Other pockets were due to rich people having their gardeners clear firebreaks behind their properties each spring, which had proved effective when the post-quake wildfires burned out of control.

Este knew of each and every one of these spaces. More importantly, she knew which ones still had fruit trees, including avocado, particularly those the 'steaders hadn't found yet. She made a quick trip to three of them, sacking up nectarines, limes, and even strawberries that had grown wild in an abandoned garden, before heading to the place with the best, most up-to-the-minute information anyone ever had on activities within the LAQZ.

The Pin Drop.

It sounded like a swanky club with overpriced cocktails, but it was actually a caravan of four large buses converted for use in the QZ to bring medical assistance to homesteaders, disaster tourists, or salvors like Este. Financed by do-gooders and a handful of researchers interested in the effects of life in the QZs, the Pin Drop's staff consisted of four doctors, six nurses, a dentist, and a small support team that included drivers and security. Aboard the buses were basic medical equipment, various pharmaceuticals, a tiny operating theater, and half a dozen examination stations.

Though they officially operated under some Médecins Sans Frontières-type name, everyone in the QZ called them the Pin Drop because of how they announced where they were going to be each day. Given the number of gangs eager to raid them for their pharmaceuticals if they stayed in one place, the Pin Drop released that day's location via GPS coordinates every morning at 4 a.m. and then for only a couple of seconds to those with satellite phones who spread the word. If you didn't have the right software to decrypt the numbers, you were out of luck. If you did, the location appeared on your app map of choice as a pin.

Hence, the Pin Drop.

There was a long line of 'steaders outside the Pin Drop this day, some seated on the ground, some leaning against the buses. As far as Este could tell, the majority of the patients' suffering was born from some kind of deficiency – iron, Vitamin C, protein-energy malnutrition, etc. – all of which came from the poor diet available in the QZ. Being a nurse, she couldn't help but scan their faces looking for what folks feared most – diseases consistent with disaster zones; diseases like cholera, tetanus, tuberculosis, typhoid fever or a hepatitis strain.

She'd heard of more than one group of 'steaders getting wiped out due to dengue fever. Luckily, not in the LAQZ.

She spotted a nurse she recognized, Astrid-something, and strode past the waiting patients to her, hefting the bag of fruit like she was making a delivery. Astrid fixed her gaze on Este, as if wondering whether her appearance was a good thing or another of the day's problems to be solved.

'What's in the bag?' Astrid asked.

'Citrus.'

'Any oranges?'

'Yep,' Este lied.

Astrid seemed to consider this then nodded to the buses. 'Surgical theater. No one's in there.'

A few minutes later, Astrid joined Este in the tiny surgical suite inside one of the buses.

'What do you need?' Astrid asked.

'Aspirin,' Este said. 'Also, you got any condoms?'

Astrid smirked and led Este to the medical cabinet in the back. She took out her keys, unlocked two doors, and went to inspect the fruit bag while Este raided the shelves. Este waited until the nurse was fully engaged, looking for oranges where there were only limes and berries, and slipped a few additional items into her pocket.

'Hey, I ran into someone yesterday,' Este said casually. 'A young woman, brunette, late twenties, Caucasian. She was all tweaked out, really bad shape. And, of course, my nurse's brain just goes straight to, "What's the ICD-9 billing code for doing drugs in the nude again?"'

Astrid snorted. 'Yeah, that happens to me ten times a day,' she admitted. 'It's like being in school again. What, you mean I don't have to fill out twenty forms before I can hand this woman a few iron supplements for her anemia?'

'"So you know, ma'am, this hospital's gonna charge you a hundred bucks for that Tylenol, but if you go over to that Rite Aid at the corner, they'll give you a whole bottle for five bucks,'" Este added.

Astrid laughed. 'The worst.'

'Where are you out of again?' Este asked.

'Charlton Methodist in Dallas. You?'

'Good Samaritan here in LA.'

Astrid went still. As Este knew she would.

'So, did you see that girl I mentioned?' Este asked. 'Just hoping she's OK.'

Astrid considered it then shook her head. 'We didn't get anybody like that in here. There was a crazy in D-Town this morning though. Not naked or anything but wandered in from the rubble and freaked out at Old Lucy. Claimed to know nothing about the quakes.'

'Surprised that doesn't happen every day,' Este said.

'Only reason I mention it is they said she was that – brunette, Caucasian, late twenties.'

Este raised an eyebrow.

'She's downtown,' Este cried, arriving back at the Blue House just past sundown. 'Gas the bikes.'

Wilfredo, who'd been asleep with Casey at his side, jerked awake. 'Who's downtown?'

'The woman with the million-dollar bounty on her head,' Este said. 'Who'd you think?'

'First off, didn't you read that thing?' Wilfredo asked. 'It made it sound like she was carrying every disease known to mankind. Gotta be some kind of Typhoid Mary. Second, you got any kind of plan? Or you just thinking you'll talk her into going for a ride with us?'

'Look, I think she might be crazy and in need of care,' Este said. 'The person I saw down there wasn't in her right mind. I feel bad. I should've done more for her. This might be my chance.'

Wilfredo eyed her skeptically. Este sighed. If anyone was going to see through her half-truth BS, it was Wilfredo.

'So, the million dollars doesn't have anything to do with it?' he asked.

'A million dollars does get us out of here,' she admitted. 'You're always saying there's a beach down in Mexico with our name on it. That much money means we never have to risk our lives out here again. I'd think, after a day like yesterday, you'd welcome that.'

'Wow, that's a fancy rationalization for kidnapping a person,' Wilfredo shot back. 'That's not what we do, is it?'

'You want to define for me what we do?' Este asked. 'How about I give it a try? We take the low-paying gigs we know we can accomplish because we're too frightened that if we actually have some success here, actually make a dime or two, we'll have to make up a new reason to not move on with our lives. If we pretend we're trapped here, we don't have to face the reality that the whole world is descending into chaos, that these earthquakes aren't slowing down any time soon. All the people who could afford to book it out of Los Angeles after the first quake did. And look at who died in the second and third ones. Those without money aren't going to survive in this brave new world. This crazy woman, toxic though she might be, could be our ticket out of here. OK?'

Wilfredo said nothing for a minute then looked at his feet. 'I thought you were looking for your sister. I thought that's why we were sticking around.'

His words stabbed into her, but Este didn't flinch.

'If you don't want to help, I'll go it alone,' she said firmly. 'But if you don't want to think of yourself, or about her well-being with all those gunmen after her, think of those people in D-Town that have no idea how dangerous she could be. I'm a nurse, so I don't have the luxury of pushing that from my mind. Yeah, I want the money, but I also don't want anyone getting hurt if there is something I can do to stop it. Stay here if you want, but I'm going.'

NINE

Alice wished she could turn off her senses for just a couple of hours. As the day progressed, she would've accepted minutes, maybe seconds. The collision of all the information she was taking in versus what her memory was telling her had become impossible to process.

She'd wandered around the encampment for much of the day looking for the cracks that would prove the dates – or anything else Old Lucy had said – incorrect. Instead, she found the opposite. Salvaged cans of food with expiration dates in the 2020s. A scrap of yellowed paper used as insulation in one of the sheds had a Dodgers box score from a Sunday afternoon game on May 22, 2022. In the glove boxes and consoles of the pickup trucks being hacked into wagons were registration and inspection forms – even tire receipts – from years a good decade and a half into the future.

Figuring there had to be a better explanation, she moved on to questioning D-Town residents.

'What year were you born?' she asked someone who looked about her own age.

'In 1997,' they replied.

'When were you born?' she asked someone else a bit older.

'Um, 1985, why?' the person sneered. 'You doing a study?'

'When is your birthday?' she asked someone else.

'April 22,' a teenaged girl replied.

'What year?' Alice pressed.

'Nosy much? Fine, 2008,' the girl shot back. 'You gonna throw me a party?'

She tried switching it up, asking about current events, natural disasters, presidents, and war. Music. Movie stars. Anything that popped into her head. But time and again, the answers were either nonsensical or confirmed it was 2025.

She finally had to walk away, burying herself in her own newly excavated memories. She was born in Boulder, Colorado, on September 17, 1975. Her family had lived at the same address – 1622 Bayless, an address she only remembered from old postcards sent to her parents – for the first five years of her life and then moved to Aurora. Her mother's name was Marguerite, her father's, Patrick. She'd wanted to be a veterinarian in high school and started out in that direction at UC before switching to sociology after a brief flirtation with art history.

Rahsaan Topbas she'd met in the fall of her freshman year in college. His parents were from Turkey, but he was born and raised in Indianapolis. He was studying to become an urban planner. They dated for a few months then broke up at winter break. The following spring, she dated a med student named Ben-something, only to get back together with Rahsaan the fall of her sophomore year.

They never broke up again.

She wasn't one of those people who believed in soul mates. By the time she got married, at the age of twenty-two – which everyone around them agreed was *far* too young – she'd probably met two or three men she could've made a decent life with. But Rahsaan just 'got' her. More than that, he grew when she grew – they grew together. She wasn't the same person at the beginning of college as she was at graduation, much less three years beyond that. Neither was he.

Somehow, that never became an obstacle.

She never tired of talking to him. They always joked they only ever had one conversation in their life, but it was ongoing, the two of them picking up the thread every morning, every midday, every afternoon and evening. As much as she despised cellular telephones, she was always happy to talk to Rahsaan.

More than wishing she could talk to him now, she wanted to know he was still alive, still out in this strange world she found herself in.

As it grew dark, Alice's anxiety over her mental condition switched to fear of what waited for her in the night. She still didn't understand what had happened to her earlier that day, still had no memory of the events leading up to her escape from the gunmen. Though the residents of D-Town seemed harmless enough, treating her more like a benign eccentric than something to be feared, she was still surrounded by strangers.

She tried to find a blanket or a cot but came up empty. She finally located a discarded piece of tarp and moved a little ways away to the courtyard of a half-collapsed cathedral a few blocks from the main mall. She leaned against a wall, covered herself with the tarp, as much for camouflage as a blanket, and fell asleep.

The next thing she knew, someone was tapping her shoulder. She bolted upright, ready to fight off whoever it was with whatever strength she could muster.

'Whoa there, time traveler!' said Old Lucy, raising her hands as she jumped back. 'Just me checking to see if you're maybe still up for some cooking. If you're planning to stay in D-Town a bit longer, of course.'

There were a hundred things Alice would rather do than stay in D-Town or cook a meal, but she was in no state of mind to make decisions.

'I'm up for it,' Alice said quietly. 'But, um . . . I just wanted to say I'm sorry about yesterday. I was a bit mixed up.'

Old Lucy nodded, resting a hand on Alice's shoulder. 'It's OK. It's overwhelming even in the best of times. There's not a one of us that hasn't had a day like that.'

Alice wasn't so sure but was in no mood to argue.

TEN

Este hated lying to Wilfredo. OK, so maybe it wasn't a *lie*-lie, but she'd deceived him and that was bad enough.

Still, she'd decided she wanted to pick up this million-dollar contract and there wasn't a damn thing anyone was going to do to stop her.

She wasn't going to lie to herself about the real *why*. Eighteen months in the QZ had taken its toll. The quakes, in fact, were *not* stopping, which seemed to indicate that there'd never be an LA again, never be a place she could call home, and Inés wasn't going to turn up and bring back even a fraction of her former, ordinary existence.

Wilfredo liked to ride fast. If Este didn't want to lose him, particularly at night, this meant she had to ride fast too, sometimes flying along at seventy or eighty miles per hour on a dirt bike designed for half that.

What kept her calm was Casey. Riding in his sidecar, doggles over his eyes, tongue lolling out of his mouth, Casey loved having the wind blast in his face.

Este smiled, remembering a visit she, her mother, and Inés had made to the San Diego Safari Park where they got to meet a real live cheetah but also its partner, a gigantic Anatolian Shepherd named Bigfoot. Cheetahs, they learned, were extremely skittish creatures. To ameliorate this, they were raised from birth alongside a puppy, like siblings. The dog would be a large breed, the kind that a thunderstorm wouldn't rattle. If there was a loud noise, or if a stranger approached, the baby cheetah – naturally nervous – would be conditioned to look to its companion for how to react. The dog never flinched. Couldn't care less. The cheetah relaxed.

These days, Casey was the Anatolian Shepherd to Este's cheetah. Growing up, however, it had always been Inés. Inés was the crazy one who saw first Houston, then Los Angeles as her playground, fearlessly exploring every corner as if no dangers lurked within. For a lot of Los Angelenos, and transplants in particular, the map of the city was something you created yourself.

My range was, um . . . Silver Lake to Downey, maybe the Arts

District and Little Tokyo, sometimes Hollywood, never the Val, never the West Side except Santa Monica and Venice like once.

Not Inés.

'There's a boutique/restaurant/outdoor music festival/street fair in the San Gabriel Valley/Baldwin Hills/Malibu/Santa Clarita I heard about from a friend/online/God knows where . . . we have to check it out!'

And they would. Sometimes it would suck, like the time they saw some play where a 'mermaid' ate fish on stage and spat water on the audience. Other times it would be incredible, like the time Inés dragged Este and their mom to a century-old castle tower on a beach in Laguna that some eccentric millionaire had built to connect his cliffside home to the sand below.

It was one of the only times they'd gone to the beach as a family. They'd had a wonderful day.

Este's reverie was broken by the illumination of Wilfredo's bright red brake light. She thought he was slowing but he'd stopped in his tracks. She pulled the brakes on her bike but had to swerve around to avoid hitting him. She came to a halt inches from the forty-two-story Talty Building in Century City, which had fallen onto its side and was now splayed across a six-lane road like a squashed bug.

'Holy crap!' Este said, terrified and awed at the same time. 'When did this come down?'

'No clue,' Wilfredo said, aiming a hand light at it. 'Couldn't have been today. There'd still be dust in the air.'

'And we would've heard it,' Este added. 'Heck, they would've heard it all over the QZ.'

'Good to know either way,' Wilfredo said. 'But it closes another major artery into the city center.'

Este nodded, adding it to her mental map of the post-quake geography. The Talty Building was one of the few skyscrapers that had survived the first three quakes and over a year's worth of aftershocks, a single shard that rose out of the city's ashes like a symbol of what had once been.

Casey barked. Este stepped back then realized it wasn't his quake bark. This was sharper and shorter. Another kind of warning.

'Lights,' she hissed.

Wilfredo clicked off his hand light and they both doused the lights on their bikes. The sound of engines came from the west, not the roar of trucks but a more strained whine, like overtaxed twin-cylinder engines.

Este looked for a place to hide then realized there was sound but no lights. Night optics.

'Wave,' Este said quietly.

The two of them waved as Casey barked. The whine grew louder until the silhouettes of four dune buggy-type vehicles appeared. Este recognized them – modified Army-surplus fast-attack desert patrol vehicles, DPVs for short, once used by the military in the Middle East.

'Who's that out there?' someone demanded. They sounded older and accustomed to being saluted.

Este was about to respond when Wilfredo spoke up. 'Uh, nobody, man,' his voice pure Point Dume surfer. 'What's that, bro?'

'DoD,' the someone shouted back. 'When'd this come down?'

Este's inner Army brat knew only two kinds of people referred to themselves as 'DoD': government agents who couldn't announce the name of their branch, like CIA, or poseurs trying to make people think they were something they weren't. She warily leaned into the latter.

'No clue, man,' Wilfredo said. 'This week? Last week?'

Este took a step forward, trying to get a look at the men, their vehicles, or any insignia or uniforms. But it was too dark.

'We're trying to get to D-Town,' the man said. 'Any suggestions?'

Este froze at the word 'D-Town'. She could see the speaker now. He was older, maybe late fifties but fit. He wore tactical gear and carried himself with a military bearing. Or maybe it was just his military haircut. They didn't seem like typical salvors, but it wasn't the same group they'd run into earlier today.

It was getting crowded in the LAQZ.

'You could try Olympic,' Este offered, suggesting the most obstacle-laden road in the QZ. 'About a mile down if you drop back to Overland.'

The man didn't say anything for a moment, then his bright white teeth flashed in the darkness.

'For a Pathfinder, you're sure bad at your job, Miss Quiñones,' he said.

He got back in his DPV and pointed to a nearby embankment. Engines whined as they drove around the fallen building. Este waited for one to lose traction and slide back down, but their speed and inertia carried them over.

'Check it out!' Wilfredo said, pointing to the last DPV. 'Those guys are AKR. Look at the blackout tape.'

Sure enough, on the last vehicle, a logo had been covered with tape already peeling away. The logo of one of the world's top security engineering and construction firms peeked from under it.

'What the hell are they doing here?' Este asked.

Ahlers, Kivel, Rayment. They were the best in the business, professionals who specialized in building secure diplomatic facilities like embassies and safe houses and did occasional work for oil companies in conflict zones. But . . . a million-dollar contract in the LAQZ? Este heard they'd been paid more than $320 million for erecting a 140-mile security wall in the Middle East. How was a million dollars enough to get a group like that out of bed, much less equipped with four vehicles and a fully armed retrieval team?

'We've been played,' Este said.

'What do you mean?'

'They're not getting paid a million. The million was meant to stir the pot. Get folks looking for her. Then they send in the big guns they already have on retainer.'

She hurried to her bike, seething.

'You think we can compete with AKR?' Wilfredo asked.

'I'm counting on it.'

ELEVEN

There was something marvelously tactile about the preparation of food. The heat of the stove, the texture of the grains under the fingertips, the combination of scents, the measuring out of ingredients. It transported Alice back to a safer, more familiar headspace.

'Spices are worth more than their weight in gold out here,' Old Lucy said, wandering through the open-air kitchen. 'Also, baking soda, baking powder. Scavenge stuff like that and you can name your own price.'

Given what she'd seen the day before, Alice figured scavenging anything like that was unlikely.

'I drove tour buses a few summers in Alaska way back when –

Skagway, Juneau,' Old Lucy continued. 'It was the same as living on an island. Not much in the way of roads leading out. During the winter, if you got hurt bad the nearest hospital was a seaplane ride away and that's *if* they could take off. Craziest thing was with all the salmon up there, you'd think they'd have fish forever. But everything they caught in Alaska gets – *got* – sent to Seattle for processing. We learned to adapt to cooking with whatever we could find. I think that's why I fit in here.'

Old Lucy had talked almost non-stop since she'd brought Alice into the kitchen. She'd always avoided putting down roots, kept her inter-action with 'the grid' to a minimum, she said. At first, Alice thought the grid referred to city services or paying taxes. Soon, she learned that it was a catch-all for anything Alice took for granted as normal – from having an address to using appliances to working a job.

'It's not for everyone,' she admitted. 'You miss the creature comforts for a few months, but then you grow accustomed to living with a parade of infinite strangers, working with your hands, rejecting a life of accumulation.'

Alice nodded idly and focused on the recipes for everything from buckwheat pancakes to various breads to beans. There was no meat, no dairy. Fresh fruit was minimal. Somehow, though, the recipes still managed to provide a modicum of variety.

'It's our fault, you know,' Old Lucy said, switching gears from her Alaska stories.

'What is?'

'The quakes. The icecaps are melting. Changes the weight load on the Earth's plates. Upsets the balance. We did this.'

Alice wasn't sure she understood but nodded anyway.

'So now we have to figure out a new way of living. A lot of people won't be able to adapt. A lot of people, well, they're just going to die.'

'You don't think these quakes are going to stop?' Alice asked.

'Who can tell?' Old Lucy raised her hands as she checked on a cauldron packed with black beans, navy beans, bell peppers, zucchini, and some corn she'd traded for. 'We used to think of plates as settling down eventually, right? But that science is out the window now. Guess we'll see.'

Alice tried to imagine living in a world of constant quakes. It was as unfathomable as everything else that had happened to her.

'Here, try this.' Old Lucy handed her a forkful of the beans now wrapped in a thin tortilla.

Alice did and was amazed by the taste.

'That's delicious.'

'All from our own gardens,' Old Lucy said proudly. 'About six months ago, we sent a small convoy of wagons up to the Central Valley where they used to grow just about everything. The fields were going fallow but we managed to collect a bunch of seeds and specimens to replant.'

'Seems like it worked,' Alice enthused.

'We're getting there,' Old Lucy said. 'I've been experimenting with a red beet hummus using those same navy beans, but it's not perfect yet.' She checked her watch. 'We're almost done. Just got a vat of oatmeal to make. Help me get the barrels from the shed?'

Alice followed Old Lucy into the dark. In the early morning hours, D-Town was beginning to stir. Individual cooking fires were being lit and the smell of coffee wafted into Alice's nose.

'Whenever you smell coffee, you know somebody's come back up from Mexico,' Old Lucy explained. 'We've tried growing the beans up here but the earth ain't having it. Most find it easier to break their caffeine addictions. But when a little comes in, everyone's drinking for days.'

The storage shed was one of three small prefab buildings, the kind purchasable from any hardware store in the pre-quake world. Each door was padlocked, but Old Lucy had a key. As she inserted it into the lock, the ground began to shake.

Alice took a small step back as the sheds gently clattered. Old Lucy grinned.

'Less than twenty-four hours and you're already a 'steader,' Old Lucy said.

Alice smiled despite not feeling like one at all.

'When you climbed out of that building yesterday, how long did it take you to find clothes?' Old Lucy asked, swinging the doors open.

Alice tensed. She hadn't told Old Lucy about that. 'Um, what building?' she asked.

Old Lucy turned back to her, the humor drained from her face.

'Sorry we can't be better friends,' Old Lucy said, her tone darkening. 'But, so you know, your finder's fee is going to help a lot of people.'

Alice felt a sharp, stinging pain in her neck. Her limbs went numb. Old Lucy caught her as she fell.

'A little help?' Old Lucy said to the darkness.

Strong hands lifted Alice up and carried her backwards. Alice couldn't move her head. Her eyes stayed fixed on Old Lucy, who regarded her with a mix of sadness and resignation. Then she turned away.

The hands laid Alice on her back on the seat of a small, open-air vehicle. It looked like some kind of dune buggy.

The dart was plucked from her neck and a syringe inserted into her arm. She fell into darkness.

TWELVE

'They got her,' Este hissed, watching the AKR men load the young woman into one of the DPVs from a hundred yards away. 'They knew exactly where she'd be.'

'Is that Old Lucy?' Wilfredo asked, pointing to the woman by the shed.

'I think so. I wonder what they're paying her.'

D-Town was notoriously off the grid. No phones, no internet, nothing. Este doubted Old Lucy had any idea there might be a million dollars at stake.

'Probably ten grand and a few bags of flour,' Wilfredo scoffed.

'Definitely on the bags of flour,' Este agreed. 'But no one in there uses cash.'

'Hydrochloric acid for meth production then. You ready to head back now?'

Este's mind raced. She shook her head. 'They're not driving her out of here in those,' she said. 'They're not carrying enough fuel. There's got to be an aerial extraction point.'

'You planning to hijack a helicopter?'

'We're not going to let them get that far.'

Este hurried back to her dirt bike, considering various landing zones. There were a hundred places you could drop a chopper in the QZ. But if they were pulling out the vehicles too, that meant transports.

So, where was the closest place you could—

'Exposition Park,' she exclaimed. 'This was last minute, so I doubt they did much scouting on their own. Exposition Park is where the big medevac choppers land. They'll use that.'

'You sure?' Wilfredo asked.

Este peered at the DPVs. Their engines revved and they headed south by southeast.

'Ah,' Wilfredo said.

'We can take the footpath, cut through the D-Town gardens,' Este said.

'Then what?' Wilfredo asked, leading Casey to the sidecar.

'I'll tell you when we get there.'

Even as they zipped through D-Town to catch up with the convoy, Este already had a good idea of what she'd try. It was risky and a little bit stupid. And would work a hundred times better if they hadn't already encountered the AKR team in Century City.

But it was all they had.

Despite her helmet, Este's dirt bike was so loud she could hear almost nothing else. So it was a surprise when she caught the heavy *whup-whup-whup* of helicopter blades. She slowed and looked up, surprised to see not transport helicopters but two low-flying tilt-rotor V-22 Ospreys.

Figuring they belonged to the competition, half of her realized the job just got harder, the other half was jealous. With that kind of tech and funding, there'd be no job she couldn't bid on.

Sigh.

She pushed those thoughts aside and kept going.

They reached the ruins of St Vincent de Paul, a Catholic cathedral near the USC campus on West Adams. The AKR convoy would have to slow down to go around it on their way to Exposition Park, making it a perfect spot for an ambush.

'Keep Casey quiet,' Este said, hurrying to the edge of the road.

She stared back toward D-Town, not yet hearing the buzz of the DPVs but knowing they'd gotten there first.

Este's mom had wanted her daughters to attend the parochial school attached to St Vincent de Paul at one point, but luckily, Ruben vetoed it. He'd gone through Catholic school and wasn't having it. Lilia *did* manage to convince him to attend Mass there in the brief window when the Los Angeles Rams played football at Memorial Coliseum before moving into their home in Inglewood. Parking was always a disaster around the area on game day, but St Vincent kept its lot open for parishioners all day.

So, they hit Mass and then walked to the games.

Este and Inés *hated* football almost as much as church by then.

Ruben seemed to understand this and gave them extra money to run around the stadium, buy whatever horrible stadium food was on offer, and try to meet the players. When Banc of California Stadium opened for LAFC soccer games, they went to a couple of those, too, but Este already had one foot out the door to nursing school. As for Inés, well, like a lot of folks her age, the last people she wanted to hang out with were ones who could see through her most recent personality makeover.

'Here they come,' Wilfredo announced.

Este got ready. She knew these guys wouldn't hesitate to kill her. They'd get away with it, too. The QZ was effectively lawless. And if they had Ospreys, they had overflight permission. This meant they were probably covered by the Pentagon's loosey-goosey 'total force' extra-legal protections. Even Garrison, the lowest-rung, one-step-above-mall-cop private security firm that ran patrols around the QZ fences even as they made extra cash overseeing much of the LAQZ smuggling trade, was part of Pentagon total force.

Or, as Este's mother put it during the second Iraq War, 'total farce'.

But something else bothered Este. When the AKR operators darted the young woman, it looked like an execution. They shot her in the neck and she just dropped. One moment, she was grinning and chatting amiably with someone she was probably desperate to trust. The next, getting carried away like one more recovered hard drive, expensive necklace, or portfolio of bearer bonds.

Este closed her eyes, shutting out these thoughts. This was not the time. She could consider the moral implications later.

'Este?' Wilfredo tapped her arm urgently. 'They're almost on top of us. If you're going to make your move, you've got to m—'

She pushed Wilfredo aside, took Casey's leash, and stepped directly in front of the oncoming vehicles. They were barely half a block away, coming fast at upwards of seventy miles per hour. Este knew they'd see her. Whether or not they'd stop was a different story.

A fusillade of machine-gun fire lit up the sky over her head. The sound was deafening, the muzzle flash lighting up the entire street. Este flinched. Casey did not. The Alsatian broke away from her and charged the convoy.

'Casey!' Este yelled.

She'd been anxious before, but now she was scared.

'Casey!' she cried again.

The dog was only a few yards from the lead DPV when the vehicle hit its brakes and swerved. Casey looked ready to leap through the sunroof at the nearest operator when one of the men aimed a mounted .50-caliber machine gun his way.

'Call off your dog!' yelled the grizzled mission leader. 'Or we will fire!'

Casey seemed to recognize the threat and stopped short, barking furiously at the men rather than attacking. Este raced to his side, threw her arms around him, and pulled him back.

'Don't shoot my dog!'

'Get out of the road!' the mission leader bellowed.

'I will, I will,' Este said, backing up, but staying in front of the convoy rather than moving to the side. 'Thanks. I owe you.'

This seemed to calm the situation. The operator released his grip on the .50-cal's trigger guard.

'By the way, Old Lucy's playing you,' Este said.

Now she took Casey by the leash and led him away. None of the operators said anything for a moment.

'What's that?' the mission leader asked finally.

'That girl you got?' Este said. 'She's from friggin' Norway. Just off the boat. But you'd know that if you did your DNA swab on site instead of waiting until you're on the helicopter. She's selling the real target to Javelin. I mean, you really thought you could buy her off so cheap when everyone in the QZ knew the real bounty? Or did you not know that "Old Lucy's" real name is Lucille Plume and she's quietly running one of the largest meth ops on the West Coast? Go ahead. Run that name. You'll see arrests in Maine, Alaska, even New Brunswick.'

Silence.

'Why're you telling us this?' the mission leader asked.

'Professional courtesy,' Este said. 'Also, a finder's fee for taking you to the real target.'

'You know where she is?' he asked.

'Yeah,' Este scoffed. 'You guys were twelve feet from her. Or did you think there was a padlock on that shed to keep out bears? You want my help or not?'

THIRTEEN

Alice came to, head throbbing. Hands pressed roughly against her shoulders.

'What's your name?' asked a gruff voice. 'Your *name*?'

'I . . . I don't know,' she answered groggily. 'Who are you? Where am—?'

'Your *name*,' the voice repeated, more angrily.

Alice wanted nothing more than to tell the man her name. But it wouldn't come.

'I'm sorry,' she said, shaking her head. 'I don't know.'

The hands tensed as if they might reach for her neck next.

'It's the propofol,' another man said. 'Once you bring her back to consciousness, the haze lasts another ten or fifteen minutes.'

The man swore and shoved her back into the seat.

'I need to speak to the client,' he said into his shoulder mic. 'The blood type matches, but we can't get verbal confirmation. Can we arrange a visual?'

Alice twisted her head around but saw only darkness, her vision blurry. Was that a dog out on the road? She saw its mouth opening and closing, but the bark sounded miles away.

'You guys done screwing around over there?' a woman's voice asked from the darkness. 'If Lucy's done selling counterfeits for the night, she'll be moving on to the main event.'

Alice recognized the woman's voice. Who was tha—

It came to her. It was the woman from the day before. The one who rescued her underground.

'You got the client on the horn yet?' the gruff-voiced man asked into a radio. 'Thanks.'

He pulled a thin metal device from his pocket and held it in front of Alice's face. She thought it was a mirror but then saw a blurry face appear on it, staring back at her.

'Where is she?' asked the person on the screen.

Alice tensed. This was another voice she knew, but not one from the LAQZ. This was a voice from her life. Her *old* life.

'You're looking at her.'

'Hey, who's there?' she asked. 'Who is that?'

The screen was too bright against the dark background for Alice to see much more than a small misshapen mass staring back at her. But she recognized the silhouette. The eyes.

'That's her,' said the person.

'You sure?' the gruff-voiced man asked, turning the device back to him.

'Hundred percent. Bring her home.'

The light blinked out.

'No, wait! I know that person!' Alice yelled. 'Let me speak to them!'

But the gruff-voiced man had already walked away. Alice sat up. A younger man came over, holding out his hands. He had a gun on his belt and another in a holster on his chest.

'Just calm down,' the man said.

Alice thrust her leg forward, kicking the guy squarely on the chin. She lunged forward but the seatbelts held her down. She ran her hands down them looking for a latch. Freeing herself with a click, she launched herself out of the dune buggy, only to fall on her face next to the man she'd stunned.

'She's out of the vehicle!' someone yelled.

Damn right, she is.

She looked for the man with the electronic device, the one with the voice she knew, but couldn't see where he'd gone.

The woman's voice cried out to her. 'Over here! Remember me? Follow my voice! Hurry!'

Alice hesitated. She didn't know who to trust.

'Turn around!' the soldier she'd kicked in the chin barked, raising a gun. 'On your knees!'

She was about to obey when the gruff-voiced man hurried back into view.

'Stand down!' he yelled. 'We're lethal force negative on this capture. Got it?'

The gun was still pointed at Alice. She ran anyway.

Though she couldn't hear the young woman's voice anymore, she heard the dog barking and ran toward it.

'Ov—'

A peal of gunfire cut off the words. Alice thought it was a warning shot from the gunman she'd kicked but saw lightning bolts of muzzle flash emerging from the darkness all around her. She dropped to the ground as bullets struck the vehicles and street behind her, kicking up gravel and ricocheting in every direction.

Her would-be captors returned fire, but haphazardly. The incoming bullets were coming in from everywhere at once. The gruff-voiced team leader drew a couple of grenades, both painted bright orange. Rather than lob them at the incoming gunmen, however, he seemed about to throw it at Alice.

Alice was too fast, though. She crawled backwards while keeping as close to the ground as possible. She fought the urge to scream, but her survival instincts took over. If she was going to live through this, she had to be cautious, methodical.

She looked back to the convoy of vehicles in time to see two of her kidnappers topple over, lifeless. Her terror was quickly becoming unendurable. Still, she kept moving. More gunfire. More gunmen hitting the ground on both sides now. More screaming.

When she finally reached one of the vehicles, she crawled behind it, balling herself up as small as she could. The keys were still in the ignition. Could she drive out of there? The gunmen who'd appeared out of nowhere didn't appear to have vehicles.

What she really wanted to do was run. She could just make out the dawn on the eastern horizon. If she could get away from the gunfight, make it a couple of blocks away, she could disappear by the time it was daylight. She could put all these people behind her, reach the ocean, and keep going until she reached safety.

With bullets flying overhead, she eyed the nearest debris pile. It was only fifteen feet away or so. It would take her what . . . four seconds to reach it? Maybe three? They wouldn't even have time to aim.

She leaped to her feet and managed a single step before a bullet struck her in the shin, shattering her tibia. She screamed, twisting backward to reach cover. The pain took over her nervous system. Her body was on fire.

A second bullet ricocheted off the ground inches from her fingers. A third struck her left hip, wrenching her body in the opposite direction.

A fourth thudded into her skull.

BOOK II

FOURTEEN

Este screamed. Seeing the terrified young woman falling forward, a fatal bullet fired into her forehead, was too horrifying, too terrible to bear.

'No!' she shouted, her voice drowned out by gunfire. '*No!*'

She needed this undone. She needed to reverse time, to step back a handful of seconds and pull this person back. Yank her to safety.

But it was over and she was dead. And, in her heart of hearts, Este knew it was her fault. If she hadn't stopped the convoy, the young woman wouldn't be dead. More than that, if Este hadn't treated her like a prize to be won – a ticket to a million dollars – but instead like a human being in distress—

No, a human being. Full stop. If she'd treated her like a human being, maybe she could've warned her. Helped her hide. Helped her escape.

Instead, gunmen on both sides lay dead. The team leader was crumpled over by one of the vehicles, fixing a half-knotted tourniquet above a ghastly and probably fatal wound in his leg. Two of the attacking gunmen, recognizable from their lack of uniforms and mishmash of weapons, lay dead or mortally wounded at his feet.

Este knew who these guys were. Or at least had a good idea. The AK-47 used by one of the first attackers to fall had belonged to Albert, a former Angeleno who ran a fuel-siphoning gang out of the Imperial Valley. He and his crew tended to take low-risk jobs, but with most of the tanks and reserves tapped out, they'd moved on to copper and batteries, cash and gold.

Like her, they were just another crew looking for a big score, and they'd do whatever it took to land it. *Exactly* like her.

The syringes of ketamine in her pocket grew heavier.

'We have to get out of here,' yelled Wilfredo, voice shrill from adrenaline even as he grabbed her arm.

'We did this,' she replied. 'This was us.'

'This was going to be a bloodbath the second they put a million-dollar bounty out there,' Wilfredo countered.

The second who *put a million-dollar bounty out there?* Este wondered.

'You're right,' she said. 'Let's go.'

She grabbed Casey's leash and followed Wilfredo as he hurried back to where their bikes were hidden in the ruins of St Vincent de Paul. Damn. She realized she hadn't cleared her lines of sight. One of Albert's men was almost directly alongside her, pulling guns off a pair of fallen AKR men even as their radio squawked out unheeded instructions.

'Use incendiaries!' someone called. 'Use incendiaries and fall back.'

The gunman smashed the radio, then ran his fingers over the man's tactical vest. Like the leader, the dead man had orange grenades as well. Este figured he just might be distracted enough for her to make a break for it.

Look the other way, she thought, willing him to ignore her. *Let us go.*

Which is when the dog with the worst timing in the world decided to bark.

'Casey!' Este shushed.

But the gunman was already looking their way. He raised his assault rifle.

Every muscle in Este's body tensed. As if in response, the cloth of the man's right sleeve went slack. His gun toppled from his shoulder as if he'd tossed it away. When Este looked closer, it appeared the man's entire arm had simply vanished.

She must not have seen right. Her mortal fear was doing something to her vision. But the man's facial features contorted next, twisting around at nightmarish angles like a wet towel being wound tight. He shrank inward, his clothes falling in on themselves as if there was suddenly nothing within to hold them up.

'Holy crap!' Wilfredo exclaimed. 'That's got to be some kind of chemical weapon.'

The man, or what was left of him, crumpled to the ground. Two of his comrades hurried over, yelling and pointing. They spotted a wounded AKR man, seemed to figure him responsible, and were about to shoot him when their own bodies began to twist and warp. They bent and buckled at unnatural angles as their masses dwindled. Their limbs stiffened into a form of rigor mortis before shrinking back entirely. There were no screams, no blood. Only faces twisted with pain followed by nothing.

The wounded AKR man had witnessed this as well. He tried to

crawl away but fell forward, rolling in a slow spiral on the ground. His radio crackled, the sound of a voice coming in and out as he turned.

'What's happening?' someone demanded. 'Report! Is the subject contained?'

Not captured, Este realized. Contained.

She remembered the post. *Hazardous materials. Take precautions. We're lethal force negative on this capture.*

Este looked at the body of the young woman still lying there. This was somehow her doing.

'Come on!' Wilfredo grabbed her arm.

Este let herself be led away, closing her eyes to the violence. Now that the gunfire had ceased, the only sounds were the running feet of terrified men and the crackle of radios.

'Clear station, clear station,' the voice on the radio said, dour as if resigned to the knowledge that something horrible had happened on the other end. 'Deploying chimeras. Clear station.'

Este managed a last look back at the young woman, now more visible in the pre-dawn twilight.

I'm sorry. I'm so, so sorry.

FIFTEEN

*T**he light. It's too bright! I've got to get to shade. This is too much.***

The young woman took a step but dizziness almost knocked her over. She tried to grab something but came up empty and landed on the ground.

This brought new pain. She opened her eyes. She had landed on a pile of rocks. They'd cut into her legs, hands, and hips. She scraped her knees and shin trying to right herself.

Fantastic, she thought.

Pain shot up from the soles of her feet. Only then did she realize she wasn't wearing shoes or socks. In fact, she wasn't wearing anything at all. She gasped.

She didn't care how much it hurt. She stood up, opened her eyes wide, and took in her surroundings. Even as the cuts burned and her eyes reddened, she processed that she was outdoors in some abandoned or rundown part of a city.

What the . . .?

She looked for her clothes but saw none. Her skin, always pale, was turning pink in the blazing sun. She had to get inside. Had to remember what had happened to her, where she was, how to get back where she belonged.

She shielded her eyes with her hand and looked up and down the block. Nothing seemed familiar. There were only torn-down buildings in every direction, like some endless construction site. She saw no signs of people. No standing structures. It reminded her of photos of bombed-out cityscapes from World War II.

A horrible feeling came over her. Had she been attacked, her clothes torn off? She looked herself over and saw no signs of trauma, then felt her body for bruising or soreness. There was nothing.

Her feet were burning on the hot asphalt. She spotted a patch of dead grass in the median of a nearby street and hurried over to it. The dirt was still hot but not like the concrete. She checked her soles. They were already beginning to blister.

How long had she been out in the sun?

As before, no answers came.

What's my name?

When this didn't come either, the young woman felt a new sense of panic rising.

She turned in a circle, making herself dizzy again. The ruined section of the city extended farther than she'd initially believed. It wasn't just piles of debris. Entire blocks were completely demolished. The annihilation was total. Only a few steel beams and concrete columns rose like splinters against the sky.

The hills in the distance were unfamiliar. Though she could see patches of pale green and brown, much of the hills' surface appeared blackened, as if scorched by a great fire.

Where am I? she demanded of her mind.

What happened to me?

What's my name?

Alice. Your name is Alice Helena Rhodes. Alix to some. Allie to none.

She breathed a little easier. It was a start.

She felt her head, wondering if she'd received a brain injury. There was no obvious wound, and despite her absent memory, she didn't feel like someone who'd taken a blow. She was still able to string together thoughts.

Unless she was crazy. Maybe she threw her own clothes off and dashed into the sunshine.

Well, that would explain certain things, but she definitely wasn't responsible for tearing all these buildings down.

Her thoughts were interrupted by a buzzing sound. She searched the sky for a plane, but as the sound neared, she realized it was on the ground. She caught sight of two dirt bikes as they raced past.

'Hey!' she cried, her voice a rasping whisper. '*Hey!*'

She ran after them but they were moving too fast. There was no way they could see her.

'HEY!' Alice tried one last time, waving her arms. 'Heeeeey!'

Her feet burned anew as did her lungs. She had the impulse to throw up but forced herself to keep going. When the bikes disappeared from sight, she finally slowed down, sweat pouring from her forehead.

'*Dammit,*' she muttered.

Then she heard something. The bikes had faded from view, but the whine of their engines was growing louder again. She looked up. One of the bikes had come around the block and was racing toward her.

Alice gave a weak little wave then bent over, hands on her knees as she caught her breath. She wondered if she'd been foolhardy. If she'd been attacked, might these be her attackers? Also, she *was* naked.

It was too late to run.

The rider hit the brakes, turned off the engine, and climbed off his – no, *her* – bike and removed her helmet. She stared at Alice, eyes wide.

'Oh my God,' the rider, a short, dark-haired woman in her mid-twenties, said, mouth agape. 'You're . . . alive?'

'Um . . .' Alice said.

'You're *alive,*' the rider reiterated. 'Holy crap.'

The dark-haired woman strode up to Alice and touched her shoulder blade. 'Holy crap,' she repeated.

The second bike pulled to a stop behind the first. It had a sidecar with a dog in it. Its rider was a twenty-something male.

'We have any clothes in the pack?' the female rider asked.

The male rider was already checking. He pulled out a pair of shorts and a light jacket from a backpack.

'All we got,' he said, tossing them over.

'Here,' the female said.

Alice didn't think twice. She pulled on the clothes, too-small shorts and too-large jacket, and stepped back onto the dirt.

'We'll find you some shoes, too,' the female rider said. 'But first, we have to get you out of here. You're not safe.'

'I know,' Alice said. 'I'm sunburning fast.'

'Um, no – the gunmen,' the rider said. 'They caught you. You were shot.'

The rider's gaze traveled down Alice's torso.

'I don't . . . I don't remember being shot,' Alice said.

'Do you remember anything from this morning?' the female rider asked.

'No,' Alice admitted. 'Are we friends?'

'You don't remember me?' the rider asked.

'No.'

The rider looked back to her counterpart, then to Alice. 'Yeah, we're friends,' she said. 'I'm Este, this is Wilfredo, and the dog is Casey. Right now, a lot of people think you're dead, but knowing this place, that ain't gonna last. We have to get you out of here.'

Not a dream, Alice thought. *Not a dream at all.*

SIXTEEN

Este felt like she was having an out-of-body experience. The person she'd seen killed not two hours earlier was now on the back of her dirt bike, arms wrapped around her waist, as they roared through the LAQZ.

Or was she? Este figured it *could* be a clone, but that felt insane and unlikely, despite the alternative being this woman she had seen getting shot to pieces was some kind of superhuman. Was 'insane and unlikely' her official diagnosis as a registered nurse, Cal State LA, Class of 2022 (Go Golden Eagles)?

Yeah, Este thought. *I guess it is.*

After the gun battle, she and Wilfredo had looped back to D-Town. Este told Old Lucy what had happened, but the crazy old lady somehow already knew something was up and had snorted a bunch of her product to push out the guilt.

'You killed her,' Este had blurted out, angry as all hell. 'Now you ain't gonna see any of your money. You happy?'

Old Lucy had kind of shrugged, all glassy-eyed. 'She's a time traveler,' Old Lucy said, slurring through the words. 'She'll just go back in time and live all over again. Maybe in a timeline without no quakes.'

Este had rolled her eyes at the time, but Old Lucy's comment about the young woman – who'd said her name was Alice – not really dying and just coming back rang in her head. She'd thought it the ravings of a meth head, but now she didn't know what to make of it.

'Where are we going?' Alice asked as they raced through the city.

'Pan City,' Este shouted back over the engine noise. 'There's a railhead there. The quakes have wrecked most train tracks, but the Army Corps of Engineers keeps repairing that line.'

'Quakes?' Alice asked. 'That's what happened here?'

'Yeah, LA, San Francisco, San Diego. And all over the world,' Este said. 'Like, dozens of cities brought down, and it's not over. Every time you check the news, it's either reporting on the destruction of the most recent quake or breaking news about a new one happening in some part of the world you've never heard of.'

'What about Denver?' Alice asked, voice quivering.

Este didn't know if she wanted to answer. Old Lucy had said something about 'a husband in Denver', but again, she'd thought it the ravings of a lunatic.

'What about Denver?' Este asked.

'I'm remembering things,' Alice said. 'I'm from Colorado. I need to get back there. My husband is there.'

There is no Denver anymore, Este wanted to say. But she didn't.

'I don't know if that's possible.'

'Why not?'

'Well, not right now,' Este corrected. 'First, it's too far to get on bikes. And right now, we need to get you to a hospital. Only, we're fresh out of hospitals in the QZ. Got to take the train to the Land of Plenty for that.'

'Land of Plenty?' Alice asked, moving away from the Denver question as Este had hoped.

'Everywhere in the world that's not a QZ. Places that still have power, running water, and Cheerios on the grocery store shelf.'

Alice fell silent. Este wondered what memories were surfacing for her now.

The truth was, Este hadn't managed to plan very far ahead. Getting out of the LAQZ was the first step, but getting through the sprawling National Guard encampment at Panorama City to the railhead was a different set of obstacles. The good news was, everyone thought Alice was dead, so they wouldn't think much of Este's passenger. The other good news was that the base commander had recently hired her on as a pathfinder at a fraction of her regular fee, to help map a route through the LAQZ for a contingent of Congressional reps and their aides junketing the West Coast quake cities, so she figured she was owed a favor.

The one thing she hadn't done – and wouldn't do – was trade on her mother's name. She figured some people knew she was a military brat just from the lingo she (skillfully, carefully) dropped to let them know just that, but using her late mother's memory to do something illicit just felt like a betrayal. The guilt her mother would rain down on her from the afterlife would be too much.

The bigger question was 'what next?' Handing Alice over to whoever put up the million-dollar bounty was the safest bet. This would keep Alice from getting shot again while simultaneously keeping . . . *whatever it was* that happened to the AKR and siphon gang from happening to other people.

Oh, and she'd collect the million dollars.

Or, she could do what Alice wanted and try to get her back to her husband. If, of course, he was alive.

Knowing what she *should* do didn't make it any easier.

In the sidecar up ahead, Casey looked up, scanning the sky. Este followed his gaze and spied a slender silver line high in the cloudless blue sky. It blinked in and out of view like an optical illusion.

A drone.

How could they have found us already?

She signaled to Wilfredo to follow her and sped up, taking a quick right in the direction of Little Tokyo.

'Where are we going?' Alice asked.

'Shortcut,' Este said. 'Los Angeles River. More of a culvert, really, but even the military isn't suicidal enough to follow us through there.'

SEVENTEEN

The LA River may have been a concrete culvert at one time, but now it was a jungle. After seeing so much bleak destruction, racing through an overgrown forest of shrubs, a handful of trees, grasses, and even flowers was exhilarating.

Alice understood she should be terrified. She could feel Este's heart racing as she leaned into her on the bike. She had no idea who these gunmen her would-be savior had mentioned were – or even if there had been any gunmen in the first place – but, for the time being, she was out of the sun, she was with people, she was wearing at least some clothing, even shoes – they'd found a pair of sneakers near the makeshift path they'd used to descend into the concrete river basin, and her memories, perhaps spurred on by adrenaline, were rushing back to her.

Except for anything that might tell her how she had come to be in Los Angeles or why anyone would want to hunt her down.

They zigzagged around a pair of palm trees – their trunks black but bright green leaves sprouting fan-like from the top – growing from a sandy mound, only to race up a small ramp to jump a wrecked car that had somehow also ended up in the river. Though they mostly drove on concrete or dirt, boards had been put down over more difficult sections of the trail, allowing the bikes to maintain speed.

As they passed an explosion of ferns the size of a small house growing near a shattered overpass, Este pointed out the equally immense pile of trash – everything from old mattresses to shopping carts to furniture – accumulating behind it.

'It's rare, but we sometimes get these heavy rains,' Este said. 'Anything that's not nailed down washes into the LA River. On the one hand, that means all kinds of nutrient-rich soil, seeds, and plant life. On the other, well . . . all this! Oh, yeah – hold on!'

Alice barely had time to react when she saw Wilfredo go airborne ahead of them, launching over a length of chain-link fence that had washed into the culvert. She gripped Este as they followed.

When they landed, a memory of an older man popped into Alice's mind. She figured him for her father but something told her she was wrong. *Grandfather?* she asked herself.

Yes. His name was Walter.

She saw a backyard. A childhood home, the second house her family lived in. This segued into a memory of a cluttered bedroom, walls papered with pictures torn from magazines. Her freshman dorm room.

She saw a young man with light brown hair and glasses. It wasn't Rahsaan. She couldn't remember his name until she saw another image of him, maybe ten years older now. Ben-something. This led to a memory of her mother sitting at her bedside, eyes filled with tears. She wanted to know the reason, but the memory didn't lead there.

She bounced to her grandfather's seventieth birthday. He sat at her mother's dining-room table surrounded by a lifetime's worth of photos. Sepia-toned ones from his childhood mixed with ones of him in his Army uniform, half-buried in the snow. World War II? No, Korea. He'd survived some famous attack. The Chosin Reservoir. He and the last remnants of his unit gathered for an annual reunion.

She'd tried to remember the date, even the year, but had come up empty. Her grandfather's story helped as she remembered he'd been twenty-one in the war, which meant he was born in 1930 or so. His seventieth birthday was in 2000 or thereabouts. This was only two or three years back which meant it was 2003.

So, when did these quakes start?

She tried to remember the last earthquake she'd seen reported on the news, but few memories emerged. The only one that stood out was an Oakland-area quake that had happened during the World Series, but wasn't that in the 1990s or something? Wouldn't she know if there was a 'plague of quakes'?

She focused on the most recent memory she could muster. Things that happened in 2003. She remembered planning a trip to the Columbia River Estuary for her and Rahsaan, with a lot of hiking, a couple of bed and breakfasts in their price range, and a debate whether to save money by driving, although it would add a travel day on each end of the trip.

She had no memory of the trip itself.

Instead, she saw a hospital bed. Boring television programs. Pills. Injections. More boring television. Drips. Preparation for surgeries. Recovery from surgeries. Tears. More needles. Doctors. More doctors. And more doctors after that. She saw Ben-something.

He was a doctor but also an ex-boyfriend. He knew her mom. Ben *Ganske*. She saw him shake hands with Rahsaan and introduce other doctors. When she saw their faces, she remembered their names.

Dr Baig.
Dr Chen.
Dr Brammeier.
Dr Kapur.
Dr McCarthy.

She felt something new. Warmth. Strength. It was Rahsaan's hand in hers. She didn't see it but felt it. He held her hand, squeezed it. Let it fall loose when she slept. Held it tight when she cried. Held both her hands in his own. Held her.

His scent came to her. An overpowering sensation. She loved how he smelled. It reminded her that she'd been loved, madly and completely. She let out a sob of frustration and pain. Este slowed the bike and looked back at her.

'You OK?' she asked.

Alice let go of Este to unzip the light jacket but the zipper got stuck. Este braked.

'What're you doing?' Este asked. 'You can't let go.'

Alice was off the bike in a flash. She pulled the jacket over her head and looked down at her right side. She ran her fingers over her skin then moved to the left. It was perfectly smooth. There were no scars.

'What's going on?' Wilfredo asked, hurrying back from his bike.

'They're gone!' Alice cried.

'What's gone?' Este asked.

'My scars,' Alice said, pointing. 'From surgery. I had multiple surgeries. Here, here, and here. They're gone.'

'Um, isn't that a good thing?' Wilfredo asked, though a scowl from Este shut him up.

'Scars fade over time,' Este offered. 'When did you get them? How old were you?'

'Twenty-eight,' Alice said. 'Like, recently. At most, a few months ago. It was serious. I was dying. Or, at least, they thought I was dying. I had leukemia. Lympo . . . lypo . . .'

'Lymphocytic?' Este asked.

Alice nodded. Este inspected Alice's torso. 'Do you remember the hospital?' she asked. 'Or a date?'

'May 23, University of Colorado Hospital,' she said, surprising even herself.

'May?' Wilfredo asked. 'Like, last year? It's only April.'

Alice shook her head. That didn't make sense. 'No, May, 2003. I'm sure of it.'

Este turned to Wilfredo as if to shut him up. He didn't seem to get the message though, covering his mouth as he laughed.

'Yeah, I don't know what to tell you about *that*, lady, but seeing as how it's 2025, maybe medical science has you a little better hooked up than you think!'

Alice went cold.

EIGHTEEN

ste didn't have to be a nurse to know Alice was seconds away from a panic attack, maybe even a cardiac incident. There were ways to deliver distressing information to a patient. This wasn't one of them.

'What're you talking about?' Alice asked. 'It's 2003, not 2025. I think I know the year.'

'No, man,' Wilfredo countered, making a bad situation worse. 'I was like five years old in '03. Check it out.'

He produced a battered California driver's license. Alice stared at it then looked away as if hoping to find an alternative answer elsewhere in the culvert. Este raised her hands.

'Hey, that's why we wanted to take you to a hospital,' she said. 'I might've put it more delicately than my partner here, but besides the we-thought-you-were-dead thing, there are actually a few more question marks in your file we'd like to get to the bottom of.'

'Like what?' Alice asked. 'You think I'm crazy?'

Este gently took Alice by the wrist, checking her pulse. 'I was a nurse before the quakes,' she explained. 'So, I can tell you that you don't look unhealthy, your vitals are strong, there are no outward signs of trauma or concussion or, luckily, cancer, but I'd need an actual blood test for that. But for reasons I can't explain, there seems to be something going on with your body on a cellular level that's not like anything I've encountered before.'

'Meaning?' Alice asked.

'Meaning, this might not just be your brain,' Este explained.

'So, you believe me about my missing scars?' Alice asked.

'For now, I do,' Este said. 'We saw you get shot early this morning in a way that wasn't survivable. Yet here you are with no sign of injury. You say you had surgery? No sign of that either. But what if I ask if you remember seeing me yesterday? We were in the sub-level of a building off Wilshire. You could barely move. I told you how to get out. You don't remember that at all, though, do you?'

Alice shook her head, bewildered.

'That's a good thing,' Este said. 'It squares with my theory. Whatever rebuilds your body seems to be rebuilding your brain as well. It wipes out your memories.'

'What?' Wilfredo asked, incredulous. 'That's nuts, Este.'

'Yeah, well, nuts is all we've got right now,' Este said.

'That can't be it,' Alice said. 'I *do* have memories. Just not recent ones.'

'Which proves my point,' Este said. 'Your deep memories, the long-term ones that are stored in your cerebral cortex, those are coming back, right?'

'I think so,' Alice said.

'That's because they're hardwired in. Part of your brain's permanent chemical architecture. That's not the case with short-term memories. You're not retaining them.'

'OK, but it's a big leap from not remembering a few things to a twenty-two-year gap in my life,' Alice said. 'I know my own birthday like I know my own name. September 17, 1975. But do I look fifty years old?'

'That I can't explain,' Este said, shaking her head. 'I can only stitch together your symptoms and come up with a half-cocked diagnosis. If I hadn't seen you get shot, yes, I'd think you were crazy. But I'm trained to believe my eyes and trust my instincts. Something we've never seen before is happening with your body. I only wish we weren't encountering it under these conditions. If you'd walked into Good Samaritan a few years back, we would've had you with the best doctors in the world within hours. But here? It's like a joke. A miracle in a wasteland.'

Alice looked down, her breathing returning to something approximating normal.

'And my husband?' Alice asked. 'What about him? Does he know what happened to me? Does he even know I'm alive? What about the rest of my family?'

The rest of my family. The words made Este think of Inés. How many times had she imagined pulling her sister from the rubble, imagined some impossible scenario that allowed Inés to be alive and intact?

Standing in front of her was proof that such things could happen.

'I don't know anything about your husband,' Este said carefully. 'But Denver, well . . .'

'What about Denver?' Alice asked, then seemed to realize what Este was saying. 'Like this?' she waved her hand.

'Yeah. On Valentine's Day of this year.'

'Oh my God!' Alice exclaimed. 'Were there any survivors?'

'Yes, of course,' Este said. 'Far more than perished. If he made it through, it just means he's been displaced. Maybe moved in with relatives in another city. Or maybe he's living in one of the displaced people's camps.'

'How can I find him?' Alice asked, terrified.

'Well, the one decent thing the government has done these days is create a national survivor database.' Este placed a reassuring hand on Alice's arm. 'If your husband's registered, we can find him.'

Este didn't want to say the database also listed the deceased. Though more people had lived than died in Denver, the deaths were still in the six figures.

'I need to see him,' Alice said firmly. 'Now.'

'Agreed,' Este said calmly, glancing to Wilfredo. 'We have anything else to do today?'

'Not a thing, Este.'

This made Alice smile a little. Este leaned close to her. 'We'll figure this out together, OK?'

'You'll get me home?' Alice asked.

'We'll get you home,' Este agreed.

'OK,' Alice said, nodding. 'Why is all this happening? These quakes, I mean?'

'No one knows,' Este said. 'There are theories, but most of us have had to spend our time worrying about surviving rather than puzzling it out. It's our present reality. So, we deal with it.'

Este turned to Wilfredo. Time to go. Before she could reach her bike, however, Casey barked. His P-wave bark.

'Seriously?' Este asked, annoyed.

'What is it?' Alice asked.

'LA's still getting rocked by endless aftershocks. That's why no one's even considered rebuilding it,' Este said. 'Casey's our early warning system.'

Alice looked frightened. Este took her hand.

'Sit with me,' she said, indicating a spot in the middle of the culvert.

'Don't we have to get out of here?' Alice asked.

'No time,' Este said. 'Also, we're probably safer here than anywhere else in the city.'

Alice eyed her with uncertainty.

'We're not going to get very far if you don't trust me,' Este warned.

Este sat down alongside Wilfredo and Casey, the latter putting his head on her lap. Alice hesitated a moment longer then joined them.

The quake was a strong one. Chunks of concrete that had somehow stayed in place on the culvert wall through earlier quakes shattered on the ground, sending shrapnel in every direction. A broken telephone pole rolled down from street level, splintering as it bounced off the rubble, yanking dead power lines with it.

Alice gasped. Este held her hands tighter. Like the aftershock the day before, this one was taking its time.

'We can't stay here!' Alice screamed, as pebbles of cement ricocheted off her back.

Este put her arm around Alice's shoulder and drew her close. 'It's OK,' she whispered.

The ground bucked and the branches of the nearby trees swayed as if in a gale. Casey, looking bored, rolled on his side inviting a belly rub. Este accommodated the request.

After a third minute passed, an eternity in seismic time, the quake shuddered to a stop. The trees stilled and the hollow thunder echoing down the culvert quieted.

'Is it over?' Alice asked.

'Yes, and you survived – congratulations,' Este said. 'You good?'

'Not really.'

'Correct answer,' Este said. 'But come on. We've got a train to catch.'

NINETEEN

There was a second aftershock about ten minutes later. Casey barked. They were barely off the bikes when it started and back on less than forty-five seconds later when it turned out to be barely more than a hiccup.

'Better safe than sorry,' Este said, starting down the culvert again.

'How do you live like this?' Alice asked.

'Oh, we don't live in the QZ,' Este said. 'We're out in the high desert. We still feel them out there, but not as much.'

'So, why do you come here?'

Este explained about being a pathfinder and the various wildcat salvage operations around the QZ.

'What kinds of things do people want?' Alice asked.

'Oh, anything – rare antiques, personal items, important documents,' Este said. 'Anything that can't be replicated in the LoP.'

'Why aren't you there?' Alice asked.

'Money to be made here,' Este said. 'Lots of it. In the LoP, I'm a refugee living off the government. Here, my job skills are much more valuable.'

'Were you on a job when you came across me?' Alice asked. 'You said we were underground?'

Este hesitated. 'Yeah, pathfinder gig for out-of-town clients. Which means we were escorts, not extractors. Turns out, they were trying to rob a group already working the site. A heavily armed group. A fight broke out. We barely got out with our lives.'

'And then you found me?'

'In the middle of it, yeah. I thought you were just some squatter down there,' Este admitted. 'You were naked then, too, and totally out of it.'

'What about memories?' Alice asked.

'We didn't have much of a chat,' Este said. 'But it didn't look like you knew where you were.'

Even as she told it, Este mentally pieced together what she now knew about Alice and what she'd seen down there. Her clients hadn't known much about what they were after, but the other ones had. They wore hazmat suits and came loaded for bear.

No, not bear. They were darts. Tranq darts. They must have understood what could happen if you killed Alice. What might be unleashed.

Retrieving her and whatever her body's abilities were was worth every bit of the millions they'd shelled out. A human being that could survive past death? When millions had died in just the last few years? The secrets locked in these regenerative cells of hers could be beyond priceless.

Wilfredo slowed. Este followed.

'Another quake?' Alice asked.

'No, we're going the rest of the way on foot.' Este indicated a dark, gaping hole in the culvert wall.

'You've *got* to be kidding.'

'Eh, it's not so bad,' Este said. 'It's a short walk through the old sewer system, but then you're in the Metro tunnel. The ground's uneven – watch your step.'

The group moved to the hole in the wall. All except Casey, who stared back down the culvert.

'Come on, boy,' Wilfredo said, tugging his leash. 'Let's move.'

But the Alsatian didn't twitch. He also didn't bark. His nose gently bobbed up and down, then went still, his body tensing as he gazed into the thick foliage they'd just driven through. Then he began to growl, a low rumbling sound from deep within his throat.

Este shot a look to Wilfredo. Casey *never* growled. If something alarmed him, it had to be bad news.

'*Go*,' Este said.

Wilfredo turned first, pulling the dog behind him as Este and Alice followed. Alice was terrified, unsure what scared her more – the dark of the tunnel, the quake that might bring the whole thing down on them, or whatever lurked in the culvert.

'Take this,' Wilfredo said, thrusting a flashlight into her hand. 'Stay straight then take a right at the dead end.'

Alice nodded and ran. The flashlight did its job. Barely. The floor was cracked but mostly intact. The crumbling, broken ceiling, however, had strewn the path with cracked tiles and broken brick. Alice was so glad they'd found shoes. Otherwise, her feet would be in tatters.

'Go right!' Wilfredo yelled from behind her.

Alice didn't know what he was talking about until she almost slammed into a looming dead end in front of her. She headed right a couple hundred yards before reaching a large break in the tunnel wall.

'Through there!' Este cried from somewhere behind her.

Alice did as instructed and found herself in a subway tunnel. The brick and tile floor had been replaced with wood, multiple rails, and packed earth.

'Which way?' she yelled back.

'Left!' Este said, now only a few feet behind.

But Alice heard something else. Something from farther back in the tunnel.

They weren't the only ones down here.

She flew down the subway tunnel, pumping her legs up and down like pistons. She'd never run so fast in her life. Her muscles, numb before, surprised her by how well they responded. She felt like an athlete but knew it was fear-fueled adrenaline.

A platform appeared beside her and, after a couple of false starts, she managed to vault up onto it. She saw light streaming down from somewhere above and sprinted up multiple flights of stairs to get at it.

The exit was around a corner and up yet another stairwell, this one three-tiered. Now Alice was beginning to tire, but the promise of daylight made her run ever faster. She took the steps three at a time. She emerged into sunlight seconds later, another ruined, sun-bleached cityscape in front of her.

But there were also six men in black uniforms and tactical gear, all with machine guns leveled at her torso. It was as if she'd surfaced in front of a firing squad.

'Where's the fire, girl?' the apparent leader of the squad, a young man with the name Chernov stenciled over his pocket, asked, lip curling into a grin. 'Or didn't anyone tell you this is a toll station now?'

TWENTY

Este was three steps behind Alice when she heard the man's voice. His tone suggested that whatever this 'toll' might be, he expected to collect. She froze in place, yanking back Casey's leash as he tried to join Alice.

'No, no,' Chernov's voice called from above. 'Y'all come up, too.'
Dammit.

Este knew they'd run into somebody on the way to the railhead,
but she'd hoped it wouldn't be a random Garrison squad. If it was
the National Guard, they'd at least get inside the wire before they'd
have to answer to somebody, possibly with a bribe or calling in a
favor.

But Garrison? They were corrupt from start to finish. If somebody
was coming into the QZ, they'd get tariffed. Coming out? Also
tariffed. Smuggling supplies in or out? Also tariffed. This especially
included anything coming off the trains. Worse, they had a piece of
the LAQZ drug trade, which made it almost a monopoly. If you
bought from them, you paid their markup. Sold to them, you did
so at cost. Did either with another crew? They just might shoot you.

'What do you want to do?' Wilfredo asked quietly.

'Like we have a choice,' Este said, tugging Casey's leash and
leading him up the steps.

'Hands where we can see 'em!' Chernov demanded more urgently.

Este twisted Casey's leash around her wrist and raised her palms.
'Right here, Keith.'

She remembered his voice. He'd been on the escort team of some
corporate outfit, looking to reopen some LA City oil fields and had
introduced himself as being from Georgia. He'd hit on her. She'd
blown him off.

'Estefania Quiñones!' Chernov exclaimed. 'It's like I had a hunch
. . . no, a *premonition* you'd be involved with this. On your knees,
guys. 'Sup, Fredo?'

'What's up, yourself?' Wilfredo asked, kneeling beside Alice and
Este. 'Mind lowering the guns?'

Chernov responded by aiming his gun at Casey. 'Casey, right?
Bet you'd love to take a chomp out of my butt about now, huh?'

Este shot a look at the Alsatian. To her surprise, he seemed to
barely notice the Garrison patrol. His focus was on whatever was
coming up the tunnel behind them.

'OK, you caught us,' Este said. 'How much to let us go? We're
burning daylight.'

'No can do,' Chernov said. 'There was some incident outside
D-Town last night. Big gun battle between AKR and Albert what's-
his-name's outfit . . .'

Husti, Este thought.

'And there might've been a biohazard spill to boot. So, we have to quarantine anyone coming through and bring them back to base.'

'We don't know anything about that,' Este said.

'And who's this?' Chernov asked, nodding to Alice.

'Molly Thoft,' Este said. 'Vineland homesteader. Her parents got caught up in the New Brunswick quake a couple weeks back and she can't get in touch with them. So, we were helping her get out and get to a phone.'

Chernov laughed. 'You're quick with the *caca de toro*, Miss Quiñones, I'll give you that,' he said. 'But we heard from Old Lucy that you not only witnessed the shooting, you knew something about the target. A girl.'

He eyed Alice. Este scoffed. 'If you talked to Lucy, then you know that girl was killed. Besides, that was yesterday's job. This is today's. So, why don't you take us to the base commander and we'll get this over with.'

'You telling me my business, girl?' Chernov said, advancing on Este. 'Oh, hello – what's that?'

He indicated the canister in her pocket.

'If you must know, it's for Casey's heart worm pills. But we're out,' Este said. 'Hoping to pick some up on the way back in.'

'Wow!' Chernov said. 'Lying is like a superpower to you, huh? It's a sight to behold.'

He reached for the canister, but Este punched him in the jaw. It wasn't much of a hit, but he was surprised enough to punch her back, toppling her onto her side.

'Shouldn't have done that!' Chernov said, reaching for his sidearm. 'Suspect in a mass shooting striking a government contractor while attempting to escape custody. That justifies lethal force right there.'

As he raised the weapon to strike Este, Wilfredo rolled onto his feet and lunged at Chernov. He had the Garrison security guard pinned to the ground with a couple of punches to the face before two of the others managed to drag him off.

'Jesus Christ!' Chernov shouted, spitting blood. 'The hell you think you're doing?'

'Knocking you down,' Wilfredo shot back. 'What did it feel like I was do—?'

Wilfredo's words were cut off by one of the men smashing him in the head with the stock of his rifle. Wilfredo raised a defensive hand that froze mid-air, as if losing its train of thought. Blood trickled from a wound on his scalp and he fell, sprawling out onto the ground.

'What the hell'd you do that for?' Chernov asked his comrade.

The young man looked surprised and shrugged. 'Thought he was going for you.'

Este raced to Wilfredo's side, inspecting the laceration. It was bad.

'You want to draw an excessive force report, well, that's how you do it,' Chernov said, shaking his head. 'Guess we need to come to an understanding, Este.'

Este barely heard him. There was already swelling where Wilfredo had been struck. Este felt for a depression underneath but found nothing. The blow had probably fractured his skull. A wound like that could cause a brain bleed or even swelling. Without surgery to relieve the pressure, Wilfredo could die.

'You really hurt him,' Este said quietly.

'You know that was *not* our intention,' Chernov drawled, eyeing his men.

They looked scared. Like boys playing a game that had suddenly turned serious.

Casey growled. Chernov's finger went to his rifle's trigger guard.

'Oh, what? You're going to shoot my dog, now?' Este asked. 'So you know, there's been a drone following us all day. Pretty sure this is all on camera, but if you're looking to make things worse, I guess that's one way to do it.'

That part's not bullshit. There was a drone, Este thought. Though she had no way of knowing the intentions of the people tracking them.

Chernov paled. He looked ready to speak when one of his men indicated the Metro entrance.

'Um, boss? What is that?'

Everyone turned. Two eyes peered back at them from just over the top step of the Metro stairs. They were gold, retinas tiny and black in the bright sunlight. Este couldn't quite make out the head until it moved. It was massive.

'Jesus!' Chernov exclaimed. 'Is that a cougar?'

As if in answer, a large, dusky mountain lion took a single tentative step out into the daylight. Its ears were pinned down, its head low, as if unhappy about being seen. Este knew there were big cats like this in LA, but she'd never seen one this size. It looked over 200 pounds, easy. More like a giant tiger than a Griffith Park puma.

Its tail, black with a white tuft at the end, flicked back and forth. Este could just make out matching white tufts at the tips of its ears. Casey was on his feet now, rigid as stone, staring at the newcomer. The cat eyed him for a moment, as if assessing his threat potential, then padded slowly around the group.

Until it spotted Alice.

'What's it doing?' Chernov asked.

'I don't know,' Este shot back.

A low, ferocious growl rumbled from its mouth, followed by a roar. Chernov and the Garrison men stepped back. Casey, however, got between the mountain lion and Alice.

'Casey . . .' Este warned.

But it was too late. The cat took a step toward Alice, and Casey leaped at it, jaws open. The lion batted the dog away like he was nothing, only for the Alsatian to roll back onto his feet and launch himself at the cougar again.

'Casey, no!' Este cried.

'What's going on?' Alice asked, terrified.

Chernov nodded to his men. 'Light 'em up.'

His men raised their weapons, some aimed at the lion but others at Casey. Este waved her arms.

'No! Not my dog!' she yelled.

But before she could get in front of their guns, a second mountain lion leaped from the Metro station stairs and sank its teeth into Chernov's throat.

TWENTY-ONE

The machine gunfire was so loud Alice couldn't think. She saw blood but didn't know whose it was. She caught sight of Este, mouth open in a scream, but the fusillade drowned out her cries. One of Este's hands was on Wilfredo's shoulder. The other reached for Casey's leash even as it whipped through the air – the dog was riding one of the mountain lions like a bronco.

The Garrison men had panicked and were firing in every direction. Their leader, in the jaws of the second mountain lion, struck the animal lamely with his fists before blood loss sapped away his strength.

It wasn't as if all the bullets missed. The lions both bled from wounds stitched across their torsos. It was just that no one had managed a kill shot yet.

Even as the chaos reigned around her, Alice knew it could only get worse. If there was going to be any rescue for her friends, it would have to come from her. She was scared, but an odd conviction emerged from the back of her mind.

I can't die. I come right back. I only lose my memories.

She jumped to her feet and ran over to Este, keeping low to avoid the bullets. She grabbed Este's hand and turned her around.

'We have to go!' she yelled.

When Este stared at her blankly, Alice gently lifted one of Wilfredo's arms as if to carry him away.

'Help me,' Alice commanded.

This got Este moving. She lifted Wilfredo's other arm, getting him to his feet. The two women took a couple of steps to get accustomed to the weight, then looked back at Casey.

'Come on, Casey!' Alice yelled.

To her surprise, the dog seemed to hear her. Not only that, he abandoned his fight with the mountain lion to hurry to his masters' side.

'We need a medevac!' one of the Garrison men yelled into his shoulder mic, paying no attention to the retreating group. 'We're under attack!'

Alice glanced back in time to see the first lion go down in a hail of gunfire as the second tore into the leg of another of the security guards. If it wasn't so brutal, she'd be incredulous.

How on *earth* did they end up with a pair of mountain lions on their tail?

'We've got to get to the railhead,' Este said, nodding to Wilfredo. 'They barely have a medical staff at the base and they're not going to call in a helicopter.'

'Understood,' Alice replied.

They'd just made it across the Metro station's empty parking lot to a neighboring street when a group of National Guardsmen, weapons at the ready, hurried toward them.

Rather than seek cover, Este waved to them.

'There's a mountain lion!' she yelled. 'It attacked us, then attacked the Garrison patrol when they tried to rescue us! They need help!'

'Identify yourselves,' one of the guardsmen ordered, though he was already directing his men toward the sound of the shooting.

'Estefania Quiñones. Call Major Chester. She knows me.'

There was a new burst of gunfire followed by a scream. The guardsman signaled to Este.

'Get to the aid tent,' he ordered, indicating the base half a block behind him, before grabbing his own shoulder mic. 'Medical teams to the Sepulveda Gate.'

'Thank you!' Este said aloud, then turned to Alice and muttered, 'Railhead is at the back of the base. We'll leave Wilfredo in the hospital tent and catch the next train.'

Alice eyed her with surprise, but Este wore a sly smile, even as Wilfredo tilted his head toward her.

'You're not leaving me anywhere,' he protested weakly.

'No, I'm not,' Este said, squeezing his hand. 'Just wanted to do a quick hearing test. You passed.'

The National Guard base at Panorama City was huge, extending over several acres and marked by dozens of hard plastic Quonset huts. They were more permanent than tents but could survive most earthquakes, as they tended to bend rather than crack and were easily repaired.

Este found the sick bay and stole a wheelchair, not a difficult task given the base was on high alert due to the gunfire outside the wire. She and Alice lowered Wilfredo into it, then rolled him toward the railyard in back as quickly as they could, Casey bringing up the rear.

'I think we might get lucky,' Este said, despite worrying that she might jinx it. 'Should be a train heading out of here about now. It'll be freight cars not passenger cars this time of morning, but that's probably better.'

As the wheelchair bumped over obstacles, Wilfredo groaned in pain.

'Sorry, Fredo. We're almost there.'

She led them between two huts and through a narrow gate. The railyard, with ten tracks, multiple loading ramps, and tents large enough to house a circus, was on the other side. The yard was one of the only places in Southern California that had been brought back to its pre-quake operational status. Though half the tracks were bent out of place, five sets were up and running, used to supply the tiny outpost.

A number of freight cars rested on the tracks, waiting to be loaded. Este cursed her five feet five inch frame that she couldn't see above them, but Alice could.

'There's a train moving,' Alice said, pointing. 'Can't tell if it's coming or going though.'

Este hurried along a set of tracks to a gap between the resting cars. Sure enough, the train in motion was exiting.

'That's us,' she said. 'But we have to hurry. They keep it slow in the yard but the second the last car clears the gate, they throttle up.'

Alice nodded and ran faster.

'Hey, where are you going with that?' a soldier shouted from one of the nearby loading ramps.

'This corporal's due to rotate home but slept in!' Este yelled back. 'Got to get him on the freight.'

The response confused the soldiers just long enough that Este knew they wouldn't be able to catch up.

'That Chernov guy was right,' Alice said. 'You're good at that.'

'Bullshit artist is practically my job description,' Este agreed.

They bounced over several more tracks, Wilfredo gripping the arms of the chair as best he could. They had almost reached the last car of the moving train when one of the wheelchair's wheels began to wobble and shake. Afraid it might give way and tumble Wilfredo onto the uneven concrete, Este decided to ditch it.

'We'll have to carry him!' Este said, taking his arm.

The train was only about twenty yards ahead of them but was gaining speed. Este could just make out the car code chalked on the back: RTSBWO. She didn't know what the last four letters stood for but the first two told her it was operated by Rawlins Tellis, which meant it was heading for Salt Lake City.

Good. Anywhere but here.

A potent combination of panic and adrenaline drove Este and Alice. They caught up to the final freight car only to find it locked.

Damn military efficiency.

The second was locked as well. There was a lock on the third, but Este could see that the latch on the pull gate was broken. When she gave it a yank, it slid right open.

'Casey!' she called, reaching inside the freight car to bang on the metal floor. 'Up!'

Casey, the only one whose energy wasn't flagging, made the leap – however gracelessly – and was soon inside.

'I think the train's speeding up!' Alice said.

Este looked ahead. The front of the train had reached the yard gates and was slowly accelerating.

'We can still make it,' Este said. 'Just gotta be quick!'

Her words were answered by a burst of gunfire coming from behind them. They spun around, expecting to see their pursuers but no one was there. Este squinted, seeing movement on the loading dock where the soldiers had been. Only now, one was being thrown to the ground.

By a large mountain lion.

'How'd it get through all those soldiers?' Alice asked in disbelief.

'No clue,' Este replied, voice shaking. 'Lift Wilfredo up!'

They hoisted the injured man as high as they could, even as they ran alongside the accelerating train. Casey did his part by grabbing onto Wilfredo's pants leg as Este and Alice shoved him into the car.

When they were done, Este turned to Alice.

'You're next!'

Alice didn't demur. Este helped her grab the handrail alongside the pull gate and gave her a boost. Alice almost missed her footing but managed to catch herself and roll into the freight car alongside Wilfredo. Este prepared to follow her when Alice pointed back toward the railyard.

'Look!' she exclaimed. 'They're following us!'

The mountain lions, having finished with the soldiers at the loading dock, were now galloping toward the train. They were much faster than Alice or Este and had closed the distance in seconds.

It was baffling, but Este didn't have time to think. She grabbed for the handrail, only for it to slip from her fingers as the train lurched ahead.

'Come on!' cried Alice, extending a hand.

Este reached for it, but it was too late. The freight car was pulling away. Este tried to run faster, tried to find that last burst of energy that would get her inside, but her legs wouldn't respond.

'Look out!' Alice yelled.

The mountain lions were now only a few yards behind Este. They ran like greyhounds on a track, pouring on the kind of speed their large frames should have denied them. The second she tried to get inside the car, Este knew they'd pounce.

She had to come up with a different plan.

'Close the door!' she yelled to Alice.

'No!' Alice cried. 'Are you crazy?'

'They'll get in!' Este said. 'Close it!'

Alice hesitated. Este glanced back to the lions. One eyed her. One eyed the open gate. Both were ready to leap.

'Now!' Este yelled.

The closest mountain lion jumped, sailing past Este toward the freight car. Alice slammed the door closed just in time, nailing the beast in the head as it landed half-in, half-out of the train car. Though hardly injured, the blow was enough to daze it, and it slid out. Este ran right up and over it, the second cat right behind her.

Este spied the service ladder at the rear of the freight car. Without a second thought, she jumped at it even as she felt the lion's hot breath on the back of her neck. Her feet missed the lower rungs, but she managed to grasp two of the higher ones with her hands. Almost falling, she curled her left arm painfully around the steel handrail to keep from sliding off.

'*Gnh*,' she groaned, her shoulder feeling torn in two.

She looked down at the mountain lions as they ran alongside the train, running and staring but not attacking. They moved like no predator she'd ever seen.

The white tufted tail and ears of one of the creatures told her it was the mountain lion that had emerged first from the Metro station. But that one had been shot a couple dozen times. This one didn't have a wound on it, save for what looked like a dart or two. She blinked. Could she be mistaken? Or maybe all mountain lions had markings like this and she didn't realize it? There'd been so much gunfire, so much blood. It could've been the other cat that got hit.

But this one got through without so much as a scratch?

She met its gaze. It stared back at her, unblinking. Mindlessly determined. More drone than living creature. For wild animals, there was something very unnatural about them.

TWENTY-TWO

Alice woke with a start in dim light. She was seated upright, head resting against metal. The air was cool and a light breeze blew around her. A dull and repetitious drumbeat of clanging metal rang around her like poorly tuned bells. She reached to her left. Her hand landed on fur.

A dog. Casey. The dog's name was Casey.

'You OK?'

She could just make out a woman's silhouette opposite her. Este. The door beside her was slightly ajar, revealing a forest flashing by in the night. They were in a freight car on a train.

'Fell asleep,' Alice said, noticing Wilfredo lying beside Este, his head in her lap. 'Forgot where I was. How is he?'

'Resting, but he's got a fever,' Este said. 'That's never good.'

'How much longer are we on this train? Where are we headed?'

'The train's going to Salt Lake City, but we're getting off before then, closer to Yosemite. Whoever's after us will be waiting at the depot. Check it out.'

Este nodded out the half-open freight car door. Alice rose to take a look. They were somewhere in the mountains, surrounded by the tallest pines she'd ever seen. The sky was so clear, she could see thousands of stars.

'What am I looking at?' Alice asked.

Este pointed to one star in particular that seemed to blink in and out of view.

'An airplane?' Alice asked.

'Airplanes have position lights,' Este said. 'That's another drone. There's a tunnel in a few miles. We're going to disembark there and pick up a car.'

'In the middle of nowhere?' Alice asked, dubious.

'While most of the towns out here shut down even if they weren't hit by quakes, a few survived,' Este said. 'There's a big tourist trade in Yosemite. It's expensive, but there are a handful of lodges and bed and breakfasts running these "roughing it" experiences for the morbidly curious from the LoP.'

'Not just camping?' Alice asked.

'Oh, no – not for what they're paying,' Este said. 'They've got roofs overhead, fuel-fed generators to power lights and refrigeration, even running water.'

'Wow, sounds . . . absolutely ridiculous,' Alice observed.

Este laughed. 'It is. I've taken some folks like that into the LAQZ – tourists who want selfies in front of the burned-up Hollywood sign or what's left of Dodger Stadium. They're always the first to tell you how much they've donated to relief efforts. They know it's ghoulish. There are a few, though – locals mostly – who come back looking for closure. They want us to take them to their house or school or somewhere familiar. More often than not, it's a pile of bricks. They come seeking something identifiable, at least, and instead receive an unasked-for lesson on impermanence.'

'*Jeez*,' Alice said. 'Are you always this dark? Or is this like a train thing?'

Este grinned. 'Sorry. Been an odd couple of days.'

'Yeah, I was just starting to get used to living in a futuristic hellscape when we were attacked by giant killer mountain lions,' Alice replied.

They shared a laugh. Este shook her head while idly stroking Wilfredo's hair. Alice nodded to the young man.

'How long have you guys been together?' she asked.

'If you mean as business partners – driver and pathfinder – just over a year,' Este said. 'But if you mean friends with benefits, that plus a few months.'

'That's serious.'

'Except it's not somehow?' Este questioned. 'Easy not to think about the future when it no longer feels you've got much of one. How was it with your guy?'

'Easy,' Alice said with a shrug. 'We have a routine – get up, work out, make breakfast, head to work, go adventuring on weekends. We would sometimes hang out with friends, but we still go on dates. He grew up with almost nothing but classical music playing in his house, so he likes all these bands and drags me to shows. I like seeing dance, so I drag him with me to those.'

'What, were you a ballerina as a little girl or something?'

'Not at all. I just like watching it, I guess,' Alice said. 'People in motion. Strength, precision, choreography, music. Not you?'

'Dance was forced on me,' Este said. 'When I was fourteen, half my friends started having these quinceañeras. We'd have to rent dresses like we were bridesmaids and go to church to learn all these formal ballroom dance steps.'

'I thought those were supposed to be fun parties.'

'I'm sure some are, but mine were all church related and kinda sucked.'

'I think you're skirting the real issue,' Alice said. 'I'm going to need to see some of those steps.'

Este twisted her face through several phases of frown. Alice laughed.

'While you were out, I got to thinking,' Este said. 'You get a good look at those mountain lions? The one that tried to take me down had these white tufts on its tail and ears. Pretty sure I saw it getting blasted to hamburger by the Garrison guys.'

'I didn't see it,' Alice said. 'Not that I remember anyway.'

Este reached into her waistband and extracted the canister.

'You ever see this before?' she asked.

Alice looked it over, straining to read the alphanumeric string by starlight. The first numbers read 30022250252180 before it trailed off into a dark blur.

'No, why?'

'The building where I found you the first time? This was down there. I think it was what my client was looking for. And they weren't the only ones looking. The guys that swooped in and took those bozos away had more of these things. Lots more.'

Este absently toyed with the canister in the palm of her hand. *Were they looking for you too?* she thought. Este was certain she knew the answer and briefly turned away to avoid Alice's gaze.

Alice eyed the canister more closely, then shook her head. 'I wish I could tell you, but it feels like one more missing piece. Thanks for getting me out of there, by the way. And for rescuing me off the street. And for getting me on this train.'

'No problem,' Este said.

'Are you my guardian angel or something?' Alice asked.

Este wondered if she should mention the million-dollar bounty then decided against it. She felt a momentary pang of guilt but swiftly let it pass.

'People with means got out of LA when the quakes began,' Este said. 'But those that were left behind – the old, the sick and disabled, all the people in prison – when LA-2 and LA-3 hit, all of those people were wiped out. Kind of shapes your feelings about such things.'

'I'd imagine,' Alice said.

'But it's also personal,' Este admitted. 'Seeing you die like that and then come back . . . I don't know. If you can do it, somehow that gives me a little hope for my sister. She's still missing some-where out there. I know deep down that she's dead. But if you made it back, maybe there's hope for her, too.'

'I'm so sorry about your sister,' Alice said. 'But yeah, if there's anything I can do to help you get her back, I'll do it.'

'Thank you,' Este said idly. 'I will need your help the next little while but not necessarily with that.'

'With what then?'

'The LoP and me, well, we don't exactly see eye to eye,' Este said, looking out into the night. 'When you've gone through a quake or worked a QZ, you know how bad it is. You live with it every day, waiting for the next one. So, being among people who have no idea, who go about their lives oblivious as they careen into a future they're not remotely prepared for – it's a bit much. You get the impulse to scream "Do you not understand what's happening?" on every street corner.'

'And you need someone to pull you back from the brink?'

'A bit that, yep.'

'I'll do whatever I can,' Alice assured her, touching Este's shoulder. 'Despite being a brain-damaged time traveler who attracts mountain lions at will.'

'And I'll do whatever I can to get you home and back to your husband,' Este said, putting her hand on Alice's. 'Despite needing to tell you we're going to have to jump off a moving train into a narrow tunnel in about thirty seconds alongside a dog and a guy with a head injury.'

'Bring it on,' Alice said.

TWENTY-THREE

Alice hadn't been certain Este meant the whole 'jumping off the train' thing literally until she leaned Wilfredo aside, slid the pull gate open a little wider, leaned out, and looked down the track for the tunnel.

'It's right there,' Este said. 'Luckily, the town where we're boosting the car is just down the hill. We won't have to go far. Also, the train'll have to slow down for the tunnel.'

Alice moved to the open door. The train was moving much faster than she'd ever feel comfortable jumping from.

'How do we do this?' she asked.

'Sit down and scoot off,' Este said, rousing Wilfredo and moving him into a seated position. 'Like pushing yourself off the edge into a swimming pool. But once you're on your feet, press yourself against the tunnel wall as tight as you can so you're not yanked backward by the train's draft.'

Alice eyed Este dubiously. Este shrugged.

'Hey, you're the one who can't die, so you can do what you want,' Este said, putting her arm around Wilfredo. 'You go first though.'

'You're going to jump with Wilfredo on your own?' Alice asked.

'Got a better idea?'

'Well, yeah.' Alice sat next to Wilfredo as well.

Este was surprised but nodded. 'Cool. Casey? You come down after, OK?'

The dog stared at her as if this was all big fun.

And then they were in the tunnel.

Este closed her eyes and felt Wilfredo's weight on her arm. 'In three. One . . . two . . . *three* . . .'

It was almost a disaster. Alice disappeared into the darkness first, Este not even hearing them land over the racket of the train. She pushed herself and Wilfredo off next, falling forward until not her hand but her head struck the tunnel wall. Dizzy, she pressed her body against Wilfredo's back like a buttress as the train raced past.

'You OK?' she yelled down the tunnel, not sure Alice would hear.

'Barely,' Alice called back. 'I almost lost all my teeth.'

Este glanced to the disappearing train and could just hear Casey's bark. He was still in the freight car.

'Casey! Come on, boy! Come!'

But the dog stayed put. The silhouette of his head was barely visible as the train headed to the far end of the tunnel.

'Casey, come! Come!'

But seconds later, the train was out of the tunnel and gone from view.

'Oh my God, Casey!' Este shouted, lowering Wilfredo to the base of the wall. 'Casey!'

She ran down the tracks, more distraught than she'd been in months. She'd lost so, so much. She couldn't lose her dog. That would be too much.

'Casey!' she cried.

This time, she got a woof in response. She stopped short. From the darkness of the tunnel, the Alsatian came bounding over to her from the shadows. She dropped to her knees.

'Casey!'

He leaped on top of her, licking her face. She collapsed under the weight and stroked his fur.

'You guys OK?' a groggy voice asked.

Wilfredo, with Alice's assistance, stood over her.

'Can't complain,' Este said. 'You?'

'Same.'

'He sounds better, no?' Alice asked.

'Just means he's had rest,' Este said. 'You can't tell a cerebral edema from external signs.'

'Should we get going?' Wilfredo asked, glancing down the tunnel.

'We need to wait five,' Este said. 'Make sure that drone is gone with the train.'

They waited ten. Este finally poked her head out of the tunnel, scanned the sky, and saw nothing.

'Let's go,' she said.

Twain Harte was half a mile away, down a narrow half-dirt road through a grove of towering sequoias. The forest was illuminated by moonlight, and the lights of the town sparkled in the distance. As they got closer, they heard music and smelled a campfire.

'Are they having a party?' Wilfredo asked.

Sure enough. Behind one of the motels, a number of people had gathered around a bonfire to eat and drink. Despite the late hour, a couple of children roasted marshmallows as a trio of singers harmonized over a folksy ballad accompanied by an acoustic guitar. Fairy lights twinkled overhead, connected to a loudly humming generator.

'Looks festive,' Alice said, voice tinged with irony.

'Should mean we'll have our pick of vehicles in the parking lot.' Este gestured toward several SUVs lined up around the corner on the town's main drag.

They waited until the revelers had doused the fire and retired into the motel for the night before slipping over to the row of cars. The older vehicles with keyed ignitions were a no-go, as were the couple of self-driving cars – Este knew these were equipped with the most elaborate security systems.

'Self-driving cars?' Alice asked, amazed.

'The future we were heading into might've been pretty interesting,' Este said, then pointed to a 2019 hybrid SUV. 'That's our ride.'

She and Alice stole four gas cans off the back of a nearby Jeep and swapped the license plates with a pickup across the street. Este then felt around inside her pack until she found a small black fob.

'What's that?' Alice asked.

'Manufacturer's universal remote key,' Este said. 'Watch.'

She hit the opaque button on the end, praying as she did every time she used it that the battery still worked. The fob cycled through frequencies until the SUV's doors unlocked.

'Piece of cake,' Este said, opening the back doors. 'Everybody in.'

The SUV was a treasure trove of supplies – food and clothing, even a tablet still holding a little charge. There were homemade snacks, thermoses of water, and multiple pairs of shoes. Este drove them a mile or so outside the city with the headlights off before stopping to take an inventory.

As she and Alice put on clean clothes and passed around food, they exchanged a guilty look. It was one thing to steal a car, but raiding the owner's personal items felt like another level of skeevy. Still, Este checked the tablet to see about loading a map. There was no signal at all.

'What is that?' Alice asked.

'Computer of the future,' Este said, handing it over for Alice to inspect. 'We shrank everything.'

Wilfredo slept in the back of the SUV with Casey's head in his lap.

'Where to now?' Alice asked as they set out again.

'Straight into the park. We'd lose too much time backtracking and we'd be seen if we used the main highways. We exit out the northeast side and pick up the freeway to Reno. That's the nearest big hospital.'

'Let's do it,' Alice agreed.

The road into Yosemite was treacherous, a narrow, two-lane road carved into the sides of high cliffs. Este navigated the unlit path as best she could, imagining themselves getting this far only to tumble over the side into the valley below. She doubted they'd ever be looked for, much less found.

It was almost morning by the time they reached the park itself. Though Este had managed to sleep for a few hours on the freight train, she was still exhausted, and it would be several more hours before she'd be able to rest.

'You want me to drive?' Alice asked, as if reading her mind.

'No, I'm all right,' Este said. 'Besides, it'll be slow due to the switchbacks and uncleared back roads.'

After playing with the tablet for a while as its battery life waned, Alice fell asleep. Half an hour later, Este rolled past an abandoned ranger station and into the park.

The drive was as difficult as expected, but sunrise made it easier. One by one, the glorious vistas of Yosemite revealed themselves, from verdant valleys and impenetrable thickets to great rock formations and a waterfall so high Este couldn't believe what she was seeing. Water cascaded from a high cliff, dropping hundreds upon hundreds of feet before hitting rocks and starting a second, lower waterfall.

'Would you look at that?' she whispered to Casey, the only other one awake in the SUV.

The Alsatian poked his head up to the driver's seat, happily accepted a scratch on the head, then retreated to Wilfredo's side.

It was fully morning by the time she drove them out of the park. Several small towns fanned out from the exit, but all were long since abandoned. There were no signs of life for miles to come.

As she neared South Lake Tahoe a few hours later, however, this changed abruptly. From a quarter-mile away, she spied a gas station all lit up, inside and out. *Yes, We're Open!* was posted on its blazing marquee. There was much more electricity being wasted than could have come from a single generator. As she passed, Este could just make out a clerk behind the counter watching television.

A shiver went up her spine. The station was on an electrical grid. They'd entered the Land of Plenty.

She was disgusted by the waste. Sure, she'd grown up in two of the most wasteful big cities imaginable, Houston and Los Angeles. But after spending so much time in the LAQZ, it was hard to stomach, like someone from a land of perpetual drought dropped into one of endless rain.

She thought about the food on the gas station's shelves. The fuel used to truck it out there. The multiple brands that allowed shoppers to luxuriate in variety and choice. Then that same food, when it passed its sell-by date, was thrown in the trash, and more fuel used to truck it to a dump somewhere.

She understood this was the norm for 'civilized society'. That the way folks who hadn't been through a quake yet dealt with their fear was to keep right on consuming, right on living as if it'd never affect them. But her brain had been rewired by her experiences over the last two years. She didn't belong in the LoP. She didn't think she ever would again.

A tractor-trailer appeared on the highway, approaching from the opposite direction. Este pulled as far to the right as possible, fully expecting to be hit despite the four shared lanes of highway. It was an irrational thought, but it filled her with terror nevertheless. She slowed the SUV, her hands slick with sweat and her heart racing. Her breathing grew rapid and ragged and she forced her eyes away from the oncoming vehicle, suddenly fearing she'd drive right into it.

The truck passed without incident. Este drove on, waiting for her body to relax. It didn't. Instead, her eyes lost focus. The steering wheel grew slippery under her hands. She could no longer catch her breath. It was as if a great weight had settled on her chest. For every tiny breath she took, the weight grew heavier.

A hand touched her shoulder.

'You OK?' Wilfredo asked, leaning over from the backseat, newly awake.

Este responded by spinning the wheel counterclockwise. The SUV careened into the oncoming lanes. This was a bad idea, Este knew, so she took a sharp left, bouncing off the highway onto the opposite shoulder.

Except there was no opposite shoulder. Just gravel, grass, and soon – trees.

'Este!' Wilfredo yelled, grabbing for the wheel. 'Hit the brakes!'

But Este couldn't do it. She understood logically that she should but had no idea where the brakes were, much less how to use them.

A hand joined her own on the steering wheel, another touched her wrist. It was Alice. She smiled at her.

'This is fun but stop the car,' she said without a hint of judgment or fear. 'Right foot, center pedal.'

Este stepped on the brakes with such force it felt like they might flip. Gravel fired in every direction as they fishtailed to a stop. Alice immediately pulled the emergency brake, turned off the car, and hopped out. She came around and opened the driver's side door. Este waited for a lecture but got a hug instead.

'Come here,' Alice said, holding her tight.

Este unsnapped her seatbelt and climbed out. The treetops were lit up gold with the morning sun and she inhaled the rich scent of the surrounding forest. Though it was summer, the air was crisp at this altitude.

'You OK?' Alice asked.

'I don't know,' Este said, looking around. 'Probably just need some rest.'

'I can drive,' Alice said.

'I'm . . . I'm sorry,' Este said.

'It's OK,' Alice said, hugging her again.

Este scoffed.

Alice hugged her again.

The nearest trees weren't the old-growth kind they'd passed in Yosemite. They were young, thin. The ground below wasn't bare but overflowing with flora – the tree canopy wasn't broad enough to block out the sun. This sparked a memory.

'I want to say all this burned at one point, maybe in '06 or '07,' Este said. 'All the hundred-year-old trees were destroyed, but the pines are already coming back. You can't even tell there was a fire.'

'Growing up in Colorado, they talked about that a lot,' Alice said. 'Fire as an agent of renewal. Nature doesn't tear anything down unless it has a plan for what comes next.'

Este nodded, considering this in terms of the quakes. She hoped this was some kind of window into the future and wanted to allow her senses to absorb the beauty, a rare optimistic forward glimpse.

TWENTY-FOUR

Alice liked the cars of the future. Though the concept was the same as what she remembered from the 90s and early 2000s, everything – *everything* – was electronic. It was like being at the helm of the Starship *Enterprise*. Instead of turning dials and pushing clunky buttons to adjust the air conditioning, they were choices on a touch screen like Este's tablet. Even the odometer and mileage counter were digital, something she had to keep an eye on to make sure they didn't run low on fuel.

Este slept as they left Lake Tahoe, but Wilfredo stayed up and chatted with Alice. He'd grown up in an LA suburb and was living at home while finishing his undergraduate degree, hoping to get into a good law school in the spring. Unlike Este, both his parents – second-generation Chicano dad, first-generation Korean mom – had survived the quakes and were now in Arizona.

'They got lucky,' Wilfredo said. 'They had friends in Flagstaff who not only took them into their home but also helped my dad get a job.'

'How come you didn't go with them?' Alice asked.

'At the beginning, there wasn't any room for me,' Wilfredo said. 'Also, I wasn't ready to leave LA. Then I met Este.'

'How was that?'

'Like inviting a good hurricane into your life if that makes sense,' he said, nodding to Este asleep next to him in the backseat. 'I'd never met anyone like her before. She's tough, but she really cares about people. Nothing makes her angrier than people getting screwed. *Nothing*. And a lot of people got screwed in the LA quakes.'

Alice wondered what Rahsaan would say about her if asked. She pictured him. The first memory that came to mind was of him in his home office, bent over his computer, working on a report relating to the expansion of a local elementary school. She wondered how different he looked now. Could he really be fifty years old? And if so, would he even remember her, much less how much they loved one another?

It suddenly felt like a fool's errand, this racing to her husband's side. She'd thought about what it would mean to her but not him. And if he rejected her out of hand, if he'd moved on, remarried, had a new life and new love, how would she feel then?

She still had to find him. If only to learn what had happened to her.

She turned to voice as much to Wilfredo, only to see that he'd fallen back asleep. She returned her gaze to the narrow highway through the Sierra Nevada range ahead of her.

It wasn't until Reno came into view a couple hours later that Alice saw Este stirring in the backseat. Alice had never been to Reno but could see even from the highway that the city was expanding rapidly. At least a dozen tower cranes rose over a cluster of buildings she took to be the downtown area, and another half-dozen rose on the far side of town.

'That's Sparks,' Este said. 'Like a sister city. When people moved inland from the West Coast to escape the quakes, a bunch settled here.'

'Makes sense,' Alice said.

More and more cars and trucks crowded the highway now, despite gas prices listed on the marquees of the stations they passed that appeared astronomical to Alice. She caught sight of another one in the side-view mirror but ended up seeing herself, too. She realized she hadn't seen her reflection clearly up until this moment.

'What?' Este asked.

'Nothing,' Alice said quickly. 'Just another memory.'

'Of what?' Este prodded.

'Getting this haircut? It sounds random, but it's the last outing my mother and I went on that I remember. I was in treatment. I was getting really sick to the point I could barely get out of bed.'

'This is the leukemia?' Este asked.

'Yeah, but one day I was well enough to go downstairs to the hospital cafeteria, so my mom asked if she could take me out on a field trip to get my hair cut. This is the same haircut. I got it on . . . May 20, 2003.'

'You remember the exact date?'

Alice cocked her head, considering this. 'Yeah, my diagnosis was on March 4, 2003. Radiation started maybe two days after that. I don't remember the specifics, but I was in bad shape from it by April 22. That's my mother's birthday. I know I was in the hospital on May 3 because that was my and Rahsaan's anniversary. We celebrated in the oncology ward. My last haircut was maybe two or three weeks later. I cut it shorter than I ever had before, knowing I might not be able to take care of it.'

'Like that?' Este asked, indicating Alice's current hair length.

'Yeah, I didn't recognize it at first. Then I remembered why it was that short.'

Este went still. 'How sure are you?'

'One hundred percent,' Alice said. 'When you're counting down, dates tend to stand out. Will I make it to my dad's birthday? To the Fourth of July? To my own birthday? To my parents' anniversary? Oh, and please don't let me die on Christmas or Easter or something that would be ruined forever for my surviving family members.'

'What was your daily routine like then?' Este asked.

'Tests and more tests, I guess?' Alice said. 'Checking protein levels. And, if I'm remembering right, white blood cells.'

'To check for abnormalities,' Este explained. 'Lymphocytic leukemia is all about white blood cell build-up.'

'Ah. That. There were lots of needles.'

'And the tests were in the morning?'

'Yeah. How'd you know? Oh, yeah. You're a nurse.'

But when Alice glanced in the rearview mirror, Este had the canister in her hand.

'The number on here is 30022250252180,' Este said. 'But read backwards it's 08:12:52 on 05, 22, 2003 or May 22, 2003. Hospitals use codes to obfuscate things from patients, but not so complicated you can't decipher them later.'

Alice almost laughed at the coincidence. But Este wasn't laughing.

'You think that canister has something to do with my disease?' Alice asked.

'I don't know,' Este said warily. 'I'm grasping at the same straws as you. But that number has to mean something, right? You say you only ever cut your hair that short a few days before this date, this May 22, 2003, right?'

'Right,' Alice agreed.

'Yet you have no surgical scars. No signs of cancer.'

'None,' Alice said. 'What're you getting at?'

'That maybe if your body can resurrect itself without bullet damage, it can do the same without cancer. Resurrecting itself as it was on the morning of May 22, 2003,' Este said, holding up the canister.

'That's . . . insane, right?' Alice asked.

'A week ago, I would've said insane, but now that I've seen not just you but a giant, white-tufted mountain lion come back to life, I'll go out on a limb and say the line between what I think is sane and insane these days is on the move.'

'So, I'm not a time traveler,' Alice said. 'Not a clone. Not a what – a zombie? Wolverine from the *X-Men*?'

'No. You, my friend, are a ghost.'

TWENTY-FIVE

A ghost. No sooner had the word left Este's mouth than both women laughed.

Then stopped, considering it.

'A ghost,' Alice said. 'But I can't move through walls or anything. I'm not haunting a house.'

'No, but maybe you're some kind of afterlife facsimile of a person who lived at the end of the twentieth century,' Este said. 'The treatment you describe is for late-stage cancer, so I think we can safely assume you probably died not long after this May 22 date. But instead of, say, a reincarnation or a genetic clone, you walk the Earth as the person you were when you died. But without the cancer.'

'Does that mean I don't age?' Alice asked.

'I doubt it,' Este said. 'I mean, you eat, you sleep, you have normal biological processes, so I'd imagine you're aging right now. But if you were to die, I'd guess that you'd start back over at the

May 22, 2003 you. Everything you'd experienced up until your death, any aging your body did, would be reset.'

Alice didn't know what to think. If it hadn't been a nurse telling her this, she would've found it easier to dismiss. A *ghost?* It was a strange word to use, but broken down as Este had done, it made some sense. If that was the case, what had she been doing for the intervening decades and why couldn't she remember?

This weighed heavily on her mind as they took the exit for the hospital in downtown Reno. Este pointed out a large gray building.

'The emergency room drop-off is around the corner,' she said. 'I'll take Wilfredo in first to get him situated, and then we'll decide what to do with you, OK?'

'OK.'

Leaving Casey with Alice, Este walked the newly awake but still bleary-eyed Wilfredo into the hospital. It was like stepping into the past, leaving the quake-riven world behind to slip into a fully functional, well-staffed hospital. There were Kleenex boxes. Indoor bathrooms. Actual magazines. A television broadcasting not just endless news but soap operas (reruns now, given the state of Hollywood).

It was probably as mind-blowing to Este as, say, the tablet was to Alice.

'Hi, my friend took a bad fall out past Virginia City,' Este told the receiving nurse at the front desk. 'He's dizzy and has a fever. He was unresponsive in the car on the way over with low breathing. Before that, he said he was having severe and acute onset pain in his head. He said his vision is blurry, too.'

It was a hodge-podge of nonsense but included the seven or eight buzzwords Este knew would be necessary to bump Wilfredo to the front of any waiting line. She was handed a clipboard of paperwork as an orderly hurried over with a wheelchair for Wilfredo. They moved from the waiting room to a glassed-in cubicle.

'Someone will be right in,' the orderly said, heading back out.

'Thank you.' As Este turned back to Wilfredo, she noticed his eyes were having trouble focusing. She took his hand. 'Hey, you OK?'

'Not really,' he slurred. 'Can you call my parents?'

'Of course. Um . . . do you have their number?'

'It's in the survivor database,' he said, head lolling back. 'What's going to happen to me here?'

'They'll X-ray you, which'll spark an MRI, then likely surgery,'

Este explained. 'You'll be in recovery for a few weeks but then good to go. You'll be driving like a maniac through the LAQZ in no time.'

Wilfredo grinned and shook his head. 'I, well, I don't think I'm going back,' he said. 'If this isn't a wake-up call that it's time to start dealing with the present instead of playing dress-up in the past, I don't know what is.'

Este bristled. 'Fredo, the LoP is on borrowed time. It's *all* falling apart. It's just a question of when.'

'I know.'

'You really want to live like that? Never knowing when the life you've built is going to be yanked away again?'

'You're right,' Wilfredo said. 'The LoP will keep shrinking until it's gone completely and the whole planet is Quake Cities. But, we've got a choice. Keep thinking life as we know it will come back. Scientists or the government or whoever will wave a wand and suddenly we're back at Staples for a Lakers game like nothing happened. *Or*, figure out what you and the people close to you need and put in the work to make it happen. Otherwise, what does it matter if you survived? You might as well be back in one of those mass graves in the QZ.'

Este had never heard Wilfredo talk like this. 'What about "us"?' Este asked.

Wilfredo chuckled. 'Us? The only time you say anything about an "us" is when you mean it the least. Sure, we made a great team, but that's not because of me. It's because you're driven way past what's normal. Part of that, sure, is you blame yourself for your sister. Part of it is you feel responsible for not getting more people out alive. But the biggest part is that part of *you* is still buried in the LAQZ.'

'Oh, and you think I'll never be able to find myself without your help?' Este asked, agitated.

'It's not that. Not at all. I think you should leave it buried. Learn to walk away. Build a new life. Put stuff behind you once and for all.'

Este scowled. 'I know I'm a screw-up,' she said evenly. 'I know I'm stuck out there, half-scared, half-full of crap. But I own that. At least I'm not a tourist who could go home to his family at any time. I don't have that luxury. You do but, for whatever reason, you stuck around anyway, playing cowboy. Now, the going gets rough for once and you're the first to pull out. Why not? You have that option. But it's why I knew I could never fully rely on you. You say I only use "us" when I mean it the least? Well, you're the one who's decided I'm expendable, not me. Good luck out there.'

Este turned to leave, almost running into a nurse.

'Excuse me, are you family?' the nurse asked. 'Or someone authorized to make medical decisions on behalf of the patient in case of emergency?'

Este looked back at Wilfredo. He suddenly looked much younger, a scared teenager. She turned back to the nurse and shook her head.

'I'm not,' she said, halfway out the door. 'Sorry.'

She found Alice walking Casey through a park across the street. She forced a smile so Alice couldn't tell how distraught she was.

'How is he?' Alice asked.

'Fine for now,' Este said. 'They're taking him in for X-rays. Should know soon how bad it is, and then they can figure out a course of treatment. Now, what about you? Am I walking you back in there? Or are we going to see about this husband of yours?'

Alice looked down as if Casey was holding onto the answer for her.

'The latter,' she said quietly. 'All I want to do is go home. If that's with Rahsaan or if that's somewhere else, I need to know where to start looking. Does that make sense?'

'More than you could know,' Este said.

TWENTY-SIX

Este led Alice and Casey through the heart of Reno. Despite all the expansion and construction, the center of the city was still anchored by a warren of casinos and their neighboring hotels. Garish signage and the promise of loose slots and cheap longnecks appeared to draw a steady stream of people.

'It's not what you think,' Este said, watching Alice's gaze. 'There are still gamblers, but the government subsidizes the hotels to open up rooms to construction workers and displaced people. They're at capacity.'

'I thought we were looking for this database.'

'That's the thing,' Este began. 'I'm worried about alarm bells. The national survivor database is monitored from Washington, but those servers can probably be accessed by all kinds of people. Whoever came after you would have those resources.'

'Meaning what?'

'Meaning, as soon as we log in and look for someone like your husband, I bet they'll be pinged. They trace the IP address back to Reno and suddenly we're on the run again.'

'They can *do* that?' Alice asked, surprised.

'Oh, I guess the internet was more fun when you were around,' Este said. 'There's no privacy anymore. Zero. You're online at your own risk.'

'How do we avoid that?'

'By hiding in a crowd,' Este said.

Este selected one of the casinos and led Alice to a side door that opened directly onto the gaming floor. Dozens of people milled around, though few seemed to be playing games. Some drank, many chatted, others watched television.

Este eyed the various signs pointing the way to the concierge desk, parking garage, restaurants, and more before spying the one she wanted.

'Upstairs,' she announced.

The casino's second floor housed its vast conference rooms and banquet halls. They were currently empty, though the tables inside made the setup look like a large cafeteria. Este wondered how many people they must feed every day. When she glanced at Casey, whose nose was twitching, she figured he was wondering the same thing. She'd have to find him some food soon.

'There,' Este said, pointing to a glassed-in business center at the far end of the floor. 'Just what we need.'

The business center, three long tables with four computer stations set up on each, was devoid of people. Este sent out a silent prayer of thanks to the Universe and gestured to a chair.

'More computers of the future?' Alice asked as she sat, nodding to the flat screens with keyboards in front of them.

'Yeah, but these are connected to every other computer on earth just about,' Este said, tapping the keyboard to bring the screen to life.

'Yeah, we had the internet way back in 2003,' Alice said.

'Oh. Duh.'

Este opened four new windows and tinkered with the computer's admin tools.

'What're you doing?' Alice asked.

'Some light hacking to mask our identity. It won't hold up, but to casual observers it'll look like we're operating out of the hotel's corporate offices in Atlanta.'

'Why?'

'Two things – first, to access the survivor database to grab Wilfredo's parents' phone number,' Este explained.

She opened up the national survivor database website, a spare but user-friendly directory, and typed in Luis Lugo. The image of a man who looked like a forty-year-old version of Wilfredo appeared on screen together with contact information.

'Next, I go into the encrypted site Wilfredo and I use to communicate with clients.'

'Should I be writing this down?' Alice asked.

'Given your memory, you should be writing everything down,' Este said, scoffing.

She opened a new window that was simply a black background with a flashing green cursor. As she typed, different letters from the ones she keyed on the keyboard appeared on screen. A message board appeared with several notes on it. Este opened one.

Hey, looking for a good pathfinder team for LAQZ job. You came highly recommended. Contact for details.

'That sounds promising,' Alice offered, absorbing the new technology.

'It's fake,' Este said. 'The people who are after you know you're with me and are hoping I slip up and give away our location.'

She indicated all the messages down the screen. 'It's all of these,' she said before deleting them. 'But if it wasn't, I'd be worried they were closing in. Now hang on. Gotta call Wilfredo's dad.'

She leaned over to a telephone in the middle of the row, typed the number listed on it into the encrypted window, and waited. The phone rang a second later. She picked it up, typed Luis's parents' number into the keyboard, and waited. When someone answered, she moved away.

'*¿Es este Luis?*' Este asked. '*Mi nombre es Estefanía. Soy amiga de Wilfredo. Él está bien y recuperándose, pero tuvo un accidente.*'

Alice turned to the computer next to her and clicked on the hotel's website. Gorgeous photos of resorts in different locales appeared, no indication whatsoever of the current spate of disasters. *Life in the LoP*, she surmised. At the bottom of the page, however, a news ticker ran through the day's headlines.

Twin Quakes Rock Straits of Magellan, Interrupting Trade.

São Paulo Without Power After 300 Days.

Nigerian Oil Production Rises to 60% of Capacity Following Post-Quake Reconstruction.

Charleston Braces for Hurricane Sarah Following Minor Quake.

She looked back at Este's computer, catching sight of the national survivor database URL. How easy it would be to type Rahsaan's name. But she trusted Este. If she thought this would lead to her capture, she had no reason to believe it wouldn't.

She wondered if there were other names she could try that wouldn't set off alarm bells. Her parents were probably out but what about a neighbor? A friend? Anyone whose presence in this strange future would provide a sort of safety line back to her own life. Proof that she'd existed and there might be answers.

She wracked her brain for a name that might work. Then she remembered Ben. Would they really stake out a college ex who happened to then be her oncologist?

Unlikely.

She typed in the URL, the directory appeared, and she put in Ben Ganske.

No results found. Please try your search again.

Oh, well.

She considered trying another name but had the same problem. Who wouldn't be tied back to her? There was a toolbar with an internet search icon at the top of the browser page.

Huh. Computers of the future were easy.

She typed in Ben's name again and hit Return.

To her surprise, a whole range of pages came back, including several photos confirming this was the Ben she knew. He was older, still brown-haired but graying at the temples, with sallow features and a serious expression. The first page was a college faculty director revealing that Ben D. Ganske, MD, was a Professor of Medicine (Oncology) at the Feinberg School of Medicine, Northwestern University. A short bio followed with awards, specialties, boards Ben served on, and finally, education. University of Colorado School of Medicine, 1991 to 1995.

It wasn't much but it was enough. Proof that Alice had existed. That her memories weren't completely faulty. She had been an incoming freshman in the fall of 1994, and Ben had graduated the following spring. It added up.

Este, done with her call, leaned over. 'Who's that?' she asked.

'College boyfriend,' Alice said. 'Figured he'd be safe enough to look up. Check out the dates.'

'You think this rules out time traveler or brain transplant?' Este shook her head.

Alice sighed. Este rested her hand on her shoulder.

'Kidding,' Este said. 'But I can do you one better.'

She nodded to her computer screen. It was different now, an image of a desert sunset with a dozen icons arranged to one side.

'What's that?' Alice asked.

'Fredo's dad's computer,' Este said. 'He gave me remote access so I could check the survivor database and make it look like it came from a computer at his workplace.'

'And they can't track that back here?' Alice asked. 'Or get Wilfredo's dad in trouble?'

'Nah, but we have a window of maybe two or three minutes. We have to be fast.'

Este opened a browser and typed in the database's URL. She turned the keyboard over to Alice who entered Rahsaan Topbas and hit Return.

Three pieces of information came back alongside Rahsaan's name. His date of birth – April 13, 1976. His job – urban planner. And – Camp Ben Nighthorse Campbell, Building 9, Row A, Sector 16.

'What's that mean?' Alice asked.

'It means he's alive,' Este replied. 'That's one of the big displaced people's camps outside Denver.'

Alice couldn't believe it. Rahsaan was alive. The news filled her with joy like little ever had. There was no photo, so she imagined him aged up like Ben, a man she recognized but a bit older. All she wanted to do was look into his eyes and see if there was anything there for her to come back to.

This triggered a second thought. She hesitated, then typed his last name into the database. Two names came back. Neither were in Colorado.

'What're you doing?' Este asked.

'If, well, we were separated in some way for all that time, if maybe he thought I had died for real, I wanted to see if . . . if maybe he had a new wife, maybe even a family,' Alice said. 'I mean, I know a lot of women don't change their names, but if there isn't another Topbas . . .'

'It gives you hope,' Este said. 'I hear you.'

'How far is it to Denver?' Alice asked.

'It's a long day's travel, but if we leave now, we'll be there this time tomorrow.'

'Then let's g—'

Alice's eyes fell onto the corner of the screen. One of the windows Este had opened was just visible, half a message partially obscured by the others. But what caught Alice's eye was her own face looking back at her.

'How do you have my picture?' Alice asked.

Este tried to close the window, but Alice was too fast. She clicked on the image, bringing the entire message forward. It was the warning to salvage teams. That the subject was dangerous but that the bounty on her was $1,000,000.

'Is that . . . what is that?' Alice asked.

Este was caught so off guard, she didn't know how to respond.

'Was I a job?' Alice pressed. 'You said you stumbled across me underground somewhere. Was that a lie?'

'No, that wasn't a lie,' Este said.

'So it was a coincidence? You get this notice, then *wham* you find me later that day or something?'

'Not exactly,' Este admitted.

'Huh,' Alice said, scoffing. 'Then exactly what was it? I guess hunting me down makes more sense than a perfect stranger just happening along and trying to help me.'

'Alice, that's not it,' Este countered.

'But it is, isn't it?' Alice asked.

'Maybe at the beginning,' Este said. 'But things change.'

'Whoa,' Alice said. '"Things change?" So, you're saying at one time I was a high-dollar target for you but now you're escorting me halfway across the country out of the goodness of your heart?'

Alice got to her feet. 'How do I know this isn't a trap? That you're not still planning to cash me in for a—'

Alice's words were cut off by a bark from Casey so sharp both women jumped. The dog had been so quiet tucked under the chair, they'd almost forgotten he was there.

'What is it, boy?' Este asked as the dog moved to the business center windows.

The hotel-casino's second-floor lights blinked out.

'What's going on?' Alice asked.

'I don't know,' Este said, walking to the door.

Casey put himself between her and the doorway. He growled into the darkness.

'Is it a quake?' Alice asked. 'Should we get downstairs?'

'Not enough time,' Este said. 'If the electrical grid has been hit, the building's next. We're safer to stay in place.'

Outside, dull red emergency lights glowed to life. As they grew brighter, Casey barked again, louder. There was movement in the darkness. At first, they looked like people – casino workers? – lumbering carefully through the black. But they grew larger and appeared to walk on four legs instead of two.

Mountain lions.

TWENTY-SEVEN

'Oh my God,' Este whispered, pulling Casey backwards.

'How could they have found us?' Alice choked, wide-eyed with terror.

'They couldn't have,' Este said, stumbling into the computer table. 'It's impossible. This . . . this is something else.'

The mountain lions, four now, reached the business center and glanced around. They didn't look like they were in any big hurry. Their noses twitched as they inhaled scents from within. Then they turned, one at a time, to stare at Alice.

Alice stared back, horrified. The lion nearest her reared back and slammed its head, full force, into the glass. The entire room shook.

'We have to get out of here!' Alice yelled.

Este looked around the room for any avenue of escape – an air duct, a service hatch, even a way into the ceiling. There was nothing. They were sealed in. She turned to the computers, considering their potential as weapons. Given all four of the mountain lions were now single-mindedly smashing their heads against the heavy glass, she figured pain wouldn't slow them down much.

But she had another idea. She ran down the row of computers, sweeping them all onto the floor.

'Help me raise these upright,' Este said, grabbing the empty table. 'Up on their ends.'

Though the tables were heavy, the two women managed to get

the first one vertical, the table-top facing the windows like makeshift ramparts.

'Next one,' Este gasped.

Within seconds, they had all four tables up on their ends and shoved against the windows. The mountain lions continued to smash against the glass, but even as the room shook, the heavy tables did not.

'What now?' Alice asked.

'As soon as they're through the glass, they'll attack the tables trying to get to us. But with the windows broken, we can turn the last table like a revolving door and get out onto the floor.'

'Then what?'

'We run.'

It wasn't much of a plan. The most they could hope for was getting to the fire stairs and making it down to the streets before the cats caught up. If they could get in a vehicle, they could get away. There was no fighting these monsters. Evasion was the only way to survive.

Casey kept barking, and the noise of the lions smashing their heads into the windows grew louder. There was a splintering sound now as well, the window and door frames cracking apart. Though they couldn't see the creatures, the shuddering of the entire room told the women the lions were close.

Alice took Este's hand.

'What're you afraid of? You'll just come back in a few hours,' Este said, trying to lighten the situation even as her voice quavered.

'Maybe so, but not looking forward to getting torn apart by wild animals?'

'Eh, at least you won't remember it.'

Alice almost laughed but was interrupted by the sheering of glass from one of the frames. Barely a second later, two snarling and furious lions slammed into the tables, trying to bash through them to get to Alice.

'Now!' Este said.

Yanking Casey's leash to make him follow, Este pushed the table farthest to the right to make a narrow passageway to the shattered window. There was barely enough space for her to slide through, but it would have to do.

'Come on!' she cried.

Alice moved to the window first as the next two mountain lions barreled through the next pane over, slamming into the tables. The force of their impact caused one of the tables to fall backward, hitting Casey's leash. It flew from Este's hand, and Casey lunged away to attack the mountain lions.

'Casey, no!' Este yelled.

But the Alsatian already had its jaws around the neck of one of the large cats that had managed to wedge the top half of its body between the two tables. It raised its forepaw and slapped Casey away as if he was no more than a hummingbird, the white tufts of its ears just visible in the dim light.

'Casey!' Este yelled, but the dog was now at the back of the room.

She looked to Alice, who was already edging her way out of the business center, rotating one of the tables to keep its heavy surface between her and the lions. She had to make a decision.

'Go!' she yelled at Alice. 'I have to get Casey!'

She ran back for the Alsatian, but the mountain lions were almost through the tables.

Dumb dog, she thought as she lifted Casey's head. To add insult to injury, he tried to bite her before realizing who it was.

One of the lions was only a few feet away, wedging itself between two of the tables as it clawed forward. It was only a matter of seconds before it reached them.

'Hang on!' yelled Alice, coming back into the business center.

'I told you to run!' Este cried.

But if Alice heard her, she gave no indication. Este leaped up, grabbed one of the upright tables, and brought it crashing down on the mountain lion. As the other three lions realigned themselves to pounce on Alice, Este grabbed a second table and yanked it down as well. There wasn't enough room for it to land, however, so it merely gouged a large hole in the back wall.

A hole large enough for a person to squeeze through but not a lion.

'Alice!' Este yelled. 'Up there!'

Alice spied the opportunity immediately. Using the fallen table like a ramp, she raced up it and dove through the hole. Este rolled on her side, lifted Casey as best she could, and followed.

One of the big cats roared in frustration, swiping at Este's leg as she passed, digging a pair of claws deep into her calf as she went. Este groaned in pain but forced herself to keep going. She shoveled Casey through the hole like a basketball player executing a lay-up, then followed.

At the last minute, she imagined falling into a pit of more lions.

In reality, the hole opened into one of the hotel's smaller banquet halls. Este landed on a small stage and rolled forward, coming to a stop at Alice's feet.

'Come on!' Alice said, grabbing Este's hand.

Este grabbed for Casey's leash and followed Alice out of the room, limping as blood trickled down her leg from the cut. They ran out of the banquet room, down a short hallway lit only by emergency lights, and found the fire stairs. They were through the door and down the steps before the lions knew where they'd gone.

Este was thinking they were home free when it occurred to her the lions couldn't have been the ones who turned off the lights. A person must have done that. Someone who was probably still in the building.

'Alice, wait up!' Este yelled, halfway down the stairs, her throbbing leg slowing her down.

She burst through the doors into the lobby after Alice, only to find her friend surrounded by men in hazmat suits. Tranquilizer guns were aimed at her torso. A couple more men held up the same kind of orange grenades the team in Los Angeles had brought.

'Este?' Alice asked, voice filled with fear.

Three darts flew into Alice's torso.

Este felt a tug as two darts struck Casey, causing him to flinch and fall. Este looked out the window to the street, seeing all the people who'd been on the gaming floor earlier were now outside, looking in. Reno police kept them back to allow more men in hazmat suits to enter.

Damn.

The first dart hit her in the arm, the impact like a punch. The second entered her neck, the needle tip drawing blood.

She turned to the shooter, smirking. *I'm still standing, aren't I?*

A second later and she was on the ground, head resting on Casey's paws.

TWENTY-EIGHT

Alice awoke in the most comfortable bed she'd ever been in. It was as wide as a kitchen table and covered in pillows and thick blankets. It looked like something from a catalog dedicated to outrageous luxuries for the ultra-rich.

She raised her head, fearing the onset of pain or just disorientation. Neither came. She didn't know where she was and had no memory of ever being in a place like this. But at least she didn't have the hazy, confusing feeling she'd had when she awoke naked on the hot streets of the LAQZ.

She reached for her name and found it. Alice Helena Rhodes. Alix to some. Allie to none. She was – or had been – in Reno, Nevada. After being pursued by monster lions through a casino with her friend, Este, she'd been captured.

She reasoned that if they'd wanted her dead, that could've happened by now. Instead, she was in a luxury suite, maybe even in a fancy hotel, wearing pale blue pajamas with slipper socks. She wore a wristband with a bar code and alphanumeric string on it. The sun streamed through a window overlooking a city she didn't recognize. It wasn't Reno. New York, maybe? Chicago? It was intact, so not one of the Quake Cities.

A young woman sat on a silver sofa opposite her holding a clipboard-sized electronic device in her hand.

'Good morning, Alice,' she said. 'How are you feeling?'

'Disoriented,' Alice replied.

'That's not good,' the woman said, then whispered something into a lapel mic. 'But we can do something about it.'

'Where am I?' Alice asked.

The woman looked about ready to answer when the door opened. Two men entered, one short and in his mid-fifties. The other, to Alice's surprise, was Ben Ganske.

'Alice!' Ben said. 'I can't believe it!'

'Ben! Oh my God! What're you doing here?'

'Well, until a few hours ago, wringing my hands worrying about whether we'd get you back here safely or not,' he said, leaning over and giving her a quick hug. 'It's so good to see you. I see you've met Dr Abouzeid.' He indicated the woman opposite Alice, then nodded to the man who'd come in with him. 'And this is Dr Kapur.'

Dr Kapur leaned forward to shake Alice's hand.

'Do you remember me?' he asked.

'Should I?'

'When you were in treatment in Colorado many years ago, I was one of the admittedly several doctors you saw.'

She ran a mental slideshow. She saw him alongside Ben, just twenty years younger.

'Of course!' Alice said, sitting up. 'But, where am I, Ben? What's going on here?'

'You're in Chicago,' Ben said, taking a seat. 'At the Kellner Group facility. "Profectum vitae".'

'What's that?'

'"Progress of life",' Ben said. 'This is where you were reborn.'

'I was born in Boulder, Colorado,' Alice protested.

'I know it's confusing,' Ben said. 'But I have a video for just these occasions.'

Dr Abouzeid handed him her tablet. He touched a button on the screen and gave it to Alice.

'What is it?' Alice asked.

'An introduction,' Ben said.

'To whom?'

'Well, to you.'

An image of Alice appeared on screen, smiling and waving to the camera.

'Hey!' the onscreen Alice said, a silly hat on her head. 'Guess who's celebrating a birthday?'

'Oh my God!' Alice said.

The image cut to Alice blowing out candles on a cake marked with the number twenty-nine, surrounded by doctors or technicians in lab coats, including Ben and Dr Kapur. This segued to a video of Alice, now in a lab coat herself, working on an experiment in a lab.

Then exercising in a gym. Also, sitting in a park, chatting with others. Then back at work on another experiment.

Then wearing another silly hat as she blew out the candles on another cake marked with the number twenty-nine.

'Hey!' Alice said to the camera. 'Guess who's celebrating a birthday?'

The image cut to yet another birthday cake with candles and the number twenty-nine being blown out. The image faded out.

'If the video was intended to make me less confused, it didn't work,' Alice said.

Ben laughed and put the tablet away. 'It was really just to show you where you've been all this time.'

'And where's that?' Alice asked.

'Well, here!' Ben said with a wave of his hand. 'And at our other facilities around the globe. Working with us.'

'On what?'

'Everything under the sun,' Ben said. 'Particularly now that the world is going through such tremendous upheavals, finding a way to either suspend human life until the planet settles again or resurrect a life once it has been snuffed out has become our number-one goal. It would unlock the mystery of immortality. Instead of facing our extinction, we could be looking at a new way for mankind to endure and thrive.'

'Jeez,' said Alice.

'Yeah,' Ben said. 'Leave behind one life only to find out you could be instrumental in saving the human race in the next. But we're getting ahead of ourselves. What do you remember about your last days? Once it was understood your cancer was terminal.'

'Very little.'

'Do you remember me introducing you to the Kellner Group? They're the firm that identified you, or more accurately, your cells, as a candidate for their protocols. I was on their board.'

It rang a distant bell. 'Maybe?' Alice replied. 'There were so many doctors.'

'This was a couple of months before the end. Around the same time you were making other decisions relating to organ and cornea donations.'

It came back to her. Of the many difficult days toward the end, this was one of the hardest. She remembered Rahsaan having a particularly tough time with it.

'Yeah,' Alice said. 'Now I remember.'

Ben looked ready to say something else, but Alice cut him off by rising from the bed. Her body felt good. No fatigue, no sense of injury. She looked out the window again. The building she was in was a few blocks up from a river. To the east, she saw one of the Great Lakes. Which one was next to Chicago? She couldn't remember. Superior? Michigan?

'Alice?' Ben asked. 'You still with us?'

'When did I die?' she asked. 'The first time.'

'Oh, um . . . July 20, 2003,' Ben said. 'You were at home. You died early in the morning, in bed.'

'And you took my body later?' Alice said, indicating herself.

'Oh, no – that's not how this works at all,' Ben said. 'Your body, the body that died that morning, was buried. Your life ended.'

'Apparently not.'

'Well, that was a surprise to us, too,' Ben went on. 'While we worked to save you, we routinely took various tissue and blood samples to study your cancer, including DNA, RNA, and a complete set of your RNA engrams, all of which were encoded onto bacteria for safekeeping. What we discovered was that fighting Stage Four cancer – or even Stage Three – from a genetic point of view is nearly impossible as the tumors have already grown out of control. But if we were to de-age the cells, literally flip a switch in their DNA to age them backwards into something eliminable, like you'd find in a Stage Two or Stage One patient, you could defeat their cancer.'

'My cancer,' Alice emphasized.

'Yes.'

'So, how does that lead to . . .' Alice indicated her body, 'all this?'

'That's where it gets interesting.'

'Oh, I was interested before.'

Ben and his colleagues laughed. 'Well, your cells lived on and regenerated – and not just your cancer cells. It was like a genetic snapshot of who you were on the day the sample was extracted.'

'May 22, 2003. At eight in the morning.'

'Precisely,' Ben said.

'But that's my genetic makeup, no?' Alice asked. 'Like, you could clone me or something. How did I regenerate as a twenty-eight-year-old woman with all my memories? My friend likened it to being a ghost.'

'That's a good term for it,' Ben agreed. 'For decades, it was believed memories were only stored through a pattern of synaptic connections between neurons. What I discovered was that there is also chemical memory encoded in RNA. These types of memories can be copied and thereby transferred between organisms of the same genetic makeup with ease. And cells are like any living thing. They have but one desire: to reproduce.'

Alice suddenly had a good idea where this was going.

'So, you helped them along?'

'We provided them with all the building blocks of human life. Proteins, amino acids, fats, calcium apatite, trace amounts of metals from iron to iodine, carbohydrates, and so on, including water – sixty percent of your body. The bacteria onto which your genetic "ghost" was encoded, to use your word, attacks these raw materials like swarming piranha skeletonizing a cow—'

'Vivid,' Alice interjected.

'And the bacteria use every cell they consume to reproduce until they form a new human body. You. Exactly as you – and it – remember it to be,' Ben concluded. 'From the length of your hair to the density of your toenails.'

'That's incredible,' Alice said, her mind racing with the possibilities.

'We thought so, too. But once we broke down the elemental composition of a human body, the cells did the rest, taking what they needed, leaving the excess behind.'

'Can I make new memories now?' Alice asked.

'Yes,' Ben said. 'Think of it as if your body and mind from 2003 were merely suspended – aging not a minute – until your rebirth. Rather than hit reset, you sort of "un-pause" and go back to living your life as if nothing happened.'

'But my friend Este saw me get shot,' Alice said. 'I wasn't in a lab then. No proteins or amino acids to pull from. How'd I come out?'

Ben looked to Dr Kapur to take this question.

'That's why your release out in the wild was of such great concern to us,' Dr Kapur said. 'Your genetic "ghost" can't distinguish between laboratory conditions and living creatures. It's like this. When you die – when you were shot and your brain activity ceased – an enzyme is triggered. The ghost bacterium is released into the air and, indiscriminately, seeks the organic material it needs for you to resurrect.'

This information sent shivers through Alice's body.

'Living creatures?' she asked.

Ben sighed, leaning in. 'Now do you understand why it was so important to us to get you back before anyone else was killed?'

'I . . . kill people?' Alice asked.

'Not you, your "ghost",' Ben said. 'It's a byproduct of the process. We're working on various solutions, but again, it's why our work must be so closely guarded and protected. Interest in the results means that we've become extremely well-funded over the years. But in the wrong hands, well . . .'

'How many people have to die so I can "resurrect"?' Alice asked, horrified.

'Four,' Dr Kapur said, the number ringing out as if he was a judge handing down a sentence. 'It's why, when we send out trackers, our mountain lion-like chimeras, they're genetically programmed to go after their target's DNA and no one else's.'

'How do you program an animal like that?' Alice asked.

'We alter and accelerate their natural tendency toward filial imprinting,' Ben explained, holding up a canister. 'If we inject the target's DNA into one of their special canisters, the creature is born not imprinting on some already-absent mother, but their target. It sounds complicated, but it's as simple as speeding up the development of an animal's prey drive. They're born, they're confused, they're hungry. We funnel all those instincts toward, in this case, *you*. The genetic material of the target is brought into their system in a bacterial form created by the canister, to limit their prey drive to a single genetic makeup.'

'Tell that to the guys who got eaten out there,' Alice said, incredulous.

'That wasn't supposed to happen,' Ben said. 'The chimeras are designed to retreat when provoked, not defend themselves. The situation seems to have been confused when there were both hostiles and the target occupying the same space, made even worse when they resurrected. Luckily, we had people in the field to help redirect them remotely.'

'Redirect them?'

'Their handlers were watching from a safe distance. They couldn't call them off when all hell broke loose, but they could dart the resurrections with your genetic material to get them back on target.'

'Does the government or the military know you're this reckless?'

'Who do you think paid for their development?' Ben asked.

Alice sighed. She should've figured that. 'What would've happened if they'd killed me?'

'You would die, your ghost bacterium would be released, and, in theory, it would attack the lions, killing them permanently as their mission was accomplished and giving you just enough living organic material to reform. Only, you'd be weak and without a memory. It gives us time to swoop in and collect you.'

'That's . . . extreme.'

'The alternative is much worse,' Ben said. 'If you're killed in some other fashion, you're an immediate mortal danger to all others in the vicinity. It's imperfect, but in an emergency it's about keeping others safe.'

Alice nodded slowly. It explained the hazmat suits, the empty canister that must've contained all that was her at one point, and her resurrections.

'So, what now? I mean, all this secrecy tells me you might be trying to avoid public scrutiny. And if you've gone to all this trouble to track me down, I can't imagine you'd let me just walk out that door, right?'

'It's true,' Ben said. 'What exists inside you is proprietary to this company. A trade secret, I guess? One that, as I said, has become increasingly valuable in an age in which life expectancy is up in the air. And as you donated not just your tissue but also your organs to science, in fact, you yourself are legally the property of the Kellner Group.'

Alice choked. Ben grinned.

'But that's a very gray area, you must agree,' Ben said. 'Which is why we have this.'

He removed a syringe from his pocket and placed it in front of Alice.

'Inside the syringe is a governor serum that erases not just the enzyme that activates your resurrection but the original "ghost" bacterium as well. Flushes it away as if it was never there. Your immortality can come to an end right now. You can walk out that door with a new start.'

'To go where?'

'Wherever you like.'

'To Colorado? To Rahsaan? Do you know where he is?'

'Of course,' Ben said. 'We'll even help you get there.'

'In return for . . .?' Alice asked.

'Just a blood sample,' Ben said. 'Your body has been out there in the wild for several days. How it's reacted to its environment, to microbes, to stress – that's information that would be very valuable to us.'

'You couldn't have just drawn that while I was out?' Alice asked. 'I doubt I would've missed it.'

'Well, we're also interested in your impressions and perception of what you've seen. How and when new memories were formed and the way you're able to narrativize them as that plays a lot into the development of self-perception.'

'And that's it? No more pursuit? No more mountain lions?'

'No, but also no more resurrections and no more immortality.'

Alice's gaze traveled from the syringe to Ben's smiling face and back again.

'I didn't say it'd be an easy choice,' he said.

'No, no,' Alice said. 'The choice is easy. It's whether or not I trust you that's hard.'

'Ah, fair enough,' Ben said. 'All I can do is give you my word.'

TWENTY-NINE

The Reno Federal Building was a ten-story building shaped like a half-moon encased in faux gray granite. It looked as uninviting as it did anonymous. While it didn't quite elicit the oppressive dread of a mid-century Brutalist slab of Eastern bloc all-concrete architecture, it still seemed to promise the interior was as merely functional as it was playfully labyrinthine.

From her vantage point on the tenth floor, however, Este had found a spectacular view of the Truckee River, which split the city in two, a few blocks away. She didn't know if it had been raining or if the mountains were still giving up their snow pack this late into the summer, but the river had become a hypnotic muddy torrent.

Its waters had risen so high up its banks that it threatened to swamp the well-manicured paths on either side and even the bridges that spanned it, connecting the north and south parts of downtown. The violence of the raging river stood in sharp contrast to the rest of the city, which hummed along at a leisurely pace, as if not noticing the volcanic flow tearing past just hidden by its banks.

As the tranquilizer drugs wore off, the pain in her leg where the lion had slashed her returned as a dull throb. She felt loopy. She had no idea where they'd taken Alice, what they might've done to Wilfredo if they'd connected them back to him at the hospital, or even if Casey was safe. Some animals didn't react well to tranquilizers. She had no idea whether the Alsatian was one of them.

Este had been brought to the tiny office in which she now sat maybe half an hour earlier. After twenty minutes, an officious-looking middle-aged woman in a pencil skirt, blouse and jacket that smelled faintly of dry-cleaning chemicals entered and sat opposite her, though she was absorbed with her cell phone. When Este had looked her way, the woman raised a finger as if to beg for a minute more.

Este turned to the window and saw the woman's reflection raise her eyes to study her. Este turned back quickly. The woman's eyes flitted right back to her phone.

Amateur.

'What's your name?' Este asked finally, tired of waiting.

The woman looked up, surprised. 'What's that?'

Este raised an eyebrow, unwilling to answer. She would decide the rhythm, not her interrogator.

'I'm Special Agent Monahan,' the woman said finally. 'And you're—'

'Where's my dog?' Este interrupted, insistent.

'I . . . I'm not sure,' Agent Monahan replied, flustered. 'County Animal Services, maybe?'

'So, you weren't there when we were taken into custody?'

'Um, no, I . . .'

'So, under whose authority were we taken into custody? My dog in particular. We were tranquilized. No verbal warning, no instructions. What if I had an allergy? What if *he'd* had an allergy?'

'He who?'

'My dog.'

'I don't know—'

'My dog, *Casey.*'

'I . . .'

'Under whose authority were we taken into custody?' Este repeated.

'The government's,' Agent Monahan offered.

'State? City? County? Federal?' Este asked.

'Um, I think federal,' Agent Monahan said. 'But I'm not here to answer your que—'

'Where's my dog?'

'I'm sure it's—'

'By calling him an "it", you're reducing his status to that of private property which is A-OK with me because it makes more sense when I say I want my private property returned to me pronto,' Este shot back. 'You had no right to separate *it* from me. That's a civil lawsuit to go with the false imprisonment.'

Este wasn't one to be confrontational. She preferred to use lies and obfuscation to get what she wanted, not bluster. That was more her mother's speed, something she'd seen her sister not just imitate but practically weaponize when she wanted something. Este wasn't just channeling Inés right now but felt possessed by her.

'I have no information on your dog,' the agent said, folding her hands over the file.

'And Alice? Is she in another room here?'

'I have no information on Alice, either.'

'Did you know her name before I said it?' Este asked. 'Or was she your target, meaning you're at least tangentially affiliated with the arresting body?'

The agent's phone vibrated.

'Gonna answer that?'

The agent stared back at Este for a moment then picked up the phone. She read the message on the display, then, to Este's surprise, turned it around so she could read it.

Update on Wilfredo Lugo. Tell Quiñones he's been transported to the trauma center at St Mark's in Salt Lake City. Stable condition but will need surgery.

Este read it twice. Then looked back at the agent.

'What am I charged with?' Este asked.

Agent Monahan slapped the desk with such force that Este knew her palm was going to sting for the next several minutes. The agent recoiled, sinking back into her chair while shaking her head.

'You are free to go! Right now!' the agent blurted. 'You can walk out that door any time you want! Seriously! Try it! Now! Leave! I'm asking you to.'

'Do you think they transported Wilfredo in an ambulance or helicopter?' Este asked.

'What?' the agent said, incredulous.

'Because it's over five hundred miles to Salt Lake,' Este said. 'The best helicopters only have a range of about three hundred miles, so they'd have to refuel at a time when fuel is pretty scarce. Just wondering if they're spending six figures on my boy or five.'

The agent took a second to reassess Este, then opened the file folder, looking thoroughly unnerved.

'I wouldn't know,' she said, plucking a slip of thick paper from the folder. 'I was sent in here to give you this check. That's it.'

She threw the check at Este as a sign of disdain but it landed directly in front of her, face up. It was printed, not handwritten. Estefania Quiñones was listed as the payee, the US Treasury Department as the payer. The check was for $1,000,000.

She stared at the number for a long moment. Whether it was her intention or not, Alice had been captured and she'd collected a million-dollar bounty. Alice had been right to sense a trap.

'I'm Internal Revenue,' the agent continued. 'This was supposed to be deposited into your bank account, but it seems you do not have a bank account. Nor have you filed a tax return in the last three years. This is fine given your status, but complicated when receiving monies of this size. Do you understand?'

'Why am I getting $1,000,000?' Este asked.

'No idea,' Agent Monahan said, throwing up her hands. 'If you don't want it, I'll take it. Happily. Oh, and there's also this, but you only get it if you accept the check.'

The agent slid over a thin stack of stapled pages from the file folder. There was a name at the top of the first page. Inés Teresa Quiñones.

Este felt light-headed. 'What is all this?' she managed to ask.

'Unsure,' Monahan said. 'Got e-mailed to me with instructions to print it out and pass it along with the check.'

Este put the check aside and took up the pages. They were lists of cell-phone calls made from her sister's number and credit-card charges from her card. The dates were all from late April and early May of 2024.

The days leading up to the LA-1.

Her eyes traveled down to the day itself, May 3. Sure enough, there were charges.

What time of day was LA-1 again?

Early morning, before seven. She knew this because she'd been on the graveyard shift at Good Samaritan when it struck. It had been a busy night. Heck, they were all busy nights. She'd had no idea how busy it was about to become.

Inés had made a call just past seven o'clock in the morning. Another before nine. The last charges on her credit card were from the night before, a restaurant in Chinatown and then a gas station. The second charge was $9.

A bottle of water and a pack of cigarettes, Este imagined.

Then, no more.

Of course, LA-2 wiped out the grid, toppling the cell towers along with everything else, but Inés had survived LA-1. That's the one that caught everyone unaware, the one that had the greatest number of fatalities.

Inés wasn't among them. Inés had survived.

Este's heart fluttered as she tracked back through the pre-quake charges. There was an easy repetition, almost nothing over twenty dollars, all from convenience stores, gas stations, or restaurants in a five- or six-block section of the Arts District on the east side of downtown. There were a handful of geographical exceptions that suggested a bus or car ride to a few places outside of about a two-mile radius but, through most of March and April of 2024, Inés stayed close to one area.

She went back to the phone records to see if it listed the numbers her sister had called on the day of LA-1. The first was Este's home phone. The second was the main directory at Good Samaritan Hospital.

Why didn't she try my cell?

But she had. A few rows above, Este saw bursts of calls to her cell phone, one right after another. None lasted a full second. Either the cell towers near the hospital had been damaged or the volume of calls made it so she couldn't get through.

Este's chest filled with cement. It was too awful, too terrible to consider. All she could think of was her sister, trapped and injured, trying to reach her. She had no idea if this was the case. She might've been trying to call her from the safety of one of the first evacuee buses out of town or to give her a new number or location. That just didn't seem likely.

All Este knew was that she'd spent so much of the past year looking for Inés, from scouring the remnants of the city to searching databases, but in Inés's actual time of need, Este was nowhere to be found.

'Thank you for this,' Este said hoarsely. 'I can go?'

Agent Monahan gestured to the door.

Este grabbed the file. She was halfway to the door when she heard something coming from outside the building. She moved to the window. Along the river, dogs being walked by their owners had all begun to bark. Only, they weren't barking at each other or at the river. They were barking to the south.

'Get out of the building,' Este told the agent as she dashed from the room.

'Why? What's going on?' the agent asked.

But Este was already half a flight down the nearest fire stairs. She took the steps three at a time, the nerve endings in her injured leg howling in protest with every stride. Why did the office have to be all the way on the top floor? Still, if she was quick, she could be out the front door to safety in under a minute.

If only she'd had a few more seconds warning.

Este was almost to the fifth-floor landing when the quake hit. Its strength was such that it felt like the entire building had been flipped on its head. Este was lifted straight off the steps and launched into the wall opposite with such force her shoes flew off her feet.

She sank to the floor unable to breathe.

THIRTY

A lice marveled at all she saw as she was whisked through the Kellner Group building. If her recovery suite had been like something out of a five-star hotel, the Kellner labs were like something Willy Wonka might come up with. While she understood logically that she was two decades into the future, the technology being used in station after station, lab after lab, was almost incomprehensible.

There were dozens if not hundreds of scientists and technicians, all in lab coats, some in masks, others in cleanroom suits, at work on various projects, giving the place more a feel of a university science department than the pharmaceutical company that Ben described.

'What is everyone working on?' Alice asked after getting off an elevator to find yet another floor filled with techs at work.

'When we were pharmaceuticals, food additives, cosmetics, and personal products like medicated shampoos, every lab was on a different project,' he said, whisking her down a series of long corridors. 'But now, everything – all our resources – are focused on exploiting the discoveries relating to your cells.'

'Really?'

'Absolutely,' Ben said. 'It's not just the biggest thing, it's the only thing. You don't have to imagine a future past all this anymore, as you'll be a part of it with a couple of injections.'

Alice knew Ben was right. She felt it everywhere they went, this tangible fear of what might happen next. What wouldn't people pay to get some feeling of security back in their lives that something as monumental as an earthquake couldn't take away?

So why did she want no part of it? What was that little voice in the back of her head that was telling her this wasn't the way?

'Oh, watch this,' Ben said, leading her into a lab.

Three lab technicians were gathered around a large, sealed-glass container with troughs of thick powder on the bottom of assorted colors and consistency.

'What are those?' Alice asked.

'The building blocks I mentioned. Proteins, carbohydrates and amino acids, but also trace metals that exist within living creatures,' Ben explained, picking up a small tablet to show her the information.

'Given all the disasters, are supplies hard to come by? The trace metals, I mean?'

'Not at all,' Ben said. 'You can find them in almost any all-in-one-type multivitamin, particularly for seniors. Chromium. Manganese. Selenium. Zinc. Copper. Anything too extravagant and this process becomes impractical, particularly on a large scale.'

A raccoon in a small cage sat nearby. A tech used a syringe to extract a sample from the base of its skull. This was then placed in a pressurized canister similar to the one Este had shown her.

'I've seen one of those before,' Alice said.

'It's how we preserve the ghost bacterium when in stasis,' Ben said. 'Now watch.'

The tech inserted the canister into the side of the glass case. Mist filled the space as a tech turned the dial on a nearby oxygen tank with a hose feeding into the case. The glass fogged.

'What's going to happen?' Alice asked.

'Magic.'

The tech touched the button on the back of the canister. Its contents were sent into the case as well. At first, it looked like nothing was happening. But then, the air inside began to cloud. Wisps of vertical smoke, like those expelled by an extinguished candle, traveled upwards as the cloud grew and expanded.

'Look there,' Ben said, pointing to the troughs.

To Alice's surprise, the mass of powders appeared to be dwindling as the cloud grew larger. What had initially looked like smoke became a near-infinite network of tiny, wire-like strands forming a new shape.

'Oh my God,' Alice whispered.

'Keep watching,' Ben said.

As if she could look away.

A skull appeared, followed by a backbone, veins and organs. These were slowly covered by viscous layers of tissue. The tissue formed skin, complete with hair follicles from which fur sprang. It was a mirror image of the raccoon in the cage. Once whole, it began to stir right away, lolling its head around before collapsing back to the floor of the case, half-asleep.

Yeah, I know the feeling, Alice thought.

The raccoon finally managed to stand, balancing itself on its legs. One of the techs opened the case and took it out. It curled into her arms immediately.

'Its first memory to return is of Dr Rousseau's scent,' Ben said, nodding to the tech as she gave it an injection. 'It's comfortable with her.'

'But the first thing it gets is a shot?' Alice asked.

'Yep, it introduces the bacteria that binds with the genetic material to make the ghost,' Ben explained.

'How long does it take?' Alice asked. 'Like, if it died in the next thirty seconds, would it already have the ability to generate a ghost and self-resurrect?'

'Absolutely, it's a very fast binding process. If we begin testing with it in the next hour, should it go into any kind of arrest or have any reaction to the process, we're not starting over from zero,' Ben said. 'We can recover its genetic information and determine what happened.'

Alice watched as the animal was placed in a new cage while the other techs shut down the case.

'What happens to the raccoon after the tests?' Alice asked.

'What do you mean?'

'I don't imagine you have some giant raccoon preserve out back somewhere.'

'No, following the testing there's usually, well, dissection,' Ben said. 'But only of the copies. The primary remains the immortal primary.'

Alice was still trying to process this as Ben led her away. They reached a small examination room where a nurse awaited them.

'In the chair, please,' the nurse said, nodding to Alice.

Alice took a seat. The room was spare and looked unused compared to most of the other rooms she'd seen. Alice had never liked going to the doctor even before she'd had cancer. Being a patient made her feel so helpless. It felt like the doctors were the only ones deemed worthy enough to make decisions.

'What if I was religious?' she asked. 'What if by bringing me back you're somehow denying me my audience with the Almighty?'

Ben put down his tablet and arched an eyebrow. 'You're not religious, Alice. I still remember your freshman year when you scoffed about all that.'

'Oh, I just knew everything then,' Alice said. 'But wow, good memory.'

The nurse brought in a tourniquet, a syringe and four vacuum extraction tubes.

'Hold out your arm,' she said. 'And make a fist.'

Alice did so. Ben ducked into the hallway. The nurse looked for a vein.

'Quick pinch,' the nurse said.

Alice looked away as the needle went in. It didn't hurt much. The nurse filled one vial, then a second one, then a third.

'One more,' she said.

Alice saw two things at once. Two things out of the ordinary.

The first was a reflection from a metal paper-towel dispenser. It was Ben in the hallway chatting with his colleagues. There were six people in all. Ben was doing the talking, Dr Abouzeid was listening, but beside her was . . . Dr Abouzeid, only an older version by maybe ten years. Beside her was another Ben, this one younger.

And another Ben, this one older.

And another Ben, this one about the same age as the first.

The other thing Alice noticed was the nurse switching the extraction barrel for a syringe with an injector needle, which she slipped into Alice's vein.

'What was that?' Alice asked.

The nurse looked up at her with surprise. In the reflection on the paper-towel dispenser, all four Bens turned her way. One made eye contact.

'What's going on?' Alice demanded.

Ben stepped back into the room. 'Hey, are you OK?'

'Who's out there in the hall with you?' Alice asked. 'And what did she just inject me with?'

Ben looked to the nurse then sighed. 'It's OK,' he said.

'It's not OK!' Alice said, trying to stand then feeling nauseous.

'I wasn't talking to you,' Ben said, turning to the nurse. 'I'll finish up. Thanks.'

The nurse exited. As Alice watched, the other Bens and the pair of Dr Abouzeids in the hall moved on as well.

'As I said,' Ben began, 'you're dangerous, Alice. So, when it comes time for disposal, we tend to sedate if we can't get the subject into one of the containment cases right away. They're sealed. As you'll find out in a second.'

He took one of the pressurized canisters and an extraction syringe from a drawer and moved to Alice's side.

'Sorry about this, Allie,' he said.

One more old memory surfaced. 'I never liked being called that.'

Ben grinned. 'I know.'

He slid the extracting syringe into the base of her skull and took a sample just as the tech had done with the raccoon. He inserted it into the pressurized canister and attached it to a scanner mounted on the wall nearby. He hit a button on the scanner and a bar code plus an alphanumeric string was lasered onto the side of the canister.

'Good to see you again, Allie,' Ben said. 'Usually you're in and out so fast, none of your old memories have time to surface. I'm so often a stranger to you. Nice change of pace.'

Alice felt the sedative taking hold. She felt sleepy, her eyes having trouble staying open. Her arms and legs were going limp. Soon, it would all be over.

Unless.

The nurse had left the blood samples, extraction barrels and drain on the table next to Alice. With only the bare bones of what was surely an impossible plan taking shape in her mind, she picked up the syringe, turned to Ben and stabbed it into his torso.

He screamed.

Using strength she didn't know she had, Alice fought her way to her feet, grabbed the canister and Ben's tablet, then charged out into the corridor.

'She's running!' Ben's voice cried, though it wasn't the Ben in the exam room.

It came from one of the other Bens in the hall, though Alice wasn't about to turn around to see which. She hurtled through the hallways, looking for an exit, a stairwell, *anything*, but found only closed doors and masked faces.

She wondered how many Bens were under those masks. How many Dr Kapurs? How many Dr Abouzeids?

She reached an elevator bank just as the doors slid open to allow two techs to step out.

'Excuse me!' she yelled, pushing them aside and dashing in.

There was only one button in the elevator car. Alice pushed it and the doors closed. The car began to descend.

Alice was sweating. Fighting the sedative felt akin to developing a rapid fever. Her face and hands were hot. She knew collapse was imminent, but she had to get out of the building and away from Ben – *Bens* – first.

Only, when the elevator doors opened again, Alice found herself not in a lobby, not in a parking garage, not even on another floor. She had arrived in some great cavernous room the size of several airplane hangars stretched together. The walls looked sturdy, blast-proof. Possibly fire-proof. Thousands of wires trailed down from the ceiling to row after row after row of what looked like computer server banks, all lit up with blinking LED lights indicating they were hard at work. These extended all the way to the rear wall, so far away that Alice could barely see it.

Against the side wall to her left and running back just as far as the rows of servers were sealed glass containers like the one she had seen upstairs in the lab. Only, instead of being raccoon-sized, these were large enough to allow a human to stand inside.

She moved down a set of narrow metal steps to the room's floor. She needed a way out but didn't even see a fire exit. She passed one of the servers and realized they weren't servers at all but storage units of some sort. She peered in.

And gasped.

In each were canisters. Dozens of them. Looking across the room, she estimated there could've easily been ten thousand or more stored here. The alphanumeric strings were all different though. They weren't all from May of 2003. In fact, a couple predated that.

She wasn't the only ghost.

Alice thought fast, weighing the canister she'd taken from upstairs in her hand. An idea began to take shape in her mind.

Knowing it would be mere minutes if not seconds before the elevator doors opened, she ran down the rows, quickly looking through Ben's tablet. The interface was like the one she'd tinkered with on the way to Reno. She opened a browser window and tried to remember what she'd watched Este do in the business center.

Should I be writing this down? she'd asked Este.

'Turns out . . .' Alice whispered back to herself as she worked frantically.

There was a sound. It wasn't coming from the elevators, however, but from the large glass containers along the wall. Alice angled backward until she could see them. The glass fogged just as the case upstairs had. Something inside began to form. For a moment, she thought it'd be human.

But it was four-legged, like the raccoon. Only its legs were longer. One of the mountain lions.

'Alice? Where are you?' called out Ben from some unseen loudspeaker. 'This is ridiculous. I thought we understood each other!'

Oh, we do, thought Alice, typing away, screwing up, having to backspace, retyping.

The mountain lions were almost fully formed. The elevators dinged. The doors opened and a handful of people exited at once. A hiss came from the glass cases on the side of the wall.

'Come on, Alice,' said Ben, though this sounded like the younger one. 'There's no way out of this room. It's well-sealed for reasons that should be obvious.'

'Was I kept in one of these rooms?' Alice asked, stepping halfway into the middle of a row even as she kept typing on the tablet. 'In Los Angeles?'

Six Bens, all of different ages, stood opposite her. The one closest to her age nodded.

'You were,' he said. 'After the quakes, we feared there'd been a containment break but nothing happened. We think it was an aftershock that set you free somehow.'

Ah.

'Now, hand over the extractor,' young Ben said. 'This isn't a game.'

'Oh, I know,' Alice agreed. 'Just getting used to seeing so many of you. It's—'

'Disconcerting?' the oldest Ben replied. 'Yeah, I've described it to colleagues as like viewing an Einstein ring. It's when you see the same light from the same star just at different times. It's a relativistic effect. When lights pass through multiple galaxies, each with their own gravitational pulls, it creates ellipses and curves as the light spreads—'

'Do these colleagues let you finish your grandiose analogy or throw themselves into the mouth of one of your pets first?' Alice asked, nodding to the mountain lions.

The Bens laughed in unison. It was a deranged, gull-like sound. If Alice thought this future she was trapped in couldn't get any more surreal . . .

'Now, come quietly before this gets messy,' the middle-aged Ben said.

'You never had any intention of letting me leave, did you?' Alice asked.

The Bens fell silent for a moment, looking almost reflective about this. 'You'd be surprised.'

Alice glanced to the tablet. She was almost done, or so she thought. So much rode on her absorbing not only an understanding of all this new tech but being able to use it on the first try. If there wasn't so much adrenaline pumping through her body, she just might second-guess herself into oblivion.

'How many times have I been resurrected?' Alice asked, buying time. 'How many times have I been slaughtered when I've outlasted my usefulness to . . . all this?'

'I don't know,' the oldest Ben said with a shrug. 'Does it matter? Or are you just stalling to finish doing whatever you're doing with that tablet?'

'Hundreds of times? Thousands?' Alice offered, ignoring this remark. 'All that pain you've inflicted on me over the years – on all of these people – born into servitude.'

'Oh, come on, Alice. They lived their lives. They then, *graciously*, donated their bodies to the advancement of science.'

'Is that what you tell yourselves?' Alice asked. 'This is not what I understood I was signing on for. They're slaves. All of them.'

'Are you a slave if you don't know you're a slave?' the youngest Ben asked.

Alice stared at him then back around the room at all the ghost canisters, all the technology of resurrection. That such unbelievable inventions had been the brainchild of someone so morally bankrupt, so unempathetic, felt like a historical irony. It took a certain cruelty for a person to invent eternal life at a moment of possible extinction only to suddenly see life as completely disposable. What if this future-shaping technology had been in the hands of someone altruistic and far-thinking?

Was that such an impossible thing to ask of the Universe?

With this last question in her mind, Alice checked the tablet and saw her project had reached its completion. The glass cases against the wall hissed and opened as they released their contents. The lions, still groggy, padded out and moved between the rows. Some moved alongside the Bens, who responded by petting them and stroking their fur. Others scented on Alice and began moving in.

'Last chance,' Ben said. 'There's an easy way and a hard way.'

'Something we agree on,' Alice said, raising the tablet before slamming it down on the nearest storage unit.

It snapped into two jagged pieces, the loud cracking sound causing the Bens and lions to flinch. Alice took one of the pieces and held it to her neck.

'Alice, what're you doing?' the middle-aged Ben asked, panic rising in his voice.

'Accelerating the process,' she said.

She drew the jagged piece across her neck. The last thing she saw was the Bens fleeing to the elevators in terror, the lions launching their attack.

THIRTY-ONE

Este's entire body hurt. She'd hit the wall, landed on the floor, then rolled down a couple of stairs. When she touched her chin, her fingers came back wet with blood. Judging from the amount of blood, it probably required stitches.

But that wasn't her main concern. The building was still shaking. The quake had been going for minutes now with such violence that Este couldn't believe the ground could keep it up for much longer. Was there that much potential energy bound up in the tectonic plates below Nevada?

Being trapped in a stairwell like this was pretty much Este's worst nightmare. What could be worse than being in a crucible of masonry and steel at the mercy of elements beyond your control? It was like being in the belly of a ship adrift in a typhoon. The brutality of the shaking didn't feel like the back-and-forth sway of the quakes she'd grown used to in the LAQZ. This felt animal, a savagery directed at her and everyone inside the building. Its fury was personal.

It'll be over in a minute, she told herself.

She forced herself to breathe, even tried to meditate. But the tornado-like howl of the building rocking on its foundations drowned out every attempt to organize her thoughts.

A few others had ventured into the stairwell trying to escape as well. They were thrown around like sheets in a dryer. Some screamed. Some had their voices stilled when they were slammed into the next solid object. Este could hear the panic out on the floors. Glass shattering, furniture smashing apart, people screaming. There were curses and cries to an unseen God.

As if this was his doing.

After a third minute passed, Este began ticking down seconds to calm her nerves. When a fourth passed, a manic thought came to her. *What if this is it? What if it* never *stops? What if this is the new normal?*

She was pretty sure that wasn't how physics worked, but with everything changing so fast, the normal rules no longer seemed to apply. When she counted past six full minutes of unceasing shaking, she decided she'd been crumpled in the corner long enough. She moved into a seated position and began lowering herself down the steps one at a time.

Two more minutes passed and the building still shook. She hoped more than ever that the agent hadn't been lying about Wilfredo having been transported out before the quake hit. She had no idea what had happened to Alice, but somehow, she doubted she was still in Reno.

Which left Casey. He was somewhere in this mess. She had to find him.

She knew she'd reached the bottom of the stairs when she encountered a traffic jam of other evacuees. Most were injured. All were terrified. Some screamed while others fought to keep them calm. She sifted out with them through the fire door to the bright day outside. The streets and sidewalks were flooded with people, like the residents of dozens of anthills stirred by the same event. They stared up in horror at the swaying buildings even as they stood under swinging power lines.

'Get to open ground!' Este cried. 'Get away from the buildings!'

No one seemed to hear her. A few filmed the whole thing on their phones, one turning a lens Este's way. Though her fingers ached, she still managed to flip it the bird.

Part of the problem was that open ground was in short supply. There were buildings in every direction. However, she remembered having seen a large empty plaza a few blocks north from the office window above, but that was across the raging river.

She tried to see the plaza, but from her new, lower vantage point she could only make out the parking garage that had stood behind it. It was crumpled forward now, dozens of cars spilling out of it like coins spewed from a slot machine. The plaza itself looked relatively empty. Este just had to cross the river, no easy task given that both bridges were being tossed like kites in a gale.

As the quake entered its seventh or eighth minute, Este limped the three blocks to the nearest bridge over the Truckee River. The water had almost crested its banks and was slamming into the bridge's supports with such force that it looked about ready to pull free from its moorings. Este was rethinking crossing it when the faux granite façade of the federal building she'd just fled sheared off and fell several stories to the ground, crushing gawkers amid escalating screams.

She looked up to the two buildings on either side of her, knew they could be next, and stepped onto the bridge.

Everyone knew the last thing you did in an earthquake was attempt to get from Point A to Point B. But if Este had forgotten, a great wave of cold water sweeping over her from the river below brought everything in her mind into a crisp focus. She was no longer simply wounded and in grievous pain. She was also freezing cold and wet.

Come on, Este, she whispered to herself.

She took a few more steps but lurched as something more solid than water slammed into the bridge. Este spied an SUV with park ranger sigils on the door bobbing up and down on the upriver side of the bridge. It sank beneath the waves and popped back up on the other side of the bridge to continue downstream. There was all kinds of stuff in the river now. Trees, trash; anything in its path not nailed down had been sucked into its vortex.

Este didn't see what had struck the bridge with such force, but the wires behind her had been torn from their support beams and the entire structure was beginning to collapse. Pieces of bridge that dangled into the river were caught up in the torrent, wrenching the struts back even farther. The bridge rotated and pitched like a loose porch swing.

It would be a matter of seconds before the whole thing tumbled into the river.

One of her mother's military aphorisms jumped into her head. *Yesterday was the easy day.*

Thanks, Mom, Este thought, fighting her way to her feet.

She grabbed the swaying guardrail and took four quick steps, planting her feet flat as if walking on ice. Behind her, a rumbling crash indicated another building coming down behind her. She glanced over her shoulder to look, an instinctive action, and saw a tidal wave of mud carrying logs, presumably from a mill upstream. They looked like downed redwoods, each a hundred feet long and weighing tons apiece.

There was no way the bridge would survive that.

Este gritted her teeth and ran. She slid to the ground a couple of times but fought her way forward. If she went into the river with the bridge, she knew she wouldn't come out.

She still had a good fifteen feet to go when the first log struck the bridge. She was sent flying, somersaulting forward into the guardrail as the bridge's steel supports groaned and bent. As the ground fell out from under her, Este grabbed the guardrail with both hands, blindly clawing her way forward as muddy water splashed over her body. For an instant, she didn't know whether she was in the river or on dry land. There was a great snapping sound as the last of the bridge's guy wires gave way and the entire structure fell into the waves.

Este, however, had somehow made it to the other side. She hugged the ground alongside the broken road, fingers digging past grass into dirt. She realized that the quake had stopped while she was on the bridge. She just hadn't noticed.

She turned to look back at the buildings on the other side to see which ones had survived. Only, there were no buildings left at all.

As aftershocks rocked the city – five in the first hour by her count – Este hobbled through the broken streets to retrieve her dog. A good thing about being a nurse meant she could tape her own ribs when they broke; a bad thing about a QZ was that she could find nothing for the pain.

Still, she was better off than many others in the town. Sirens echoed across the city in an endless chorus, moving close, moving away, going silent, only to rise again. It reminded her of the first hours following LA-1, parades of walking wounded moving aimlessly through the streets, unsure how to process the immensity of what they had just survived.

The animal control building, an address she found in an old school phone book salvaged from a collapsed service station, was in a part of town dedicated mostly to warehouses and auto body shops. Este was glad, knowing she would've found it impossible to pass through residential areas without stopping to help those in need.

Though the front end of the building had collapsed, a cacophony of barking from the kennels in back told Este that the canine population seemed to have survived intact. She picked her way through a side door, grabbed food and treats from a half-crushed supply cupboard, and passed them out to every freaked-out pup she came across. She debated leaving them in their kennels but figured they had a better chance of survival on the outside. One by one, she opened the gates and the dogs filed out.

Casey was asleep in his kennel because of course he was. She didn't think he was showing off to the other dogs – *this ain't my first rodeo, fellow mutts* – but he seemed genuinely unbothered.

'Casey? You ready to go, boy?'

The Alsatian rolled up onto his feet like an acrobat, beaming happily at her as if she'd arrived at the very moment he'd expected her. He took a step back when Este exploded into tears, throwing her arms around the dog and hugging him tighter than she ever had before.

'Hey, boy,' she whispered into his ear. 'You good?'

Casey licked her ear. She held him a moment longer then walked him out of the kennel to hunt down a new harness and leash.

There was a highway a few blocks away. Este led Casey toward it, unsure of their next destination. To the east, the next big city was Salt Lake. To the north, Boise.

But as she spied the steady stream of vehicles heading not away from but into Reno, Este's decision was made for her.

She flagged down one of the emergency services vehicles, a fire truck with North Lyon County Fire Protection District.

'You hurt?' the driver asked.

'No, we're good,' Este said.

'Well, we're not taking passengers,' the driver replied.

'I'm an RN,' Este replied then nodded to Casey. 'And he's search and rescue. We both worked the LAQZ. We can help.'

The driver considered this for less than a second then nodded to the rear cab. 'Get in.'

There were three more people inside, a uniformed paramedic and two more firefighters.

'I'm Mateo,' the driver said, turning around. 'Charlie and George are from my fire team. We picked up Sarah in Elko.'

'I'm Este,' Este said. 'The dog's Casey.'

'What kind of bad luck is that?' George asked. 'Work one quake only to end up in another?'

'Given the frequency, I'm sure it's an increasingly common occurrence,' Este mused.

'How's your pain?' Sarah asked, looking over Este's bandages.

'Manageable for now. Might need a stitch or two later. Wouldn't turn down some aspirin in the short term, though.'

As Sarah passed over a couple of pills, Este remembered something. She reached for her waistband where she'd shoved not only the file folder that Agent Monahan had given her but also the million-dollar check, only to find both missing. In fact, the only thing left in her pockets was the folded-up painted postcard her sister had made of the two of them.

She slumped into her seat, despite realizing that if asked to pick either the check or the card, there'd be no question she'd choose the latter.

'Long day, huh?' Mateo said, eyeing her in the rear-view mirror.

'Long day about to get longer,' Este said.

'Heard that,' Mateo shot back with a grin. 'Yesterday was the easy day.'

Este nodded, smiling for the first time in a while.

THIRTY-TWO

The young woman awoke, disoriented. She glanced around as best she could, unable to place where she was in the dim light. Her head ached and her muscles were stiff and unresponsive. She had a bad taste in her mouth, like almond oil and salt.

She was in a bed. Not a regular bed but a hospital bed. With difficulty, she sat up and pulled aside the sheet that covered much of her body. She wore pale blue pajamas and slipper socks. She wore a wristband with a bar code and alphanumeric string on it. She couldn't remember how she had gotten there.

Had she been injured? Was she hurt?

She tried to inspect her body, but her vision was fuzzy. She moved her arm and only then realized it had a tube running to a drip bag hanging on a nearby IV pole. There was a clip on her finger leading back to a heart monitor. Another machine indicated that it was tracking the oxygenation levels of her blood.

Her gaze landed on a dresser. There were flowers, cards, a half-deflated balloon and some framed photographs. One showed an older couple smiling together. Her parents? She recognized herself in another, arms around a handsome man of the same age. Her husband. His name was?

She couldn't remember.

She tried to get up but didn't have the strength. She grew dizzy and sank back onto the pillow. What was going on?

The door opened. A nurse in blue scrubs bustled in and stopped short when she saw that the young woman was awake.

'Oh, sorry, should've knocked,' the nurse said. 'How are you feeling?'

'I . . . I don't know.'

The nurse's countenance changed slightly. 'Let me get the doctor.'

She stepped back out and signaled someone down the hall. Two other nurses, also in blue scrubs, glanced in as they passed. The young woman could hear the chatter of even more people down the hall as well as the beeps and hums of medical equipment. She glanced to the window. The skyline outside was familiar. A stadium stood in the far distance, snowcapped mountains rising beyond it.

Denver. She was in downtown Denver.

Her name followed. She was Alice Helena Rhodes. Alix to some. Allie to none.

And she had acute lymphocytic leukemia. Cancer. Stage Four. A death sentence.

Terror mixed with sadness flooded her mind. She wanted to escape this flawed, self-destructing body. To leave this waking nightmare behind. Why *her*? One day, she was fine. The next, a doctor was telling her that her own body had betrayed her. It was killing her from the inside out.

Her hand shot out to the empty chair next to the bed. It was a reflex, as if she expected subconsciously that someone sitting there would take her hand. No one did.

She felt so empty. So alone.

A familiar-looking middle-aged man in a lab coat over a blue shirt and dark pants swept into the room. 'Good morning, Alice. Nurse Chester said you're experiencing some disorientation?'

'Y-yes,' she admitted as he took the seat next to her.

'Follow this light,' he said, moving a pen light in front of her eyes. She did. His name badge read Ben Ganske.

She knew that name. He was her doctor but also her friend.

'Am I OK?' Alice asked.

Ben hesitated then leaned in. 'I'll have the nurse take a look at your meds in a moment,' he said. 'But, it's actually a really good sign. I've been sitting on this for a couple of days now, but we ran your labs again this morning and I *think* I come bearing good news.'

'What is it?'

'We like to be cautious in our phrasing here, for obvious reasons, but we're in the fifteenth day of the new trial and we're seeing extremely positive results.'

'Trial?' Alice asked.

'Sorry, the new drug,' Ben said, tapping the chart in his hand. 'The Neozol.'

A distant spark of recognition ignited in Alice's mind. She'd heard the word.

'What does that one do again?' Alice asked.

'Creates a non-permissive microenvironment for existing malignant cancer cells,' Ben said. 'Or, in layman's terms, switches cancer cells off by convincing them, in effect, that they're not needed.'

Alice said nothing, not wanting to betray even an atom's worth of optimism.

'The problem with fully metastasized cancer is tracking down all the cells,' Ben continued. 'What we're trying to do is alter the chemistry of the body itself. There will be nowhere the cancer cells can travel without being affected.'

'And it's working?' Alice asked in her smallest voice.

'As your doctor, I'd say guardedly, "so far, so good, but it's early days", because that's what we're told to do,' Ben replied. 'But as your friend? Yes! Like gangbusters! We can't quite believe the results. Your cancer has regressed from a fully metastasized Stage Four to a Stage Three. We believe we can now regress that back to the original tumor, what would be considered a far more treatable Stage Two, where even surgery might be an option.'

Alice couldn't believe what she was hearing. Dr Ganske's – *Ben's* – words dissipated her mental haze. Her senses felt acute and ready for more information.

'Does . . .' she began, then found the name still elusive. 'Does my husband know?'

'We wanted to tell you first,' Ben said. 'We'd also like to do a few more tests before we pop too many champagne bottles. We're breaking new ground here.'

'Of course,' Alice said. 'But any chance I can ring him first?'

There was a flicker of misgiving but then he nodded.

'Absolutely,' Ben said. 'Do you remember the number, or would it be easier for me to write it down?'

'Could you write it down?' Alice asked.

Ben reached for a pad of paper by the phone and wrote a number on it. He handed it to Alice.

'I'll give you some privacy,' he said. 'When you're ready, call the nurse and she'll bring you to the examination room.'

Alice nodded, staring at the number as Ben headed for the door.

'Ben?' Alice said. He glanced back. 'Thank you.'

He smiled warmly. 'It's nice to deliver good news for a change,' Ben said. 'Thanks for doing your part.'

Alice grinned. He left. She wanted to laugh. She didn't know how long it had been since she'd felt this good.

She picked up the phone and dialed the number on the pad. The phone rang and rang until it was finally picked up.

'Hey, it's me—' she began.

A recording of her voice spoke back to her. 'Hey, it's Alice . . .'

'And Rahsaan . . .' a second voice, her *husband's* voice, added.

Rahsaan. That was his name.

'We're not home right now, so . . .' said a recorded Alice.

'Leave a message after the beep,' said a recorded Rahsaan.

Beep.

'Hey, it's me,' Alice said. 'Going in for some tests but maybe you want to come by the hospital when you get this? Got some good news.'

She hung up and tapped a button for the nurse.

'You ready?' Nurse Chester asked when she appeared in the doorway.

'Absolutely.'

A wheelchair was brought in and Alice was wheeled down the hall. She passed several other rooms, all like hers, all occupied by patients. Some looked haggard, others confused. She wondered if any of them would also get good news that day.

They rounded a corner and Alice caught a glimpse into what looked like a large, luxurious suite containing a regular bed and downright futuristic furniture. She grinned up at the nurse.

'When do I get a room like that?'

'Ha, when do *I* get a room like that?' the nurse replied.

They both laughed. Alice was rolled into an elevator car and brought up several floors.

The treatment room looked like the various spaces where Alice had received her chemotherapy infusions. There were large comfortable chairs, two televisions, both tuned to old black-and-white movies, and shelves of paperbacks. A dozen other patients were already in the room hooked up to IVs, some asleep, some paying half-attention to the TV.

One of the movies ended as Nurse Chester helped settle Alice into her chair. The next movie was a colorized version of a Shirley Temple film.

'Oh, I love this one,' Alice said.

Nurse Chester smiled, wheeled over an IV pole, attached a bag, and inserted the needle into the waiting port in Alice's arm. She scanned the bar code on Alice's wristband with a small electronic device she pulled from her pocket, then scanned the bar code on the bag hanging from the IV pole. Alice took in the other patients in the room, some looking not just ill but at death's door.

And here she felt like singing.

THIRTY-THREE

Este spent three weeks working the ReQZ, first as a paramedic with a search-and-rescue team but eventually transitioning onto a cadaver recovery unit with Casey. Though she'd been offered a tent in a nearby National Guard camp, she opted to stay in a displaced persons camp set up over a railroad depot in neighboring Sparks. Medical staffers were in short supply and it allowed her to be closer to those who needed help.

Also, after a day spent combing the debris piles for the dead, she found it restorative to be among the living, despite the patients' complaints taking her right back to the weeks following the LA quakes. Exposure, dehydration and heat stroke were common, particularly as the early summer temperatures soared into the upper nineties. A small hepatitis-A outbreak was traced to a single twenty-five-pound bag of almonds. Precautions were doubled to keep food from being handled with unwashed hands, but Este's training kept her on the lookout for worse diseases. Cholera, typhoid fever, dysentery. The first thing she did with any first-time disaster responders was deliver a crash course in how to decontaminate sources of water.

Her wide experience was in demand in other fields, too. She advised on meal planning and food distribution and helped set up latrines, showers and water stations. The earthquake's epicenter had been in the tiny desert town of Tonopah, Nevada, 230 miles south of Reno, and it had brought down buildings in Las Vegas as well. Although the destruction in Reno was far worse, photos from Vegas dominated the news cycles and the better-known city competed with Reno for relief supplies. Este tackled this, too, unknotting gnarled supply chains and establishing direct lines of communication with the right agencies and distribution centers.

Given the number of times those along the chains of command attempted to extract bribes to get Reno the supplies it needed, Este repeatedly kicked herself for losing the million-dollar check. But then she got the bright idea to shove Casey in front of a few cameras.

Vegas was practically crawling with FEMA-certified urban search dogs, but Casey's singularity in Reno and experience in the LAQZ made him a good story, as well as a rare beacon of hope for those in the Reno camps. Este got him onto CNN after he uncovered his fiftieth survivor in Reno. He briefly made headlines worldwide with his hundredth.

As his handler, people on the other end of the phone began to recognize Este's name. It made it easier for a few days. Keeping things running remained an hour-by-hour, sometimes minute-by-minute, challenge, but Este relished it. She had responsibilities and a purpose. Though she occasionally still had nightmares that took her back to LA, some now laced with appearances by ferocious packs of mountain lions, even these began to ebb. For the first time in a long while, she began to feel whole.

Then there was Mateo. He'd been an environmental sciences major at Boise State, in the second year of a major impact study in Yellowstone, when the quakes began. A team was assembled to keep an eye on the Yellowstone caldera, the vast super-volcano under the park, and Mateo asked to join.

'So far, so good,' Mateo told Este by the fire one night. 'Not saying it won't erupt, but it doesn't appear to be affected by the same forces that are moving the plates.'

Este marveled at how a scientist-in-training tasked with observing a super-volcano could land a side gig teaching fire preparedness to local volunteer fire departments. But in the age of quakes, this was the rule, not the exception. Everyone had these interrupted lives marked with sharp left and right turns.

The two of them shared a sleeping bag a few times the first week and began sharing a tent soon after. Este didn't even know his last name – Solis – until they received actual ID badges from FEMA. Neither were looking for romance. Just someone to decompress with after a day of stress and pain. That he made her laugh in the evenings and made her coffee in the mornings didn't hurt.

After a day spent dealing with the bureaucratic nightmare of finding hospitals in the LoP that could take the extremely ill and injured, Este made her way back to her tent, Casey at her side, hopeful that Mateo had returned first and would be waiting with a hot meal. It'd gotten harder in recent days to find beds for her patients. In the beginning, everyone wanted to help. But over time, there was a subtle shift back to isolationism and protectionism.

'We don't have the resources,' hospital administrators would say, turning away her requests.

She got it. The fear was understandable. Overburden a hospital in, say, Salt Lake or Provo now and, when their own quake came, they wouldn't be able to help their own people.

These thoughts were preoccupying her when Casey broke free, ran past their tent, and launched himself at someone moving through the rows.

'Casey, no!' Este cried, hurrying over. 'Casey!'

'It's OK, Este,' said a familiar voice. 'Who's a good boy, Casey?'

It was Wilfredo. He was flat on his back, Casey licking his face.

Este barely recognized her old partner. In three short weeks, he'd lost at least twenty pounds. It had also sharpened his features, making him appear taller, more angular. His hair was cut short to match a full shave on one side where it was just now growing back following surgery. There was a bandage, but it was small and flesh colored, as if he'd only recently had stitches out.

'How're you, Fredo?' she asked, trying to mask her surprise.

'Hey, there, Este,' Wilfredo said, still stroking Casey's neck. 'Saw this guy on the news. He's famous! Aren't you, boy?'

Este eyed the ground. 'Yeah, kept thinking I'd lose him to one of the hundreds of people calling in trying to adopt his fuzzy butt, but here he is.'

Wilfredo laughed. 'He can't deal with the LoP any more than you can, huh? He's a work dog. Gotta go where the work is.'

'I'm . . . I'm sorry I never came to see you,' Este said, unsure how best to say it. 'Things kind of got away from me here.'

'Are you kidding?' Wilfredo said, getting to his feet. 'When I heard what happened, don't you think I knew what you were doing here? The bigger shock would've been if you had rolled up. My parents were with me, anyway. It's cool.'

Este nodded. 'I'm glad you're OK.'

'Right back at you,' Wilfredo said.

Este braced herself for the world's most awkward reunion hug, but Wilfredo was already tugging a piece of paper from his pocket.

'Take a look at this.'

'What is it?' Este asked.

'I opened our old work logs to see if I could get a client referral or two,' Wilfredo explained. 'This popped up first.'

It was a printout of a message from the encrypted site they used to communicate with clients. There were only two things on it. A list of what looked like ingredients, half taken from a periodic table of elements. Then a page of diagrams relating to what looked like the canister she'd carried across a couple hundred miles. At the bottom, like a signature, was an alphanumeric string beginning 52025280547140 followed by five words.

There Is Life after Death.

'Oh my God!' Este exclaimed. 'It's her! Or, her with a more recent date. Like, from three weeks ago.'

'Day after the Reno quake,' Wilfredo agreed. 'Figured it was like an SOS or something.'

'Did you track the IP?'

'To a Chicago address. I wrote it at the bottom of the page.'

Este read and re-read the pages, trying to divine their purpose. 'She needs our help.'

'Looks like it,' Wilfredo said.

Este looked around, already thinking about what they'd need to pack. But then she caught Wilfredo eyeing her with reluctance.

'Look, I'm sorry for what I said back at the hospital,' Este said. 'I didn't mean it.'

'Yeah, you did,' Wilfredo replied. 'And I meant what I said, too. But that doesn't mean we have to go holding it against each other, right?'

'No,' Este said.

'And that guy over there who's been giving me the hard stare the last few minutes, that's none of my business either.'

Este turned. Mateo was about ten yards back, watching the interaction but staying out of it.

'Nope, none of your business,' Este agreed. 'Should you really be back in the field with your head like that?'

'Not at all,' Wilfredo admitted. 'I'm good for logistical support. Maybe some driving. But I'm out of action when it comes to the hard stuff. Cool?'

'That's what's up,' Este said, extending a hand.

'That's what's up,' Wilfredo said, shaking it. 'Now, how the hell are we gonna get to Chicago?'

BOOK III

THIRTY-FOUR

E ste really, *really* should've known better.

She'd begun feeling nauseous around Glenview, but it was so much worse now that the train was finally entering Chicago. She'd picked up the train in Spokane, a recently repaired spur that Wilfredo had tracked down, being used to funnel refugees inland from the most recent QZs, and that had been fine as long as it went through smaller LoP towns in Montana, North Dakota and Minnesota. When they'd separated for this part of the journey, she'd told Wilfredo she'd be fine. But now she was in one of the largest still-standing cities in the Western Hemisphere. Outside her window, skyscrapers rose in every direction like an impenetrable forest.

All Este could see in their seeming permanence was the sheer amount of destruction that would be wrought on the populace when everything came down. The human agony would be immense.

She turned away from the train window. Reno had been difficult but not impossible. What was different then? Oh, yeah. Alice had been there. She'd had to get Wilfredo to a hospital. She'd been swept along by the urgency of events. But there was urgency here, too, right? Why was she having such a hard time, then?

Casey stirred at her feet. The ticket clerk in Spokane had indicated the Alsatian was a larger animal than they allowed in the passenger cars, only to be told of Casey's celebrity status by a co-worker. Este reached down and stroked his head. He nuzzled her hand in return, but her anxiety remained.

The train pulled into Union Station a few minutes later, and a voice over the loudspeaker reminded passengers that this was the end of the line and to 'remove all luggage and personal items.' Este sat still as everyone else on the train packed up, as if waiting for some inner spark to lift her to her feet and carry her forward. It never came.

'Ma'am? Did you need assistance?' a porter in a reflector vest asked, poking his head in through the open doors once the car was empty.

'Oh, nope,' Este said. 'Just zoned out.'

'OK, but we gotta clean the train,' he said, his tone adding a pinch of aggression.

'Cool,' Este said, forcing herself to her feet and revealing the massive work dog under the chair.

The porter delighted Este by taking an instinctive step back, despite Casey being about the friendliest dog in the world. She grabbed her duffel, hastily packed in the ReQZ, and led Casey onto the platform.

Union Station turned out to be a beaut, its main terminal of white marble decorated with towering columns, a glass ceiling, and ornate lanterns bracketing long benches of polished wood that seemed out of another era. Sunlight streamed in from a ring of upper windows, revealing a cloudless blue sky.

Este took this all in as commuters and more than a few refugees crowded past her. All she had to do was get out of this building, hit the sidewalk, and make it the ten short blocks to the building from which Alice sent her message. How hard could that be?

As soon as the thought materialized, Este's body seized up. She couldn't catch her breath. Unlike in the SUV outside Tahoe, there was no exhilaration this time, no manic sense of invulnerability. Instead, she felt the weight of the building's stones burying her where she stood, their impossible mass locking her arms to her sides, her chest to her knees. She fell forward, grabbing onto a bench to prevent herself face-planting.

I should've stayed in the LAQZ. It's empty. No, not empty. Still.

The memory of her uncovering first her stepdad then her mother from their ruined house returned to her, unbeckoned but demanding to be seen. The cutting into the roof, the hauling away of support beams, the removal of furniture. She'd done this on so many recoveries, but this time, every scrap of upholstery, every inch of the building's crumpled internal geography, was familiar.

And even as she excavated the obliteration of those closest to her, she waited for the quake that would collapse the site and bury her in the same grave. A part of her, no matter how small, believed this was not only inevitable but welcomed an end outside of her control.

'Ma'am? You need to get your dog out of here.'

The voice was very confident in its authority. Este managed to turn her head. A pair of Chicago police officers, one woman, one man, stood over her.

'Y-yep,' Este said, hoping she didn't sound as disoriented as she was.

The cops exchanged a look. The man angled his shoulder mic toward his mouth and said something as his partner pulled on a pair of latex gloves before kneeling next to Este.

'Are you all right? Did you take anything today?' she asked.

No, just had a long day, Este wanted to say. *But thank you for your concern.*

Before she could find the energy to say it, however, the world's most endearingly protective-yet-cursed-with-an-awful-sense-of-timing Alsatian barked defensively at the officers. The two officers moved back, the male reaching for his gun, the woman her Taser.

'Restrain your dog!' the woman demanded. 'Restrain your dog or we will Tase him!'

Este knew what she should do – comply with the officers as best she could – but something inside her broke. She threw her arms around Casey's neck, as if already in mourning, and held on. In that instant, the dog was her mother, was Inés. Was Alice. Was Wilfredo.

Was herself.

'What're those?' a new voice, this one calm, asked.

The two cops had been joined by a Transit Authority officer. He was an older guy whose belly stretched his tactical vest past the point of maximum effectiveness. He was pointing at the several lime-green tags hanging from Este's duffel strap.

'Site . . . site tags,' Este said.

'Where were you?'

'ReQZ, LAQZ,' she said.

'Recovery?' he asked.

'Paramedic, then recovery,' she said.

The CTA officer straightened. 'They gave us those way back during Sandy in case we found bodies,' he said. 'Your first time back in the world in a while?'

'Yeah.'

The CTA officer glanced to the cops. A look of understanding passed through the trio and the two police officers moved away. The CTA officer leaned down to pet Casey.

'Offer you a ride somewhere?' he asked. 'Least we can do after wrecking your welcome-to-Chicago party.'

Este laughed.

A few minutes later, Este and Casey were in the back seat of an official Chicago Transit Authority Impala. The transit cop, whose name was Gus Babko, had popped by the station's Gold Coast Dogs on the way to the car and grabbed a bag full of hot dogs, which he handed to Este. She and Casey had devoured three apiece before they were even out of the building.

'You're sure this is no trouble?' Este asked, staring up at the buildings.

'Eh, I'm a shift supervisor,' Gus said. 'Besides, if they fire me for escorting a PTSD'ed hero nurse and her famous rescue dog out of Union Station, the *Trib*, the mayor's office, and half the Quake City survivors on social media will breathe fire down their necks until I'm hired back.' He chuckled then nodded to a street sign. 'Where can I drop you?'

Este handed him the address she'd tracked down online. Gus raised an eyebrow.

'You sure about the street number?'

'Yeah, meeting a friend out front there,' Este said quickly. 'Why?'

'Nothing, just this building's a bit infamous in the Twenty-fifth District,' he said.

'How come?' Este asked. 'A lot of crime?'

'The opposite. Like a black hole. Not just low crime but no crime. Every other skyscraper in Area North gets a call a day. At least. Nothing out of the Kellner building.'

'Is it vacant?' Este asked.

'No, they got tenants,' Gus said. 'Even know a couple of the former cops doing security on the lobby desk and on the cameras downstairs. People are in and out, twenty-four-seven. But it's quiet like a haunted house.'

A ghost, Este remembered. *You, my friend, are a ghost.*

Gus pulled the car up to a curb and pointed at a tall, anonymous-looking glass-and-steel monolith rising across the street.

'There you go,' he said.

'Thank you,' Este said, resisting the urge to lean forward and give the officer a hug.

'Be careful out here,' Gus warned. 'Could've gone the other way at the train station. People are jumpy. Lotta refugees coming through the Windy City, lot of them messed up, and they end up at the mercy of cops who have zero mental-health training.'

'Will do,' Este said. 'Thank you again.'

She stepped out of the car but immediately moved away from the Kellner building and down the street. The last thing she needed was to show up on one of their cameras arriving in a CTA car. The streets were packed with people, but no one seemed to be going in or out of the skyscraper's doors.

She came around a corner and saw the same thing was true of the building's parking garage entrances. Doors were closed. No vehicles came in or out for the ten minutes she watched. She didn't know what she'd expected. Gun turrets? Mountain lion sentinels?

Yet, even devoid all that, Este knew Alice was inside. She just had to figure a way to get her out.

THIRTY-FIVE

The young woman awoke, disoriented. She looked around. Nothing seemed familiar. She was in bed but not her own. It was a hospital bed. Had she been hurt? She tried to pull aside the sheets but her muscles were stiff and unresponsive. She was in pale blue pajamas with slipper socks and had a wristband around her arm, but they sparked no memories.

What was going on?

She spotted flowers on a nearby dresser, together with 'get well' cards, a balloon, and even framed photographs. She saw herself in a couple of the pictures, recognized her parents. Also, her husband, Rahsaan.

The sense of familiarity, however minor, put her at ease. She glanced out the window. The familiar sights of downtown Denver were in the foreground, then Mile High Stadium and the Rocky Mountains beyond. Her ears picked up the chatter of people in the hallway as well the beeps and hum of medical equipment in other rooms. She tried to remember which hospital she was in but couldn't. She reached for other information, but it wasn't there either.

Before she could panic, however, her name came to her. Alice Helena Rhodes. Alix to some. Allie to none. At least there was that.

A doctor swept into the room, head buried in a chart. He looked startled when he saw that she was awake.

'Oh, sorry not to knock,' he said. 'Thought you were sleeping.'

'Who . . . who are you?' Alice asked, voice ragged and barely audible.

'Dr Chen? We met a few weeks ago. I'm the new attending surgeon here in the oncology department. Dr Kapur introduced us?'

No memory of him whatsoever.

'Sorry,' she said. 'My brain is foggy.'

'Hm,' Dr Chen said, removing a pen light from his pocket. 'Follow this with your eyes.'

She did. He checked her retinas then pocketed the pen light. 'Let me talk to the nurse. Might need to work on the dosage of your meds.'

Oncology. Dosage. Meds. The rest came back to her now. Cancer. Stage Four. Dying.

She gasped, letting out a mournful sob. Dr Chen raised his hands. 'Hey, hey, don't be upset,' he said, glancing to the door. 'Um . . . we, uh . . . we have good news. Good news about your labs.'

But Alice was already crying, her body wracked with sobs. Dr Chen glanced to the door a second time as if desperate to be relieved.

'Ms Rhodes, we have good news,' he repeated. 'Good news about your labs.'

Alice tuned him out. She was terrified, inconsolable.

'Alice, are you OK? Are you all right?'

The voice came from the hall. A second man in a lab coat entered, this one familiar. Dr Ganske. Ben. A friend.

She wiped her eyes even as she continued to cry.

'I'm sorry,' she said. 'It just hit me all over again.'

Ben gave her a hug, a gesture of familiarity that seemed to embarrass Dr Chen.

'It's OK,' Ben said lightly. 'That's how it works sometimes. But we've got good news today. *Great* news. Your cancer is regressing.'

This didn't compute. Alice eyed him with confusion. 'How's that possible?'

'It's a new process,' Ben explained. 'Gene therapy that alters the cancer cells and convinces them to shut down on their own. We just need to do a few more tests, but it's looking great.'

Alice was confused. It sounded good but her thoughts were so scattered she couldn't fully understand what she was being told.

'Where's my mom?' Alice asked.

Ben straightened. 'She was here. She must've just stepped away. Might've gone home to get some sleep. I can ask a nurse. But we called Rahsaan. He's on his way.'

'He is?' Alice asked.

'On his way,' Ben repeated. 'But the reason I'm here with Dr Chen is that we want to take a more aggressive stance with the treatment. Like with the radiation and the chemo, it won't be altogether pleasant, but if the labs are any indication, the result is worth it. Do you feel up to it?'

'Can we talk about this once Rahsaan gets here?' Alice asked.

Ben hesitated. 'Well, that's . . . we could lose a day that way. We need to infuse early. Not sure that's—'

'He'll be here soon, though, right?' Alice said.

Ben turned to Dr Chen who, almost imperceptibly, gave a quick shake of the head. Ben seemed to consider this then took Alice's hand.

'If it's what you need, we absolutely can wait,' Ben said. 'We'll check back in a few, OK?'

Alice was relieved. 'Thank you, Ben.'

'No problem, Alice.'

Alice sank back into the bed as the doctors exited. She was exhausted from just this one interaction. Her eyes couldn't focus on anything. The ceiling became a blur. When a nurse came in with a tray of food, Alice wasn't sure if she'd fallen asleep.

'I'm not hungry,' Alice said.

'It's OK not to eat but maybe just drink a little water,' the nurse suggested. 'Will go a long way to clearing your head.'

Alice nodded and reached for the water. Only then did she notice the large dog that had come in with the nurse. It looked like a shaggy German Shepherd and wore a vest with a 'Certified Service Dog' patch on it. Before she could ask why the animal was in her room, the beast jumped on her bed and licked her face.

'Oh my God!' Alice cried.

'Down, boy,' the nurse said, guiding the dog back to the floor. 'Sorry about that. Can I see your wrist?'

Alice looked puzzled. The nurse nodded to her arm. Alice hadn't noticed the wristband there. She raised it and the nurse eyed its bar code and alphanumeric string.

'Hey, Alice,' the nurse said quietly.

'Um, hi?'

'I know you don't remember who I am, so you won't hold this against me, but I'm still sorry,' the nurse said.

'Sorry for what?' Alice asked.

The nurse didn't reply. She took a syringe from inside her scrubs, looked about ready to inject it into Alice's IV drip, but then came around and gave her a hug instead.

'I love you, OK?' the nurse asked.

'Wait, what?' Alice asked. 'I think I should see the doctor.'

'Which one?' the nurse asked. 'The guy who is really some kind of local actor? Or the real one who just happens to be your narcissistic psychopath of an ex-boyfriend?'

'What're you talking about?' Alice asked.

The nurse moved to the window. With some difficulty, she pried a thin, lighted screen from the window frame and put it aside. The Denver vista disappeared, replaced by a much denser forest of skyscrapers. There were no mountains.

'You're in Chicago, not Denver,' the nurse said, moving back to Alice's side. 'It's 2025, not 2003. And your cancer was cured a long time ago. It's just, they keep regenerating you to use as some kind of lab rat.'

'What?' Alice exclaimed. 'Who are you?'

'Estefania Quiñones,' the nurse said, injecting the needle into Alice's IV. 'I'm going to get you out of here. Just not . . . *you* you.'

Before Alice could ask what she meant, everything went white.

THIRTY-SIX

I t had taken Este over a week of planning to get into the Kellner Group building. If it had only been breaking and entering, a few days of bribing ConEd workers who'd been tasked with upgrading the building's access to the city grid every few months would've done the trick. But she had to hack into the building's myriad server banks to manipulate the security apparatus. That took another few days.

The building and its systems were virtually impenetrable by conventional means. Luckily, Este had spent the last two years uncovering unusual ways into buildings once all the normal routes had been cut off.

The hardest part was accessing the sub-level lab Alice had referenced in her note. Not only was it deep underground, but it had no emergency exits, no fire stairs, no nothing. The only way in or out was the elevator that descended from one of the building's upper floors.

So, not only did Este have to break into an impregnable building, she also had to go up almost to the top level to hijack an elevator to the basement. All without being caught.

Piece of cake.

All she needed was a distraction.

Once all this was done, she hacked into the building's servers and waited for an Alice to be resurrected. She couldn't believe the sheer number of ghost resurrections going on in the building: literally dozens an hour, sometimes over a hundred. Worse, she knew these specimens – these *people* – were being brought to life only to be gassed up with experimental drugs, subjected to endless and potentially excruciating tests, then 'humanely' killed, the bodies used to resurrect others.

It was madness. An endless holocaust of victims. The illusion of scientific advancement masking a factory of endless death.

She had only one death to contribute to this cycle. That someone would not only come right back to her a few hours later, but would also have only been alive for a few hours before her death anyway. Still, she agonized over the decision until the very moment she carried it out.

After bolting from the room in which she killed Alice, Este couldn't help but consider the doctors and nurses who'd likely get torn apart by Alice's ghost next. She tried to think of it as them getting a taste of their own medicine, before they were resurrected back with the sample that every employee on that floor was required to give each morning. She wished she could care less about their pain, but she couldn't. She was still a nurse. Her entire existence ran counter to this action.

'Come on, Casey!' she said, tugging the dog down the corridor.

Behind them, the first screams of terror from those attacked by Alice's ghost echoed down to her. Alarms were already going off. She could hear running feet coming up the stairwells. When the security teams arrived, carrying not only tranquilizer guns but also the familiar orange incendiary grenades she'd seen in Reno and Los Angeles, Este contorted her face in fear.

'Back there!' she yelled and pointed.

When the guards were gone, she reached the elevators, rang for a car, and stepped inside. Only when the car began to descend did she slump onto the floor in relief. Casey nuzzled her as he took a seat next to her.

'Now comes the hard part,' she said. 'You ready to do your bit?'

Casey licked her face. She took this as assent.

When the elevator doors opened onto the sub-level laboratory,

Este couldn't believe her eyes. It was a vast space, more cavern than workspace.

'All right,' Este said, grabbing Casey's leash. 'Let's do this.'

She hurried down the steel steps to the lab floor, searching the storage units for the right canister. Though she had the printout of Alice's message in her pocket, she had the alphanumeric string memorized. There were the familiar numbers that she recognized as associated with Alice alone, like a serial number. The numbers past that indicated a date that was less than a day after when Este had last seen her.

She thought this meant her friend, or at least the version she knew, hadn't lived long past Reno.

She went from unit to unit, row to row, finally locating it in a storage unit toward the back. She opened the lid and took it out, checking to see whether there were any signs of tampering. It looked like any other canister in the lab.

'You in there, Alice?' she joked to the canister.

Directly underneath it in the storage unit was a second device, one she recognized from the diagram Alice sent along. This was the real leap of faith. How much faith did Este have in Alice? This was *beyond* the right time to ask the question, but she was putting her future – no, her entire life – in the hands of a ghost and a quack doctor.

The elevator dinged. It was now or never.

She opened the second device, a two-pronged syringe-type device. One needle, the diagram had shown, would inject the bacteria that would bind with her DNA to make a ghost copy. The second, the actual extractor, would then pull the copy out to store in the canister. Este angled the first syringe around to the back of her head and stabbed into the base of her skull. The needle piercing the skin didn't hurt, but as it sunk past the epidermal layer into vascular tissue, Este's eyes watered. She felt a deep, throbbing pain just above her neck that spread throughout her head.

She waited a few seconds past the time Alice suggested the process needed for completion then pushed the button again. The second needle punctured her skin, extracted what it needed, then popped out on its own a second later.

'Holy Jeez,' Este whispered, putting her hand to her head.

'Let's see your hands!' a voice cried out from near the elevators. 'The police are on their way. Get on your knees and raise your hands over your head.'

The guard sounded ex-military, meaning he would have a whole protocol of escalations to follow before he could shoot. So Este ignored him. Instead, she leaned down to Casey and slipped the pair of canisters into his vest. She then led him to the back wall where a venting hatch, way too small for a person but just fine for the low-slung Alsatian, awaited.

'Take good care of me, Casey,' Este said, giving the dog a hug.

Casey eyed her expectantly. She opened the venting hatch, took off his leash, and pointed skyward.

'Go, Casey!'

He obeyed, charging up the dark vent before disappearing from view up the shaft. Este shut the hatch and turned back to the rows just as several security officers closed in on her.

She took out the last syringe, the one with the governor serum she'd use to give her current body a true death before, she hoped, waking to begin life anew. She stared at it for a long moment, considering all the things that had to happen next for this to be successful. She thought it'd feel freeing. Instead, she was terrified.

She closed her eyes, seeing Alice's words on the message all over again. *There Is Life after Death*. She prayed her friend was right.

'What is that?' one of the officers yelled, raising his weapon even as Este raised the syringe. 'Put it down or we'll shoot!'

'I'm counting on it,' Este said, injecting herself.

The security force fired their weapons as one.

THIRTY-SEVEN

The bed shook. The young woman awoke, disoriented. A rectangle of white light poured in from a nearby window, the only light in the small, boxy room. The fluttering drapes gave the light a strobing effect.

The woman looked around but was unable to place where she was. She grabbed the edge of the bed to keep from sliding off even as the threadbare blankets that covered it slipped to the floor. The walls and ceiling were water-damaged and the room mostly empty. She was dressed except for shoes and socks.

'Alice,' a woman's voice said from the corner of the room. 'Alice, it's OK. It'll be over in a second.'

The young woman peered through the darkness. A petite woman, face framed by curly black hair, sat in the corner.

'Who are you?' the young woman asked.

'Este, um, Estefania Quiñones,' Este said. 'Do you remember me?'

The young woman shook her head.

'We met in Los Angeles,' Este said. 'We escaped together. Went to Reno. Ended up in Chicago? You don't remember any of that?'

The young woman searched her mind but nothing came back. It was all a big blank.

'Not sure this worked,' said a man in the doorway.

'Yeah, but it's her, Fredo,' Este said. 'She's in there somewhere.'

Something large, warm, and furry launched itself onto the young woman's chest, knocking the air out of her. She tried to push it away even as it licked her face.

'No!' she said to the insistent animal. 'Get off!'

A name came to her. Casey.

'Get off, Casey!' she demanded.

The dog got down.

'You remember Casey?' Este asked.

'Y . . . yes,' the young woman said. 'I don't remember anything else.'

Este raised her hands. 'I trek a thousand miles to rescue her – to *die* for her – and she only remembers the damn dog's name.'

'What about your name?' the man asked the young woman, ignoring Este's comment.

The young woman shook her head. Then slowly the name came back to her.

Alice Helena Rhodes. Alix to some. Allie to none.

'Alice,' she said. 'I'm Alice.'

The gentle earthquake began to subside. Wilfredo, as if sensing the women needed to be alone, took up Casey's leash.

'I'll take him for a walk.'

Este nodded. After Wilfredo exited, she moved to Alice's side and took her hand.

'How're you feeling?' she asked.

'Sore. Numb. A little lost. Was there an earthquake?'

'There was,' Este confirmed.

Alice nodded. 'We met in Los Angeles?'

'We did.'

'You said you died for me?' Alice asked.

'Yeah, we may need to work up to that one,' Este said.

Alice stared at Este for a long moment. She remembered tall trees in the mountains, broken cities, a railyard. Men with machine guns. Mutated predatory animals. Then she saw Este with her through all of it.

'You always find me,' Alice said. 'And you're always so happy to see me.'

Este burst out laughing and put her arms around her. 'Yeah, yeah, and you're always like, "Who the hell are you?"'

They embraced for a long moment. Este leaned in close. 'Welcome back, Alice. I'm so glad to see you.'

Este pulled away, looking Alice up and down. 'Now, what do you remember?'

Alice searched her memory. 'That building. Waking up. All these labs, all these doctors and nurses. Oh, and Ben Ganske. He was there.'

'Yeah, found out about that,' Este said.

'He's stumbled upon this process that can resurrect human life,' Alice said. 'He's been resurrecting me over and over as some kind of lab rat.'

Este nodded, keeping the fact that it was many more people than just Alice to herself.

'How did you find me?' Alice asked.

'You sent pretty explicit instructions,' Este said. 'Though it's hard to know how much of that was you versus how much was a version of you a few minutes into the future *after* your resurrectable sample was extracted.'

Alice crossed her eyes and shook her head. 'Not following you there, Este.'

'Not even sure I follow myself,' Este admitted. 'Right now, I'm just happy to be here. Wasn't always certain that'd be the case.'

'Did you die?' Alice asked softly. Este nodded. 'So, you're like me, now? A ghost?'

'I am,' Este said. 'Though I'm only now figuring out what that means. It's mind-altering to say the least. There are so many things tied to my understanding of pain, of death, of permanence that suddenly feel like they're out the window.'

'If my math is right, I've been doing this a total of five or six days, so I don't have much of a head start on you. Guess we'll learn about it together. I guess my one big concern is how much of a danger are we to others?'

Este nodded and reached into a backpack next to the bed. 'It's hardly foolproof, but I had some thoughts on that. Talked to Wilfredo about it.' She extracted a belt of the orange incendiary grenades.

'Whoa,' Alice said. 'Didn't know it was that kind of party.'

'From what little I understand about our ghost biology, there must be a split second between the stopping of our heart or the cessation of brain activity – that actual moment of death – and the release of the enzymatic catalyst that ejects the ghost,' Este explained.

'Huh?' Alice asked, a confused look on her face.

Este sighed and held up the grenades. 'If one of us is killed, I think an explosive, all-cleansing fire, if unleashed fast enough, can consume our "ghost" before it can begin to hunt or rebuild. That's why all the doctors and soldiers carry incendiary grenades. It's like a last resort, a failsafe in case they can't subdue the patient. I can't imagine it's foolproof, but if it's between immolation and our "ghosts" going on a kill-crazy rampage, it's the best solution we have.'

Alice eyed the grenades curiously, wondering if she could immolate herself in an emergency, much less someone else. She hoped she wouldn't have to find out.

'Thank you for these,' she said. 'But in the meantime, what's our next move? I mean, I don't even know where we are.'

'Well, I said I'd get you to your husband,' Este replied. 'When Wilfredo and I cooked up this plan, we figured the Denver QZ was as good a place as any – and far enough from Chicago – to do our little homegrown resurrections.'

'You mean Rahsaan?' Alice asked. 'Rahsaan is here?'

'He's maybe an hour west of here. Since we're in the neighborhood, I thought maybe we could swing by.'

Every inch of Alice became electrified. Where her muscles were seconds ago tired or numb, they were now taut. She sat up straight.

'Oh, thank you,' she said, unsure how to respond. 'Thanks for rescuing me again, too.'

Este grinned. 'Well, it's gotta take hold for real one of these days, right? Come on. Let's go see Rahsaan.'

THIRTY-EIGHT

As they drove from the ruins of the Denver QZ out to Camp Ben Nighthorse Campbell, Este reflected on just how insane it was that Alice's plan had worked. She and Wilfredo weren't scientists and human resurrection wasn't exactly something covered by her nurse training.

They'd rounded up the ingredients Alice had listed beforehand. This included piles of protein powder, calcium, phosphorus, various trace elements and precious metals (though it was no easy thing breaking into LoP drugstores; their owners typically kept only narcotics and opioids under lock and key), and water, still scarce in some regions. But all of that still felt like a shot in the dark when it came time for the real thing.

'Still can't believe Casey found me,' Wilfredo told Este after she'd resurrected and while they were preparing to bring Alice back. 'I was two blocks away when that hound came charging out of the parking garage. I thought he'd get hit by a truck or something. But nope, he managed to make it to the truck and we hauled ass out of Chi-town.'

There's no way anyone calls it that, Este had wanted to tell him.

'We got to the motel, I put the canister through the hole I drilled in the bathroom door, then I sealed it all up. I checked the windows a second time then I hit the button and ran.'

'How'd you know it worked?' Este had asked.

Wilfredo held up a phone. 'Set up a live feed and watched from a quarter-mile down the road. Most messed-up thing I've ever seen. *Way* disgusting. I've seen your spleen, the inside of your intestinal tract, your brains – or lack thereof . . .'

She punched him for that but was glad he'd thought ahead. When it was time to do Alice, they retraced Wilfredo's steps exactly. Only, when it came time for Alice to resurrect, Este was fascinated by what appeared on the live feed. It felt like something from the Bible – a woman created from mere dust. Before the process was even complete, Este had Wilfredo drive back so she could be with Alice the moment she woke up.

As Wilfredo helped carry the still groggy Alice to the bed, Este's thoughts turned to Ben Ganske. How could anyone witness a miracle like this one and think only of how to exploit it?

The wrong man had the power to work miracles.

She glanced at Alice in the backseat of the double cab of the pickup. She was staring out the window, only occasionally speaking up to marvel with recognition at this landmark or that, remembered from her life in Colorado. Este was reminded all over again that it wasn't just being a ghost that made Alice out of step in 2025, it was that she had missed two decades of life.

Except, this wasn't true. She'd spent those two decades being resurrected, subjected to all sorts of diseases, disorientation, and experimental drugs, then dying ignominiously at the hands of those she thought were her doctors. It was almost a blessing that she remembered none of this.

'Wow, look at that,' Wilfredo said, pointing to a big rig on the same highway, its trailer filled to the brim with thousands of oranges.

'I thought there were all kinds of shortages,' Alice said.

Este pointed to a UN sign on the truck's dashboard as they passed. 'Donations up from the Rio Grande Valley, probably the Mexican side. They've had so many quakes in Mexico, they gave up on fixing the highways and railroads down from the US border. So, all the citrus there comes up to us in trucks and, in return, we put wheat and corn on boats and send it their way.'

'The quakes are uniting people across borders?' Alice asked.

'Eh, not really,' Wilfredo replied. 'You've got some trade going on out of necessity, but nobody's government is all that stable right now and they're primarily dealing with routing resources to displacement camps. Corporations are stepping up, but it's obvious they're just looking to profit. No one knows where this ride is going, so no one's quite sure how to prepare for the future. Everyone makes a big show of helping out and being in it together. But the worse it gets, the more folks' true colors come out.'

Alice blanched. Este leaned back and took her hand.

'That's why your boy Ben there is so messed up,' Este said. 'He thinks it's the quakes that'll end us all, but people will find a way to knock each other down anyway. You can't fight the future with these individualized solutions. Gotta build networks.'

Alice thought about this then nodded. 'Yeah,' she said idly.

A crop of white domes appeared on the plateau to the right, extending several square miles into the distance behind high fences.

'There it is,' Este said. 'Camp Campbell.'

She stared at the camp, feeling the kind of apprehension she felt in Chicago. It was such a strange thing to leave the battered remnants of a major metropolis like Denver to find so much of its surviving population gathered into a comparatively tiny space. With all the houses, apartments, skyscrapers and sprawl in the city, the idea that so many humans could be transferred to such tiny living spaces felt like a strange magic trick.

The camp buildings consisted of row after row after row of the same kind of Quonset huts they'd seen in the National Guard encampment at Pan City. Only, there were thousands more. They seemed to extend forever.

Although the barbed-wire-topped fences appeared intimidating, families had hung laundry on them and children played soccer on the other side, kicking up enough dust to soil the clothes and sheets all over again. The huts looked uniform from a distance, but as they got closer, they could see great murals painted on the sides, personalizing them. Next to a few of the buildings were signs of attempted gardens, though they didn't seem to have yielded much yet.

Halfway down the fence, a long line of cars waited to be checked in, soldiers inspecting each vehicle as license plates were automatically photographed. There was a second entrance half a mile down the road for deliveries. The line of trucks there was as long as that at the visitors' gate.

'Who are all these people?' Alice asked.

'Family members and friends living in the LoP,' Wilfredo said. 'They might not be able to take their refugee relatives in, but they can bring in food and supplies.'

After twenty minutes in the visitors' line, they reached the gates. Este expected to be asked who they were visiting, but all the guards wanted to know was whether they'd been on a farm recently or if they were bringing in produce.

'Outbreak control,' they said, waving them through to a large open space that served as a parking lot.

'Sector 16, Row A, Building 9,' Este said, comparing a piece of paper to a map tacked up on a nearby telephone pole. 'Almost there.'

Alice looked nervous. 'What if he doesn't recognize me? What if he's got some hot young girlfriend? I mean, I wouldn't blame him but—'

'Stop,' Este said, taking her hand. 'Why plague yourself with questions when the answers are a few hundred yards away?'

Alice squeezed Este's hand. Together they headed into the rows of huts, Wilfredo and Casey binging up the rear.

The huts were laid out on a grid. Signs at regular intervals on the pathways admonished residents to 'keep byways clear', warning them that there were 'no motorized vehicles allowed'. The camp seemed relatively empty – 'Most everybody's on work duty or at the school,' a mailman informed them when they asked – but they still had to dodge various residents on bicycles or hurrying along on foot.

'Can you smell that?' Alice asked, nodding in the direction of a few larger shelters. 'Fresh bread.'

'Yeah, like you were making in D-Town when you got hit,' Wilfredo said.

Alice gave him an odd look. Este realized these memories didn't exist within this version of Alice. Anything she'd learned or memories she'd made between her escape from the underground lab and her death in the gun battle was lost.

'We have to come up with a system to remember which memories our Alice has versus which ones were reset after she got killed,' Este said.

'Oh, yeah,' Wilfredo said. 'Sorry, Alice.'

'It's OK,' Alice said. 'Weird to think of all the memories I've created that I don't have access to. But I was always terrible in the kitchen. Probably wouldn't want to remember my baking anyway.'

Este quietly marveled at this. What if, before any unpleasant task, one could extract their own ghost-copy, do the task, then erase it from memory by reverting to their own self from an hour earlier? It would allow one to live without guilt or conscience. She wondered if this was why Ben made so many copies of himself.

'Sector 16,' Wilfredo announced, pointing up at a sign.

A group of children passed in front of them, led by a man they took to be a teacher. The kids were like so many ducklings following their parent. Alice grinned and waved but was mostly ignored, the boys jostling each other as the girls gossiped in a single group. For kids that had lost everything, Este thought they looked remarkably normal.

One of the girls, a brown-haired, blue-eyed dead ringer for Alice, waved back to Alice then stopped short as if realizing the resemblance herself.

'Mom?' the girl asked.

THIRTY-NINE

A lice stared at the little girl. Though the girl's hair and eyes were hers, the skin tone was Rahsaan's and her facial features were a blend of the two. Even the quick syllable she spoke – tight, clipped – evoked her husband.

Alice shook her head, freezing a smile on her face.

'Not your mama,' she said lightly. 'But "hi" all the same!'

'Sorry,' the girl said. 'You looked like her from farther away.'

'Come on, Katie,' her teacher said, before eyeing Alice guardedly.

Alice stepped back. Inside she was reeling. Kathryn had been her grandmother's name, but she went by Katie.

'Alice?' Este asked.

'I'm . . . I'm fine,' Alice said.

'We can come back,' Este offered, though Wilfredo looked dubious.

'Row A, Building 9, right?' Alice asked.

Este nodded. 'Um, you got your incendiaries?'

Alice patted the grenades in her waistband but held up a hand when Este tried to follow. Este understood and hung back. If she was going to suddenly reappear to her husband a couple of decades after he buried her, she'd probably want to avoid having to make a bunch of extraneous introductions first, too.

'We'll be waiting,' Este said.

But Alice's mind was already far away. As she moved down the rows in search of Building 9, her thoughts were on the little girl. What was she like? Was she scared during the quake? Was she OK there in the camp? She wanted to follow her, not go after Rahsaan.

But it wasn't her place. She wasn't Katie's mother, no matter the sneaking suspicion clawing up her spine. She was just an interloper in someone else's timeline.

She passed Building 6 and looked up ahead to confirm she wasn't walking in the wrong direction. Building 7 loomed ahead of her. She counted ahead and could just see Building 9.

Taking a deep breath, she tried to center herself. She'd spent so much time mentally preparing herself for disappointment in relation to Rahsaan, she'd forgotten to consider what life in the future might be like without him. To start over alone. To really envision what that might be like, maybe tagging along with Este and Wilfredo, maybe not.

A second big breath in and she could see it. She could turn around, walk out of here. She need never return.

She was about to do just that when she heard jogging feet.

'Alice? Hey, is that you?'

The voice was so familiar, though she couldn't remember the last time Rahsaan had said her name. Names were what they called other people. They never needed names with one another.

She closed her eyes and turned. When she opened them again, there he was. He may have been nearing the half-century mark, but he was leaner than he'd been in his twenties. His face was drained of baby fat, making his features more angular and dramatic. His hair hadn't thinned but there were patches of gray. His clothing didn't quite fit right, suggesting he'd either lost weight recently or maybe gotten them from a donation bin following the quake.

What was unmistakable was her body's response at the very sight of him. After all this time, she still felt giddy at seeing him in a way that made her feel slightly ridiculous. Wasn't that supposed to wear off after a while? They'd been together almost a decade, right? Their lives had been full of routines and habits.

But in this moment, it was like seeing a new love. This was the person for her and she for him.

'Um, hey,' Alice said. 'Surprise!'

Rahsaan inhaled sharply and did his best attempt at bewilderment. But Alice knew his body language too well, even after all this time. She could see it in his face. This was a surprise, but not a shock.

He knew.

'I was just in the neighborhood,' Alice said quickly, unsure which angle might best ease the tension. 'I didn't mean to interrupt. In fact, I was just leaving.'

Rahsaan said nothing for a second and they stood there, taking each other's measure. What Alice took to be a silent understanding passed between them. Both relaxed. A little.

'It's so good to see you, Alice,' Rahsaan said finally, moving to hug her.

Alice wished the hug hadn't felt so good, so warm. It would've made leaving that much easier. But these were the arms she wanted around her. She knew they weren't hers anymore, though, and she stepped back.

'I don't mean to intrude,' Alice said. 'I know you've gone through a lot lately.'

'Why don't you come inside for a moment?' Rahsaan asked, nodding toward his building. 'I can only imagine what you've gone through to get here.'

Another pause of mutual understanding. They moved between the rows, saying nothing the entire way to his hut. Alice had so many questions, but they felt like they were meant for someone else, not the older man beside her.

Unlike the huts with large murals, Building 9 was relatively unadorned, save for a few colorful stickers on the wall behind the tiny garden out front and several unicorns on a bed sheet being used to cover one of the windows.

Rahsaan held the front door open for Alice and she stepped inside. The interior was larger than she thought it'd be. There was a single hallway that ran the length of the hut, dividers sectioning off three rooms and then a forward common room. The residents left their shoes by the door. The rest of the common room was filled up with stuffed animals, toys and children's books. Photos of the residents were up on the walls.

'Three families share each building,' Rahsaan explained, moving toys from a chair and offering it to Alice. 'It's tight and it can get loud, but we make it work.'

Alice's eyes floated up to the pictures. She spied Katie right away in a picture with another little girl, clearly a sister. The next photo over showed the two girls with their father. To Alice's surprise, the third picture was one of her and Rahsaan taken only a few months after they'd graduated. Her mother had taken the picture. She was about to ask Rahsaan why it would be up when she made it to the last picture, one of Rahsaan, Katie as a toddler, then a woman in her late thirties in a hospital bed holding a baby.

She looked exactly like Alice. Just . . . older. Alice felt light-headed.

'Alice?' Rahsaan said, then saw where her gaze had landed.

'I don't know if you can really call me that,' Alice said. 'I mean, is that Alice to you? Is she me?'

'You are now who she once was,' Rahsaan said. 'If that makes sense. But that's where you diverge.'

'Well, yeah,' Alice said. 'But how? How is she here and I'm not? If that's even the right way of saying it.'

'How much do you remember about Dr Ganske and the Kellner Group?' Rahsaan asked.

Alice considered mentioning her Chicago adventure, then decided against it. 'Remembering more each day,' she said.

'Ben told us that though you were dying, your cells could live on due to this radical procedure he'd used them in,' Rahsaan explained. 'He said that what they were learning could one day save hundreds if not thousands of people. He was so adamant and so excited. I admit, it made us feel good for a few days. Gave us, *you*, some meaning. You died soon thereafter. But about ten months later, I got a call.'

'From Ben?'

'From you,' Rahsaan said. 'You said you were in a medical facility in Minnesota. That you were feeling well and you wanted me to come see you when you were all the way better. I asked when that would be, and you said soon. After you hung up, I spent the next day or so thinking I'd suffered a hallucination or some kind of psychotic break. But then Ben called and told me what happened. That they'd been able to regress the cancer and build back healthy cells but, somehow, this had led to reconstructing parts of your brain, even memory. They hadn't been sure if they should even pursue it, but the implications were too incredible to set it aside. After a number of starts and stops, they'd managed to bring you back completely.'

'Like a ghost of who I'd been when I died.'

'Almost,' Rahsaan said. 'Who you'd been when they took the final cell sample, so a few weeks prior. Which explains why you might not remember those last conversations.'

'Ah, makes sense. What was it like? Seeing me again, I mean.'

'Just . . . insane yet incredible,' Rahsaan recalled. 'I'd never been more grateful for anything in my life. I'd never stopped grieving and then here you were. All the pleading I'd done with the Universe seeming to pay off in extraordinary fashion.'

'And me?' Alice asked.

'You wanted to come home right away, but it was another year before Ben let you leave the lab,' Rahsaan said. 'He said that if you died again, it'd be deadly for those around you. He had to come up with this governor serum to make you safe.'

'Did my parents know?'

Rahsaan fell quiet. 'I'm so sorry, Alice. Your father passed away soon after your death,' he said softly. After giving Alice a moment, he continued. 'Your mother had become too frail, so we decided not to tell her. It was agonizing for you, but if the process reversed itself and you passed away again, we knew it would be too much for her.'

'Did she die?' Alice asked.

'Yes, about ten years ago. We stayed in touch. You were always prodding me to keep up with her. She actually dated again and was considering remarrying when she died.'

'What about our friends? And other family?' Alice asked. 'You couldn't just one day waltz back in with me on your arm all, "Surprise!"'

'No, but selling the house and moving across town was the easiest thing in the world,' Rahsaan said. 'If you remember, we never had that many close friends and few from my work pried into my affairs after I'd lost my spouse. They knew I'd found someone "new", but that was it.'

'Wow,' Alice said, thinking hard about how to ask her next question. 'In all that time, did you know about, well, me? Or about all the versions of me up there with Ben?'

Rahsaan's look darkened. 'We knew he continued to use your cells,' Rahsaan said evasively. 'That was implicit in our agreement, the one that let you come home. There was always this threat hanging over it that if we said anything, he'd find a way to come and take you – my Alice – away again, possibly even our daughters after they came along. So, we were cowed. I couldn't risk losing you again.'

'But you knew he'd resurrected other versions of me, right? Or did you not?'

'Yes, Alice, we knew.'

'How?'

'Can't you guess?' Rahsaan asked. 'You're the fifth Alice now to come looking for me.'

FORTY

Este and Wilfredo walked Casey around the perimeter of the camp in silence. Este couldn't stop thinking about the little girl, about the heartbreak Alice was likely experiencing. She wanted to be there with her but knew she couldn't. She just hoped Rahsaan had as good a heart as Alice remembered and was handling the situation well.

What that would actually look like, she had no idea. How do you tell a ghost that has fought its way back to life, to you, to the future, that, oops, sorry, you've moved on?

Hearing more and more people, they reached the end of the residential areas and came to a dining hall, a medical facility, various supply stations, administrative buildings, and several open-air workshops with large sections of wall haphazardly cut out to let in a breeze. Refugees from the Denver QZ moved in and out of the buildings, shuttling boxes and paperwork back and forth. Deliveries from the trucks were recorded, medicines were distributed to waiting residents, food was prepared for the first of several lunch-hour shifts.

They reached a long, wide trench being dug and filled with pipe large enough a car could be driven through it.

'Will this be freshwater?' Este asked one of the workers.

'Yeah, we're hoping to connect up with the South Platte, Blue and even Fraser Rivers,' the workman said. 'It's a big project, but going out east, north, then northwest, we hope to have at least one line still intact should there be more quakes.'

'Smart,' Este said. 'How soon until it's ready?'

The workman shrugged. 'Hoping to get the South Platte line finished in the next three weeks, but that's only if our supply line holds, you know?'

'I feel you. Good luck.'

'Thanks.'

The more they saw, the more Este took mental notes. Admittedly, it had been up and running for longer, but it worked more efficiently than the Reno camp.

'It's a good setup, better than we had in LA,' Wilfredo commented as they moved away. 'They've already got a large-scale septic system in the ground. They're getting good at these.'

How sad is that, Este thought.

They passed a garden, as large as two or three of the expanded shelters, where residents worked. The plants here appeared to be spices. She supposed the food crops were elsewhere. She knelt and saw handwritten signs at the end of the rows for wild mint, dwarf sage, horehound and oregano de la sierra.

It was the Colorado version of what the LAQZ homesteaders were doing, cultivating native plants. She hoped it worked. She imagined some great turn back to agrarianism emerging from the quakes, but it felt like a fantasy. Given the needs of such a large global population, it felt wildly optimistic. It solved certain issues for those in agriculture-friendly climates, but what about everyone else?

She'd heard someone at the Reno camp say that when they'd worked hurricane disaster relief in the Caribbean, there were always two waves of death – those that died in the initial storm and flooding, then those who passed due to disease and privation in the following months. She imagined this happening in a different way to each population affected by the quakes.

It was almost too much to bear.

But she forced her mind back to the trees around Lake Tahoe. A renewal, Alice had said. Humans had to learn to readapt themselves to the planet and stop trying to adapt it to them.

'Hey, Este? You need to see this,' Wilfredo said.

Este got to her feet, shading her eyes to see what he was pointing at. A dozen yards away, a group of schoolchildren ran around a makeshift playground. She looked for Katie, figuring that's who Wilfredo had seen, but then saw a group of teachers looking back her way. One of them wore a light blue dress, brown hair piled on top of her head and pinned in place. She appeared to be in her late forties. Este had never seen her before, but her eyes – no, the intensity of her gaze – was immediately familiar.

She broke away from the other teachers to approach Este and Wilfredo. Este immediately turned to walk the other way.

'Wait!' the teacher called out in a voice as familiar as her looks, hurrying over.

Nope, thought Este.

But the teacher was too quick and was soon by her side. 'Hey,' she said. 'My daughter said she saw you.'

The teacher's appearance had been enough to throw Este. That she also sounded like Alice blew her mind.

'Yeah, sorry if we freaked her out,' Este said, finally turning back.

'No, not at all,' the teacher said. 'She liked your dog. Our neighbors had an Alsatian. She used to play with it.'

'Oh, Casey would love to play with her if she's got a few minutes,' Este said without thinking. 'He loves kids.'

'That's very kind of you, but she's in class right now,' the teacher replied. 'I just wanted to say thank you.'

'For what?' Este asked.

'You seem like a nice person,' the teacher went on. 'Probably been through the wringer, a bit like the rest of us. Like all of us soon will be.'

'Yes,' Este said.

The teacher touched her arm. 'So, it's nice that our, well, what – mutual acquaintance? – has people like that looking out for her.'

Wow, now this *was a conversation for the books.*

'Oh, I know how weird that must sound,' the teacher said, smiling. 'But they keep moving the goalposts for what's normal, so I just ride the wave at this point. Just, thank you for keeping an eye out for her.'

The teacher eyed Este more closely as if seeing something new.

'Maybe you need some keeping an eye out for, too, no?'

Este grinned. 'Don't we all?'

'Yeah, but you try and run from trauma and it doesn't dissipate or remain static,' the teacher said. 'It builds.'

Coming from anyone else, Este would've felt patronized or condescended to. But as this seemed to come from the mouth of an older, wiser version of someone she trusted, it felt different. The teacher seemed to recognize exactly what was going on in her mind.

'I know,' Este said. 'My mom was military. I've been around it all my life. I'm going to deal with it. I just have a couple of other things I need to put away first.'

The teacher nodded. 'Don't wait too long, OK?'

'OK.'

But the teacher held her gaze a moment longer. There was a knowing urgency behind what was an otherwise innocuous suggestion. Este saw that she wasn't quite looking back at her but through her, a dust cloud pluming up from the highway reflected in her eyes.

'Go,' the teacher, the older Alice, whispered.

Este ran.

FORTY-ONE

Alice marveled at what Rahsaan was saying. Five Alices had escaped through the years? Five versions of her? It was too much to process.

'It was all so long ago – four over the first ten years or so. There hasn't been one in almost a decade,' Rahsaan admitted. 'I'd assumed Ben had changed his protocols.'

'How'd they find you?'

'Well, the first two both showed up at the old house,' Rahsaan said. 'They were told I'd moved. It wasn't as if I was that hard to find once they gained access to the internet or a phone book. The third went to your mother's house.'

'Oh, God.'

'Yeah, but luckily your mother wasn't home and you . . . Sorry, *she* was picked up for vagrancy,' Rahsaan explained. 'The fourth showed up at my new office and everyone just thought it was, well . . .'

'Your wife,' Alice offered.

'Yes,' Rahsaan admitted. 'She was very confused when I wasn't surprised to see her. The fifth, I actually misspoke. She didn't come looking for me. She'd gone down to Florida, down in the Keys. She got a job, got a house, started this whole new life.'

'How'd she get caught?'

'Would you believe she was at some protest? It was related to the Kellner Group sponsoring some research lab at Florida State. She had an alias but her fingerprints were in the national database. They called me when her real name came up, thinking it was a mistake or some bizarre case of identity theft.'

'Your wife now, she doesn't use her name?'

'No, Ben provided her with a new social security number, passport, last name and everything to avoid complications,' Rahsaan explained. 'The government has an interest in his work, so they've helped out with things like that.'

'What happened to all the other Alices?' Alice asked.

'The Kellner Group came and got them. Took them back to wherever they'd been before.'

'Rahsaan,' Alice protested. 'He euthanized them. I'm sure. That's what he planned to do with me until I escaped.'

When Rahsaan said nothing, Alice touched his knee. He flinched.

'I'm sorry,' Alice said. 'But how could you do that to us?'

'Are you joking?' Rahsaan asked. 'What do you know about your own body? You know you're a danger to anyone who comes anywhere near you, right?'

'I do, but—'

'The world has never been so unsafe given these quakes,' Rahsaan said. 'If you have an accident, if you die, that thing escapes your body and kills the nearest four people. At random. So yes, of course I called Ben. If I didn't, I'd be as guilty as him should anything happen to you.'

'That's not the case with your wife, I assume?'

'No, that's why they had to keep her in the lab for so long,' he said. 'They gave her some kind of serum. It turns it off.'

'So, why didn't you just ask Ben to give Florida-Alice that? Or the Alice that came to your office? By turning them over to Ben, you condemn them to death. They had no chance. He considers life utterly disposable. How could you not know that?'

Rahsaan stared back at her blankly.

'Oh,' Alice said. 'You did know that. Do you know how many of me have died over the past two decades? Thousands. You traded all that death so that you could go right on living your old life – *our* old life – with one of us. You're complicit in this.'

'Alice—'

'Thank you for calling me by my name,' Alice said. 'But you've dehumanized me in almost every other way imaginable.'

'You think it's easy for me?' Rahsaan asked.

'I'm not sure I care.'

'I keep this secret – we *all* keep this secret – and maybe there's a future for all of us,' Rahsaan said lamely.

'You sound like Ben,' Alice replied, then realized something. 'What do you mean by "we all" keep this secret?'

'Our family. Our daughters,' Rahsaan said. 'All the surviving loved ones who've already benefited from this science.'

Alice stared at him in horror. 'I'm not the only one,' she said slowly, a realization more than a question.

'You thought you were?' Rahsaan asked.

'How many others are there? Ghosts, I mean, like me. Ones under his control.'

Rahsaan considered this. 'There were hundreds of donors when he was working with you,' he said. 'But I know he meant to grow that to thousands to increase the sample size.'

Alice paled. '*Thousands?*'

Rahsaan nodded, but guiltily now, as if these weren't his secrets to tell.

Alice felt dizzy. Thousands of ghosts? All subject to his whim? Suffering death after death after death? And if even *one* of them escaped, so many more could die? If she could escape and resurrect, so could they. Given the instability of the planet, this didn't seem so far-fetched.

A development meant to save the human species could just as easily be the author of its destruction.

'This is madness,' she said. 'Do you have any idea how much agony he puts those subjects through? How much he put *me* through?'

'But it's not you!' Rahsaan exclaimed. 'It's like a fingernail of you. You've only been programmed to think you've lived this whole, full life, but actually you've only been alive a few days or weeks. I'm sorry, but you're a copy. Not the real thing.'

'Do I look like a fingernail to you?' Alice managed through gritted teeth. 'Did the ones who found you before? And what about your wife? She's a copy, too, just an older one. You have no idea.'

Rahsaan sighed and shifted his weight. Only then did Alice see the tranquilizer gun in his waistband.

'Did you already call him?' she asked.

'Call who?' Rahsaan asked guiltily. Alice stared at him. 'Of course I did. My kids are over in the school a few buildings west of here. I have my neighbors to think about. My wife. Our friends.'

'All their lives are more important than mine,' Alice said.

'Yes, they are,' Rahsaan said frankly. 'All of them are more important than you. You're the one taking their safety for granted, not me. You should be asking yourself whether *your* life is more important than all of theirs. Or even *one* of theirs.'

Alice didn't know how to respond. Instead of saying anything, she rose and moved to the door.

'Where are you going?' Rahsaan asked, fumbling for the tranq gun.

'Just let me go,' Alice said. 'You'll never see me again. For old times' sake.'

'I can't. What if four people – or more – have to die just because a copy of my wife is asking me for a favor and I'm sentimental?'

'But what if they don't?' Alice said. 'What if no one has to die and I can get away? Figure out a way to really live again in this strange future?'

Rahsaan's hand wavered, but he shook his head. 'I can't take that chance.'

Alice nodded. Of all the outcomes she'd imagined, this certainly wasn't one of them.

'I'm sorry, Alice.' Rahsaan raised the tranq gun a little unsteadily.

'It's OK,' she said.

As Rahsaan raised the weapon, the hut was filled with bright white light. Alice thought he'd accidentally pulled the trigger before aiming and this was the effect of her nerve endings receiving the tranquilizer dose.

But a furry blur launched itself past her field of vision, flying directly into Rahsaan's chest and sending him back over his chair.

FORTY-TWO

Este surveyed the scene. Alice on her feet, Rahsaan on the ground with a dog on his chest. The noise alone would bring onlookers.

'We have to go,' Este said, reaching for Alice's hand. 'Now.'

Alice nodded but was shaken. 'I thought that was one of the lions,' she admitted.

'No, but I'm pretty sure they're on their way,' Este said.

Alice turned back to Rahsaan one last time.

'I'm sorry,' he repeated.

This time, she didn't reply. 'Come on, Casey,' she said, grabbing the Alsatian's harness. 'Let's go.'

They hurried through the camp as the plume of dust outside of camp began to settle. In a camp this size, it would take time to organize any kind of response. If they were lucky, they could just slip out in the confusion.

But when they reached the parking lot, Wilfredo shooed them back.

'Guards,' he announced. 'Garrison security types. Blocking the exit, checking all the cars.'

Este peered around, eyeing the trucks. There were cages in the backs of two of them though both were empty.

'Lions?' Alice asked.

'Yeah, but they'll probably only release them outside the camp,' Este said. 'Too many civilians in here to send them in blind.'

'Are you sure about that?' Alice asked.

'Not at all,' Este replied before turning to Wilfredo. 'You get the truck out of here. They won't have your DNA.'

'What're you going to do?'

'No clue,' Este admitted. 'But I'll ping you our coordinates when I figure it out.'

As Wilfredo hurried away, Este grabbed Alice's hand. 'Hope you feel like running.'

Together, the pair raced past the seemingly endless rows of huts, dodging only a handful of people on their way to the back fence.

'We'll need a vehicle,' Este said. 'Keep your eyes out for anything. A motorcycle, a work truck.'

Alice nodded and kept running. But when they reached the back fence, they saw a group of locals gathered and staring out over the scrub. They pushed in to get a view and saw not one but two of the mountain lions out on the plain, patrolling around. One lifted its head, bobbing its nose as if scenting on Alice's approach. The two young women stared at the beasts in fear.

'New plan,' Este said, leading Alice away.

This time, they hurried to the area by the administration huts where the water lines were going in. Este nodded to the same workman as before.

'Hey, we're just over from the Reno QZ checking out ways we might improve our own setup and were wondering if we could get a closer look at your pipeline,' she said, already dropping into the trench with Alice close behind. 'Cool?'

'No, no, no,' the workman said. 'It's dangerous down there. Can't send you without an escort. Also, there's been no stress testing—'

But Este and Alice had already taken off running, leaving the workman and the camp behind.

They ran as fast as they could down the pipe, though this wasn't easy as there was no real floor. If they were pursued, they'd be easily caught. Also, there was no light, and occasionally even stretches where sand and water had pooled, causing them to slip. Este used the flashlight on her phone judiciously, conserving the battery.

Every time they came to a ladder leading up to a service hatch, Este's adrenaline spiked. She fully expected one to open at any moment and a snarling lion to drop down. She imagined hearing its huffing breath, smelling its fur mottled with wet sand, feeling its claws tearing into her flesh.

Yet still she ran.

When they reached a three-way split in the tunnel, she glanced to Alice, having no idea which way to choose, though understanding the wrong direction could cost them dearly. Alice squeezed her hand and smiled.

'This way,' Alice said, taking on the responsibility of the decision and leading them straight ahead.

The farther they ran, the more Este worried they'd run out of pipe and hit solid rock – or worse, water – and have to backtrack. So when they spied light up ahead and found that the pipe let out just on the banks of a wide river, they were thankful.

'Do you see any lions?' Alice asked as the two of them crested the bank to look back over the plain in the direction of the camp.

'None,' Este said. 'Doesn't mean they're not there, though. Let's keep moving.'

They had to pick a direction again and chose to follow the river south but not before taking a drink.

Este waited a full hour before pinging Wilfredo, and not even then until they'd come across an abandoned fire road. They took shelter next to a stack of boulders as Wilfredo texted back to say he was on his way.

'How're you feeling?' Este asked as Alice slid down onto the grass.

'Like crap? Worse than crap? Mainly because I can see Rahsaan's point.'

'Which was what?' Este asked.

'From where he's standing, he's just trying to protect his family. It *was* reckless for us to come here. I know we've got these little firebombs, but that feels like something to make us feel better. A Band-Aid, not a solution.'

'Is that cause to sign your death warrant?' Este asked.

'I don't know, maybe? It's a simple equation. If we die, we take others with us. We can say we plan for accidents, but we're kidding ourselves.'

Este didn't reply. She knew Alice was right.

'What bothers me even more, though, is that we're not the only ones,' Alice went on. 'Rahsaan said there were thousands of others. All of us being resurrected against our will, lied to, fed poisons, then euthanized.'

'I . . . I know,' Este said. 'I saw it when I came to rescue you.'

'And it never enters Ben's mind that it's wrong,' Alice continued. 'All he cares about is what we can do for him and his mad vision of the future. He doesn't care when we die. He doesn't care if, God forbid, there's some accident like what happened in Los Angeles and I'm freed. Did I kill four people to resurrect out there? Or did it happen because I was in a lab? I don't know and I'll bet he doesn't either. It's not right.'

'No,' Este agreed. 'But you're talking about the ghosts like they're real people. They lived their lives. They died.'

'What do you think we are? And anyway, does that make their pain – this afterlife of potentially endless agony – OK?' Alice asked. 'And just as bad, at any time, an accident could happen and they'd be unleashed on the world, mindlessly killing four other people to arrive in a world they don't know, possibly even without knowing what their bodies are capable of. Can one person really be trusted to safeguard all this?'

'No, not really,' Este said. 'But what can we do?'

'I don't know,' Alice said, looking away. 'All I know is we can't do nothing and no one's safe – not the ghosts and not other people – as long as Ben has all those canisters.'

They sat in silence.

'I mean, we could steal them,' Este suggested finally. 'It'd be a huge job, really, the heist of the century, but we could do it. I've already broken into that building once.'

Alice shook her head. 'There's ten thousand canisters if there's one.'

'Yeah, they are about eight inches long and an inch in diameter. A standard elevator car is about eight feet by eight by seven. Pack them in tight enough and you could get them out of the lab in a single ride.'

Alice stared at Este in surprise. 'Are you serious?'

Este's mind was moving fast now. 'Well, yeah. I mean, you couldn't exactly walk them out through the lobby, but there's that parking garage. Get in there, break through the wall in, say, the third or fourth sub-level by the elevator shaft and take them out. You'd need *complete* control of the building. I mean, all ins, all outs, all security, *everything*. But I've managed worse. The question is, then what? Now we've got the potentially life-ending unstable nuke.'

'First, get somewhere remote, far away from any human population,' Alice said. 'Then, before starting any possible resurrections, ring the entire area with all those proteins and amino acids you brought me back to life with.'

'Like a buffer zone?' Este asked. 'I'm not sure I follow you.'

'If a canister gets damaged and a ghost accidentally released, should it not immediately devour one of us and start, I don't know, floating off toward a population center, the buffer zone would act as a wall, like when you sealed the bathroom before bringing me back. My "ghost" didn't try to escape or just float in the air, it was biologically attracted to the waiting proteins. That stuff acts like a magnet. A few barrels of that stuff – OK, so maybe more than a few – and any escaping ghost won't be able to float past it without resurrecting.'

'Trapping a ghost by forcing it to become human again,' Este said. 'Interesting idea. Completely insane, but very interesting. Then what?'

'Then we get to work on a version of their governor serum, the drug they use that flushes the "ghost" bacterium and makes one mortal again,' Alice said. 'For this to be safe, we have to find a way to replicate it. Then give everyone who is resurrected the choice of whether they want to take it and head back out into the world or remain, well, *posthumous*.'

This brought Este up short. 'No way,' she said. 'We're not going to have the skill or the technology to pull something like that off. Better to burn the canisters or bury them somewhere, no?'

Alice considered this. 'What if we could steal a sample of the serum? We couldn't replicate it ourselves, but there must be someone out there who could. I'm not saying it'd be easy, but we're talking about people's lives here. After all they've been through, we owe it to them to try.'

Este still wasn't sure about this but relented. 'No one gets to be immortal?' Este asked.

'Not until we can make it safe,' Alice replied. 'I'm not saying there aren't incredible applications for this science Ben's created. It could change the world. It just fell into very reckless hands.'

Este nodded. 'First things first,' she said. 'We've got to get back to Chicago. The longer we wait, the more likely they'll realize how I broke in and close all those backdoors.'

'Also, the more likely there'll be another accident,' Alice said. 'So, are we going to do this?'

Este extended her hand. Alice took it.

The world might be tilting toward a terrifying future, but Este was still haunted by that parade of resurrections and death. If she could somehow end even just that, maybe it would help make sense of so much of the other chaos she'd endured to get here.

FORTY-THREE

They spent the next several days on the road. In case the roads were being watched, they made a big circle west, first driving south through Colorado then west through New Mexico and Arizona. Fuel was a constant problem. They were in the LoP and couldn't just scrounge or steal it. Wilfredo was able to get money from one of the accounts the government set up to subsidize displaced people, but they blew through most of the cash in a week.

When they headed north for Utah, everyone in the car felt the shift in direction. They'd discussed Alice's plan with Wilfredo and he'd agreed to help, but it was all in theory up to that point. As they headed north and the pull of Chicago became a living, breathing thing, it snowballed into an inevitability.

'You'd be surprised how easy it could be to get some light demolition equipment into that parking garage,' Wilfredo said from behind the wheel as they neared Provo. 'Couple of forged city permits and a fake court order about a gas leak and they'll let you drive a tractor trailer down there. Should be easy.'

Alice laughed. Wilfredo's confidence was contagious.

'And if we shut off the power, the elevator is on a counterweight system and would still work manually,' Wilfredo continued. 'Starting to think Casey could pull this one off by himself!'

Este wasn't as convinced. 'There's still a time issue,' she said. 'Removing the canisters from their storage units and moving them to the elevator will eat up at least a couple of hours. Also, we've got to handle them like ten thousand bottles of nitroglycerin, so safety's an issue, too.'

'We've pulled off crazier jobs,' Wilfredo shot back. 'But if it's that dangerous, you'd think the FDA or somebody might be better off handling it.'

'At this point, the government can barely respond to the quakes,' Este said. 'Something Ben's taking advantage of. Also, he wouldn't have gotten this far unless he was well connected in the government. Who do you think they're going to listen to?'

Wilfredo sighed and nodded. 'As usual, it's on us.'

When they were in an area with WiFi signal again, Este went online and began hunting for equipment. By the time they checked into a still-up-and-running motel the next morning in Watertown, South Dakota, only six hundred miles out of Chicago, she'd found a truck and a backhoe with a hydraulic hammer. It was a bit much, but it'd punch through the wall in under five minutes. It was worth considering.

She began to wonder. *Could this actually work?* There were matters of security, timing and transport they had to work out, but in these days of magical thinking, why not?

Wilfredo headed out with Casey to look for food. Este sat with Alice as they turned on the motel room TV and tried to find news. They'd heard on the radio that there'd been a quake in the heart of Europe that day, but details were scarce.

'This would be a lot easier if we had a sample of the governor serum,' Alice said at one point, clearly working the job over in her mind with the same determination as Este. 'Think we'd have time to grab a vial or two?'

'No idea, but it'd probably be more useful to take five minutes looking for the serum's formula, don't you think?' Este said. 'Also, one thing at a time.'

'That's the hard part,' Alice said. 'I keep jumping ahead from a mere break-in to how to accommodate the needs of an entire population of resurrectees.'

Este laughed. 'Yeah, the after-party is going to be something.

One ethical dilemma after another. To say nothing of the large-scale urban planning we'll need to do once we've got the serum in hand.'

'I know,' Alice said, shaking her head. 'But . . . any other solution is monstrous. Leave them there and they have only two fates – kill others or allow themselves to be killed over and over again. Or find a way to free them and let them decide what they want to do.'

Este nodded. It was a monumental undertaking and required uncompromising commitment. But Alice was right. It was also the only humane thing to do. She eyed her friend appraisingly.

'What?' Alice asked.

'It's cool,' Este said. 'Before, you were trying to adjust this future version of yourself to some familiar past you were trying to get back to. Now it's like you flipped a switch and are building a future you actually want to participate in.'

Alice liked this. She glanced back to the TV as images of a European quake appeared an instant before the picture faded out. Este reached for a lamp but it wouldn't switch on.

'Power's out,' she said.

From outside came the distant sound of Casey's bark. It was the earthquake bark, short and sharp.

Este rose. 'Guess we should get to the parking l—'

The quake hit with such force that Alice was lifted from the bed and thrown to the ceiling, her head narrowly missing the light fixture before she slammed onto the carpet. Though Este had only been tossed off her feet and thrown to the floor, she was still dazed as she reached for Alice's hand.

'Come on!'

Before Alice could grab hold, however, the quake began in earnest.

Less like a seismic event and more like a series of explosions, it tore the building apart. Furniture was dashed against the walls and ceiling, splintering into tiny pieces. The walls were next, the upward force exerted on the building's foundation, causing support beams to crack and smash through the drywall like badly shattered bones. The television swung wildly on its wall mount until it broke free and flew not to the ground but horizontally through the room's front window.

Alice knew the ceiling would be next, but she couldn't get to the door. The ground bucked her into the air like a rodeo bull. She tried digging her fingers into the carpet to keep her in place, maybe even gain traction for an escape, but it did nothing.

The room's door remained firmly closed but the entire wall

separating the room from the parking lot broke apart, the remnants of the roof hanging down like tufts of hay under a scarecrow's hat. Este tripped her way to the sidewalk. In front of her, cars and trucks in the lot bounced comically off the ground like ping-pong balls, apparently weightless.

'Alice, now!'

Alice waited for the room to throw her skyward and landed back in a crouch. In the instant before the ground lifted again, she lunged forward, tripping through the wreckage of the wall until she could reach Este's hand. Este pulled her the rest of the way out just as the ceiling in the bathroom behind her fell in.

No sooner was Alice out than a van rolled straight for her from across the lot. She leaped out of the way as it bounced onto the sidewalk and smashed into the room she'd just left.

Alice looked around for Este. Rather than heading to safety, she was already knocking on the doors of every room, trying to get people out. Alice could barely stand, much less help. Wilfredo, for his part, was already carrying a man who'd sustained a head injury out of one room before going back in for someone else.

'Alice, help me!' Este called.

Este had found an elderly couple and was helping them crawl out through the bottom half of a crushed door. Alice somehow managed to make her way over and lifted the woman to her feet. She looked around for somewhere safe, then spied a stretch of grasslands on the other side of the highway that ran past the motel.

'The field!' she yelled to anyone who might hear.

Even as the quake thundered on, the trio managed to get the two dozen or so guests of the motel out of their rooms, across the parking lot, and to the field without further injuries. But even then, the ground continued to not so much shake as buck with such ferocity that Alice wouldn't have been surprised to see a mountain come stabbing up from the depths.

'Everyone lie down!' Este commanded. 'Grab onto anything you can. Plants with roots especially.'

Alice found this only half-worked. The ground jolted her upwards, but her grip slammed her right back down. She wasn't sure if it was better or worse. Casey couldn't grab onto anything even if he wanted to. He appeared to be dancing as the quake tossed him into the air time and again, only for him to drop back to the earth with bone-shattering force.

Wilfredo finally crawled over to him and put his arms around the dog to cradle him in place. The ferocity of the quake seemed to plateau with fewer massive jolts, but the ground refused to stop moving.

'When will it end?' the elderly woman Alice rescued asked, her voice a plaintive wail.

No one had the answer. As the quake entered its twentieth minute, Alice's body black and blue, bruised down to the bone, she feared it might never stop.

FORTY-FOUR

When the ground stopped moving ten minutes later, no one trusted it. Everyone lay still a while longer, waiting for an aftershock that never came. Wilfredo was the first to stand, only to fall again, his muscles exhausted from fighting the unruly earth.

'You OK, Este?' he asked, crawling to her side.

'Been better,' she admitted, barely able to speak. Her jaw had hit the ground more than once, making even opening her mouth a chore. 'Alice?'

But Alice wasn't moving. Este realized in a panic that she didn't have any of the incendiary grenades with her. All that planning and worry, but when an actual life-and-death emergency arose, they were completely unprepared.

They could've killed everyone they'd worked so hard to rescue, as well as one another.

'Alice!' Este said, hurrying to her friend's side. 'Are you OK?'

The young woman stirred a little, her eyes seeming to focus only with great difficulty.

'Peachy keen,' Alice muttered. 'How's everyone el—?'

Her question was interrupted by a cry. One of the other motel guests was alongside the elderly couple, checking them over. The older woman was dazed but speaking. Her husband, however, had grown pale and wasn't moving. Este hurried over and attempted to revive him, only to determine that he'd likely suffered a heart attack during the quake.

She attempted CPR until she felt one of his ribs crack, but there was no response to her efforts. She moved on to the wife. Though her breathing was ragged, her heartbeat was so strong that Este almost cheered.

'She needs a hospital,' she told the others, even though she knew how unlikely this was.

Miraculously, however, as Este checked on the others – some suffering from broken bones, others looking like they'd either gone twelve rounds with George Foreman or been dragged across asphalt – a tribal police officer down from the Pine Ridge Reservation pulled up in a truck. It was just past dawn and the first vehicle they'd seen since the quake.

'I only have room for a couple,' he announced, looking over the group. 'Already got six folks packed in the bed, two more in the cab.'

Este led him to the older woman and together they carried her to the truck.

'Her husband died,' Este said. 'Better to make sure she's out of the woods before anyone tells her, OK?'

'You got it,' the officer said.

'Where was the epicenter this time?' Este asked. 'Felt like it was right under our motel.'

The tribal policeman's face changed. He shook his head. 'No, it was south of St Louis. Bad one.'

'St Louis?' Este asked. 'That's over five hundred miles away.'

'Yeah,' the officer said. 'It got the whole Midwest and into the South. Texas, Oklahoma, all over Arkansas. This . . . this one was really bad. New record for the longest duration, too. Thirty-five minutes.'

Este couldn't believe it. Five hundred miles from the epicenter? If it was this strong in South Dakota, she imagined St Louis was little more than a crater. But if it hit St Louis, it must've also hit—

'Do you have a map?' Este asked quickly.

The officer handed her one from his glove box as he situated the older woman. It was a state map of South Dakota, but there was a small US map on the back. She used her fingers to measure the distance between St Louis and where she estimated she stood five hundred miles away. She traced an imaginary circle around St Louis with a five-hundred-mile radius.

Chicago was not only well within the circumference, it was closer to St Louis by almost a third. What had happened to them had certainly happened to Chicago, only much worse.

'What is it?' Alice asked, moving next to her.

'Chicago.' Este pointed to the map.

Alice blanched. Both turned to look for Wilfredo. He was in front of his parents' truck, looking under the hood. It had flipped on its side during the quake, but he'd been able to right it with the help of a couple of other survivors.

'Will it work?' Este said after hurrying over.

'Maybe? I won't know until I start it, but it looks intact.'

'We have to get to Chicago.'

Este explained about the quake radius. Wilfredo's eyes went wide.

'Are you crazy?' Wilfredo asked. 'If even a handful of those containers cracked open, you're going to have a trail of death through there. Chicago's just about the last place we should be going.'

'Even more reason why it should be us,' Alice said. 'We know there's a real danger of that happening. If it didn't happen already, it still could.'

'Exactly,' Este added. 'Besides, if anything crazy like that *did* happen, it'd already be all over the radio. We have to try.'

Este waited for the dubious look, the one asking, *When did this become our fight?* But Wilfredo simply nodded and closed the hood of his truck.

'Let's get started.'

They were on the road within the half-hour. It was only fifteen minutes later that they saw how profoundly different the St Louis quake was to all the ones that preceded it. Towns that would've been merely crippled by LA-1 or the Reno quake had been obliterated by the most recent tremblor. It was as if the towns they passed on the broken highways had been placed in a giant sifter and ground to dust.

In several spots, they would barely have known there'd been a town, if not for the fires that had broken out from severed gas lines. Black smoke cut through the clouds of dust, making the early morning visibility that much worse.

'How could anyone survive this?' Alice asked, putting to words what they were all thinking.

They soon came upon survivors. However, all were fleeing west and north. They saw plates from Iowa and a multi-lane exodus out of Minnesota.

'It must've reached Minneapolis–St Paul,' Wilfredo postulated.

To avoid traffic snarls, several vehicles hopped into the eastbound lanes and went against traffic, figuring – rightly for the most part

– that no one would be crazy enough to head *toward* the quake-affected areas. Wilfredo had to swerve and dodge out of the way of these folks time and again, only to eventually stay off-road where the pickup could handle the uneven ground.

'Hard to blame 'em,' were his only words on the subject.

And the farther they drove, the harder it became. Overpasses had collapsed onto highways requiring long detours. Bridges that had stood since the New Deal had tumbled into waterways. Roads were as pockmarked with craters as the moon. Anything still standing was suspect, likely to fall at any moment.

Este worried about finding fuel, but then remembered the siphon gangs in the LAQZ. All they had to do was get off the highway, locate an abandoned vehicle, a post office or police garage with its own gas pumps, or even the remains of a gas station, and there'd be plenty of fuel, although that wouldn't last.

They slept in two-hour shifts, though when roadblocks began cropping up, Este would be woken to present her bona fides.

'I'm a nurse,' she would say. 'We're search and rescue out of the Los Angeles and Reno QZs.'

'A lot of places around here could use your help,' she was told, time and again, by state troopers and civilians alike.

This was hard for Este to answer. This need was immediate. The needs of the ten thousand in Chicago felt abstract in comparison. But what had she told herself about the plan taking uncompromising commitment?

'I'm sure,' she'd say. 'But my whole family is in Chicago. I have to get to them.'

She kept waiting for it not to work but, repeatedly, they were let through. It was only when they finally reached Wisconsin, angling around south of Madison for a way east, that they were stopped in their tracks.

'You'll have to turn back,' an exhausted-looking Wisconsin State Patrol officer told them. 'Nobody's getting into Chicago.'

'We have to try,' Este protested. 'We've got people there. My whole family's there.'

'There are no roads,' the patrolman said. 'You go down there, you tie up my men with some kind of rescue half an hour later. Can't have it.'

Este looked to Wilfredo and Alice then back to the patrolman.

'I'm a nurse,' Este said, hoping she didn't sound too rehearsed.

'And my dog here is search and rescue. We worked the LA and Reno quakes.'

He raised a hand to cut her off. 'Follow me,' he said, opening Este's car door.

She cast a dubious look back to her friends then followed the patrolman to his squad car. It was covered in a fine, white-gray dust.

'That's Chicago,' he said, dipping a finger into the ashes. 'The entire place is on fire, top to bottom, North Park to Calumet City. It's been burning for twenty-four hours straight. There is no search and rescue right now. You want to do some good, head back up to Madison. They need people there.'

The entire place is on fire. Este's mind reeled. All those people, all those buildings, not just shattered by a quake but cast into an inferno. She felt someone by her side and turned. Alice had joined her.

'No one's fighting the fire?' Alice asked.

'They had some fire tugs and barges with fire-fighting equipment down from Thunder Bay, but there's not a lot they can do,' the patrolman said. 'They ended up mostly just evacuating folks who jumped into Lake Michigan to get away.'

Este winced again, imagining the confusion and madness it would take for people to abandon the city and leap pell-mell into the lake to get away.

'Where are they off-loading survivors?' Alice asked.

'Sheboygan,' the patrolman said. 'I guess if you're looking for folks that got out, that might be a place to start.'

FORTY-FIVE

I f the LAQZ recalled images of bombed out cities from the Second World War, the South Pier in Sheboygan, usually reserved for sailboats and cabin cruisers, recalled the aftermath of Dunkirk. Everywhere Alice looked, survivors, their skin and clothing blackened with soot, huddled under blankets, sipping from bottles of water. Their faces told the story. They'd seen something monstrous. Something they'd never thought they'd witness in their lifetime. And they continued to relive it, most looking as if they now knew for certain nowhere was safe and maybe never would be again.

She thought of Ben's words. That though it was difficult to see the outcome from 2025, a changing world maybe meant disposable lives weren't a bad thing. If firefighters racing to battle the flames in Chicago knew they had nothing to fear from death, that their bodies could be regenerated after, would they save more lives? Maybe not. Fear was instinctual. But after the first few times, maybe they'd be reconditioned.

She had no idea. All she knew was that her fear of going where these people had come from was very real.

Este hurried up to her from the shore. 'We got a barge,' she announced, pointing to one being loaded with supplies. 'They're a support craft, bringing water and supplies to the fire boats still trying to get people out.'

It was night, so they couldn't see the smoke, but even a hundred miles away, Alice could taste the fire. She'd passed a couple of people watching video on phones and had caught glimpses of the entire city ablaze. Fire running up buildings hundreds of feet in the air. A sky gone orange and black like a nightmarish Halloween spectacle. There were screams and emergency sirens but also a tornado-like howl as the notorious Chicago winds drove the flames on like a mad coach driver.

'OK,' Alice managed to say. 'When do we leave?'

'Now,' Este said, pointing to where Wilfredo was already loading crates. 'They're leaving in five.'

Alice looked around for a reason not to go. She'd never been more scared in her life. Este was the opposite, apparently raring to go. To Alice, she resembled a racehorse in a chute waiting for the starting gun. As if she'd been bred to charge in where angels fear to tread.

'OK,' Alice said. 'Be right there.'

The barge was named *Goddess of Winter*. Its first mate introduced himself as Scott and identified the captain as simply 'Big Time'.

'Big Time's already made three round trips,' Scott told the group as he hurried them to a spot below decks where they could avoid the smoke during the trip. 'We're only on there for a few minutes. The water and supplies get offloaded in seconds and people pulled on right after. First trip, it was people just floating in the water on anything that could take their weight.'

'And the second trip?' Wilfredo asked.

'Either they made it to one of the tugs or, well, went under,' Scott admitted. 'I don't mean to scare you, but it's bad down there.

Like something out of Greek mythology. It's also *hot*. But that's what happens when a billion tons of steel are set ablaze, I guess.'

Alice tensed. Este nodded. 'We just want to help. However we can.'

'Great,' Scott said. 'Just wanted you to know what you were in for.'

As soon as he was gone, Alice turned to Este and Wilfredo. 'We can't do this,' she said. 'It's way too dangerous. We can't just walk into fire.'

'Hey, no one's mentioned ghosts once,' Este said. 'Or anything like that. And I've been listening – radios, gossip, everything. The quake was bad, the fire's worse, but that's got me thinking your buddy Ben knew what he was doing making that place fireproof.'

'OK, but getting in there? If the entire city's on fire?' Alice asked.

'You have to put that fear away,' Este said, touching Alice's arm. 'You had it right from the start. They aren't just canisters. It's people. Probably thousands of them. And the fire isn't an obstacle, it's the best gift the Universe could've given us. The city's going to be *empty*. The streets are going to be *empty*. Security cameras? Security guards? Heck, some guy walking by with a GoPro . . .?'

'What's a GoPro?' Alice asked.

'Never mind,' Este said. 'The important thing is, we've got Chicago to ourselves. It's gone from trying to do a real-life heist in the LoP to one more quake zone salvage op. This is what Wilfredo and I do best. It's all we do.'

'You're not worried about the smoke and fire?' Alice asked.

'Not a damn bit,' Este confirmed. 'With the sheer number of first responders around, it won't take much to find a Nomex fire suit and an oxygen mask and put it on. *Done*. Biggest fear is the building coming down on your head while you're in it.'

'No, my biggest fear is me dying and immediately killing the four people closest to me, in this case you or Wilfredo,' Alice said. 'We were totally unprepared back in Watertown. Sure, if you died, you'd come back, but Wilfredo doesn't have that luxury. We're taking people's lives into our hands.'

'That's been our brief for a while now,' Este said. 'But standing by and doing nothing endangers even more. We just must put our fears behind us and get this done. A single elevator car of canisters up to the surface, then those canisters four blocks over to Lake Michigan. One elevator car of canisters offloaded, into the back of Wilfredo's truck, and we're gone into the night. The danger? That's just your mind running scenarios based on information we don't have. We take it a step at a time and we'll get it done.'

This was a side of Este that Alice hadn't seen. The one who was firmly in command of a situation, calm and deliberate in the face of emergency. She nodded.

'Thanks, Este.'

Alice took a short nap then worked on the top deck with Scott, prepping the boxes of water for distribution as Wilfredo and Este slept below. They wore masks to keep out the smoke and had put one around Casey's mouth as he insisted on coming up as well.

They'd only been at it half an hour when the Alsatian began to bark.

'Great,' Alice said. 'Aftershocks.'

But Casey was looking to the shore. Alice peered through the darkness and saw movement. As her eyes focused, she saw a never-ending line of people shuffling up the bank of Lake Michigan, ghostly apparitions coming in and out of view. When they saw the barge, they called out in one voice, asking for water. Alice was about to throw them a couple of bottles when Scott shook his head.

'It sucks, but if they're walking, they can get to water,' Scott said. 'Even the lake is freshwater. Got to keep the bottles for the folks further south.'

Alice nodded and returned to work.

It wasn't long before she spotted the first dappling of orange to the south. It appeared like a single, isolated fire – a mere flare – in the distance. The piles of ash accumulating on the deck told a different story. The closer they got, the larger the orange glow grew, from a single distant campfire to a vast rising star that looked ready to engulf the planet. It expanded until it ran the length of the horizon, a line of flames separating the heavens and earth.

'Dear God,' Alice whispered.

The barge shuddered. Alice reached for Casey to keep him close. Scott nodded to the water.

'Debris,' he said. 'Floating up from the city.'

Alice looked over the gunwale. Sure enough, floating detritus bounced against the hull, though she couldn't identify any of it. Logs? Construction barrels? She couldn't tell.

Scott's walkie-talkie beeped. He put it to his ear. Alice could hear Big Time's voice coming over from the shack.

'The fire boats are saying we can't go in farther,' Scott reported after clipping the radio back onto his belt. 'Too much trash in the water. Got to put in here.'

Alice nodded but was staring at the burning Chicago skyline. She was just able to make out the silhouettes of individual buildings amidst the distant flames. The fire reflected in the water south of them, giving it an orange, sinister, oily look.

'Here,' Scott said, passing her binoculars. 'You can get a better look.'

Alice stared through the lenses, now able to see the tiny fire tugs blasting streams of water into a lakefront inferno that rose a dozen stories above them. Their actions looked comically hopeless, less than tossing grains of sand into the ocean. Yet, there they were, pumping water from the lake into their tanks to pour against the fire.

'Why don't they retreat?' Alice asked.

'A lot of them are Chicago PD, Chicago FD,' Scott said, looking away. 'If there's even a chance someone can get through all that to them, they're not going to leave. They're determined to be the last ones out.'

Alice understood. It was also probably the last time they'd experience anything that resembled their own life – fighting a fire in Chicago. To turn their backs, to leave the area, was an acknowledgment that Chicago had been lost.

Goddess of Winter found anchorage as close to shore as possible and extended the gangplank into the shallows. People on shore began to gather. Scott's radio beeped. He listened for a moment then nodded to Alice.

'We lucked out,' Scott said, then pointed into the dark. 'One of the main staging areas is about half a mile that way. They're sending a couple of trucks over to pick up our supplies for redistribution.'

'Staging for what?'

'Pathfinder teams, it sounds like,' Scott said. 'Get some firefighters close to the hot zone and assess the damage, determine next steps.'

Scott headed off to confer with Big Time. Alice went to the steps leading below decks. Este was curled up next to Wilfredo with Casey across both their laps, all in a deep sleep. It was in that moment that Alice realized her fears weren't for herself. They were for her friends.

She retreated back to the top deck as the first trucks arrived. She helped offload the boxes as the severely injured made their way on board. She directed them to where they could rest for the trip back then followed the last two paramedics down the gangplank. She followed them to a pickup truck that had traded its injured passengers for piles of blankets – a makeshift ambulance – and climbed in next to them.

'You coming with us?' one of the paramedics asked.

'Looks that way,' she said.

They hadn't gone a hundred feet before Alice found it difficult to breathe in the dense smoke. One of the paramedics handed her an oxygen tank and mask, which she used liberally.

The staging area turned out to be a high school parking lot complete with a small triage station set up by volunteers trying to accommodate the needs of what looked like thousands of people on foot. They were all blackened with soot and ash, and many of them twisted in agony as they waited to receive medical attention.

Alice helped unload the blankets and glanced round. Almost all the people were survivors looking to get away. She wanted to find the ones heading back in.

Her eyes finally fixed on a team of smoke jumpers. They had assembled behind a pair of large military trucks, the kind Alice had seen in the LAQZ. They wore yellow Nomex suits and carried their own fire equipment. She hurried over, locating the team leader, a tall woman with a deeply tanned face and the name Barnes stenciled on her suit.

'My name is Estefania Quiñones,' Alice said. 'I'm an RN out of Los Angeles. I was search and rescue during LA-1 and 2, just did three weeks in the Reno QZ.'

'And you just happen to be in Chicago?'

'Was coming home,' Alice said, trying to channel Este as best she could. 'Now I'm just looking to help out.'

'This isn't search and rescue or recovery,' Barnes said. 'At this point, we're just trying to determine what we're dealing with.'

'I hear you,' Alice said, stretching the lie past the breaking point. 'But I know the city. I'll be able to guide you. And help out if you find survivors.'

Barnes looked unconvinced. Alice leaned in.

'My mom was Army,' Alice pleaded. 'She taught me to go where we could be most useful.'

'You ever worked fire?' Barnes asked, hesitant.

'No, but that just means I'll do exactly what you tell me.'

Barnes sighed but then nodded to a nearby pile of equipment.

'We don't have a lot of choices when it comes to boots, but draw what works for you. Helmet, oxygen tank, suit, light, pry bar, aid packs. We leave for the city in five. Welcome to the team.'

FORTY-SIX

Este awoke to warm sunlight on her face. She was below decks but the light, tinged orange from the smoke, streamed in through every porthole. Casey was lying in her lap, but his eyes were open, keeping vigil while trying not to disturb his mistress.

She put a hand to her waistband. Her incendiary grenades were there, reminding her all over again of her new status as a ghost, though she still didn't feel physically different than before. The idea that there could be multiple Estes felt like yesterday's dream, far away and forgotten. That her life expectancy had so increased, this ghost DNA carving a passage through time that would let her live to see a future denied to most others, also felt foreign and unreal.

The only thing that felt urgently present was the danger she represented to others.

She craned her neck to peer out the window. The water around the boat was littered with debris, though none, thankfully, was burning. The Chicago skyline was just visible in the distance. A thousand ribbons of smoke rose from the still burning city like a skeleton dance in the sky.

'Ma'am, can you give us a hand?' a voice asked.

On the steps leading below decks were two women escorting a third whose arms and legs were wrapped in bandages.

'Of course,' Este said, clearing a spot on the bench. 'What's your name?'

The girl in bandages didn't respond. Este checked her vitals.

'She's in shock,' Este said. 'We need to lay her down, elevate her feet. She needs to be kept warm. Are you friends? Relatives?'

'We only met her on the road,' one of the women said. 'She hasn't said a word. Are you a doctor?'

'A nurse,' Este responded. 'Let me look for a blanket.'

She headed to the top deck only to find at least fifty people already there, some on stretchers, all injured. Wilfredo was directing traffic on deck, utilizing every square foot of surface for the journey up the lake.

'Hey, Este,' he said. 'You good?'

'Think so. How long was I out?'

'A *while*,' he replied. 'I figured you could use the sleep, so I didn't wake you for the load-out.'

Este glanced to shore. A steady stream of people continued to move north from the Chicagoland area. Most were on foot, though some had found bicycles, while others carried survivors or belongings in what looked like hastily modified carts. Several more stood by, waiting for space on a barge.

'There've been people waiting since last night,' Wilfredo said, indicating the deck. 'Big Time told them we might not be back if we ran out of fuel. They stayed anyway.'

Humans had faith in the improbable when faced with the impossible.

Este surveyed the scene. 'Sun'll be bad once we get away from the smoke. Got to get some tarps up for shade, especially for those already with burns.'

'I'll see what I can find,' Wilfredo said.

'Where's Alice?' Este asked, realizing everyone else on the deck had an unfamiliar face.

Wilfredo inhaled sharply then glanced around. 'Follow me.'

He led her to a bearded fellow sitting alongside the starboard gunwale. 'Hey, this is the real Estefania Quiñones. Could you tell her what you told me?'

'I met your doppelgänger,' the bearded man said. 'We were being off-loaded at an aid station near Evanston. A young woman had just introduced herself to a bunch of firefighters as a nurse named Estefania Quiñones, said she'd gone through the quakes in LA and Reno and wanted to help out. Mentioned it to the first mate here and he said you were already aboard.'

Este looked to Wilfredo with surprise. 'Alice?'

'Sounds like she dumped us to join a fire team heading into Chicago,' Wilfredo said. 'Can you believe it?'

She wanted to protect us, Este realized. *That lunatic.*

'You know this Alice person?' the man asked. 'She nuts or something?'

'No, she's just trying to help,' Este said. 'Probably figured using my story would get her there faster.'

'She wants to go toward the fire?' the man asked. 'So she *is* nuts!'

Wilfredo laughed. Este didn't. Once they'd walked away, Wilfredo leaned in.

'Are we going after her?' Wilfredo asked.

Este stared in the direction of the burning metropolis. She knew what had happened. In a misguided attempt to keep them safe, Alice had set off to the Kellner building on her own. Now she was someplace in that vast labyrinthine inferno, though where, Este had no idea.

'She's got way too much of a head start,' Este said, shaking her head. 'And there are a hundred different roads into the city. We'd never catch up. Besides, she's got a whole team of firefighters with her.'

'You sure?' Wilfredo asked.

'Yeah,' Este said, though unconvincingly. 'Besides, there's plenty for us to do here.'

Wilfredo nodded. 'OK. Cool. Good luck, Alice, wherever you are.'

The next time she was alone again, Este allowed herself to feel anger. She realized she wasn't mad at Alice for going on without her into the fires of Chicago so much as for leaving her behind to face this strange new existence on her own.

She understood. There were far more lives at stake than her own. But it didn't make it any easier.

Good luck, Alice, she told the wind, then went back to helping people climb aboard.

FORTY-SEVEN

No one on the fire team seemed to suffer any delusion that there was any way to save Chicago, not even a tiny piece. As they dutifully moved from block to block, grid to grid, in concert with a handful of other teams hunting for survivors, they knew without being told that this wasn't an assessment and there would be no 'next steps'. They would canvas for survivors, evacuate any they found, and turn out the proverbial lights on the town when they were the last to exit.

'These old houses didn't stand a chance,' remarked one of the older smoke jumpers – who'd mentioned surviving the Storm King Fire in 1994, a blaze Alice actually remembered due to its evocative name – as they passed several rows of burned-out wooden structures on Chicago's

South Side. 'Modern houses have Tyvek or something woven between the walls to slow a blaze. When there's nothing but wood, you can burn through the whole thing in seconds like it was old newspaper.'

Alice nodded. The air tasted toxic. A brackish, orange-red haze filled the streets like a fog. The heat was nigh on unbearable, adding to the feeling that they were traversing the surface of Mercury rather than America's third largest city.

She felt lucky that they hadn't run into anything by way of a medical emergency. They'd come across a few survivors, but no one needing much more than a ride to an evacuation point. Other teams reported about the same.

But after twelve hours of listening intently to the radio chatter, what relieved Alice the most was not hearing a single report that sounded like it was about ghosts. While she knew this might not mean much, it was enough to hang her hopes on. They'd gotten close to the Chicago River at one point, near enough that they could see several of the skyscrapers were still standing, albeit choking out smoke from shattered windows. Alice couldn't tell which one was the Kellner Group building.

The radio beeped twice up front and Barnes answered it.

'They're pulling us back,' she called back to the team. 'Gonna rest a shift.'

Most everyone nodded, relieved. Alice, however, waited until she spied one of the other trucks ambling through the city. She reached for her pry bar and signaled Barnes.

'I'm going to stay in if that's OK,' she said.

Before anyone could protest, Alice hopped out. She waved to the smoke jumpers then hurried off after the other truck. She waited until her team was out of sight then took a sharp right, heading down a side street.

The problem was she didn't know the city and she didn't have a map. Este had made a map, but Alice had forgotten to bring it along. Still, she remembered enough of it to know where the river should be and hoped that would be enough to guide her. The city was surreally quiet. Though many of the larger fires had burned themselves out over the course of the day, smoke continued to billow from every building, sewer drain, and subway tunnel, embers coating surfaces like newly fallen snow. Alice was thankful for her Nomex suit, gloves and boots, however ill-fitting, which insulated her not only from the heat and smoke but from many of the smells.

The intense heat had done strange things to the city. Everything from street signs to car tires and bicycle frames had melted into the concrete. The few intact windowpanes had warped and twisted in the heat as well. It gave her reflection a funhouse-mirror quality as she passed.

To her surprise, she came upon the river in only three blocks. She'd had a pipe dream of navigating it with a boat but found it clogged with debris. Still, it gave her a point of orientation. She began to follow it north.

Her mind wandered to Este and Wilfredo. She didn't *think* they'd try to follow her into the flames. Este was too smart for that. Still, she worried about leaving her friend in such a vulnerable state. But given the monumental scale of the destruction, and the very real possibility that the ghosts might already be loose in the city, she couldn't bear to risk their lives. Not when they were so busy saving others.

It took her twenty minutes to reach the Kellner Group building. It looked oddly neutered in its post-quake, post-fire state. She'd expected to feel trepidation, even fear at the sight of where she'd spent the past twenty years being resurrected only to die again, but those emotions felt unrelated. Her deaths were in the abstract. This smoking hulk was functionally anonymous, despite what lay deep below the ground.

But from it, she would extract so much life. This thought practically lifted her off her feet. After a day spent seeing nothing but the evidence of human suffering, how wonderful to not just see the opposite but to make it come to fruition.

No demolition equipment was needed now. No dodging security cameras. Sure, there were no stairs down to the underground lab, but that just meant making the arduous journey to an upper level in order to catch the elevator down. Of course, there'd be no running elevator either – she'd have to descend the service ladder, find a way to carry or pulley up the canisters in bags, but even this felt doable.

How would she get the canisters out once she'd brought them back to the surface? She'd meant to hail one of the fire team trucks circling the city, but this might invite too many questions. Instead, she'd taken a note from those pushing their possessions out of the city in makeshift carts. She would do the same. Like Noah's Ark except, instead of a great ship and animals, it'd be a couple of shopping carts pulled from the Chicago River and filled with ghosts.

At this image, she closed her eyes, pushing out the voices that told her it was too insane, too mad. That she'd sent herself on a fool's errand that could never work no matter how much time she had to accomplish the task.

She stepped into the building, took off her hood, and gagged. The colliding odors were unbearable. She quickly put the hood back on. The door to the fire stairs had melted to the frame, but she tore it open with her pry bar and began her ascent.

She expected to find bodies in the stairwell, but there were none. The place was completely deserted, the exception, not the rule, given what she'd seen with the fire team that day. Also, it hadn't fallen like so many of the others.

Ben built his skyscraper well.

Este had told her which floor the elevator leading down could be accessed from, but Alice had forgotten. She tried the eleventh floor, only to find a car in the way, possibly stuck in transit when the power died, blocking the shaft. She went back down to ten, forced the doors open and began her descent down a service ladder. Only, she did so knowing that at any moment, the car above could come loose and drop on top of her.

She'd have to be quick.

The journey was treacherous, but doable even though the only light was from the small hand-light clipped to her suit. The first few floors were fine, but her hands quickly grew tired and stiff. The thought of carrying all the canisters back up this way, likely across multiple trips, gave her pause.

But then it would be over. She knew what the relief would feel like once she'd slain this dragon. As Este had intimated, Alice was cutting a path toward her own future by not only leaving her past behind but finding something meaningful to do with her present. Part of that included descending over twenty-some-odd flights on a rickety iron elevator-shaft service ladder, but she'd been through worse in the previous few days.

When she finally reached the bottom, she used the pry bar to crank open the elevator doors and stepped into the cavernous lab, lit only by dim emergency lights. The distant hum of generators filled the room. The air tasted not of smoke but of stale, recycled air. The lab had been hermetically sealed.

She descended the steps to the lab floor, the hum growing louder as she neared the storage units. There they all were – the 10,000 people she'd come to save. Part of her was relieved to find the units intact. Another part quailed at the monumental task ahead of her.

She spotted something out of the corner of her eye. Teeth. Sharp teeth.

'*Gah!*' she exclaimed, clumsily spinning around as the jaws of not one but *two* of the mountain lions came into view.

One of the beasts was on top of a storage unit, the other on the floor. Alice staggered backward, looking for a weapon, though she knew it was too late. When they attacked, she'd be defenseless.

But they didn't attack. Neither moved nor even seemed to notice her. She took a step closer and saw, even in the low light, that they were dead.

She was gripped by a new fear. That somewhere in the lab, the ghosts of these two chimeras were approaching even now to tear her apart. She felt foolish. She should've known this was a possibility. Even as she stood still, any tingling of nerve endings from her toes to her scalp sent fear rushing up her spine.

Somehow, though, she remained whole. There was no threat, neither from ghost nor lion. She stepped closer to the big cats and spied a mess of empty canisters and syringes nearby. Picking them up to turn over in her hand, she tried to piece together what must've happened.

The chimera – or at least some of them, as their killer seemed to have been working quickly – had been resurrected, sure, but then must've been given the governor serum to prevent any further revival. They were then euthanized. Put down for good this time.

She almost felt sorry for them. Still, when she found one of the canisters that hadn't been opened, she put it in her pack to keep it separate from the others. It was far too dangerous to keep with the others.

She looked back across the storage units, puzzled now. Why leave all the other ghosts in safety but without their most potent sentinel?

A terrible realization came over her. If Ben had realized a Chicago quake was inevitable and spent the money to keep his lab safe from it, she doubted his contingency plan ended there.

She turned to the nearest storage unit and threw open the lid to peer inside. It was empty. She ran down the row, opening one after another. There was nothing inside.

All the canisters were gone.

FORTY-EIGHT

'Are you getting me a helicopter or not?' Este yelled into the radio. 'If not, get off this frequency. If so, I need it in Sheboygan right now. But while you're burning fuel, put a few boxes of penicillin, lidocaine, iodine and aspirin in it. Cool? Thank you.'

She handed the radio back to Wilfredo.

'Who was that?' he asked.

'Office of the Canadian Prime Minister,' Este said. 'We're getting two choppers and two more barges. It's all good.'

Wilfredo laughed. Este smiled. A day that had begun with a two-horse operation taking survivors in need of medical care up the lake a few dozen at a time had expanded greatly. She'd found boats, recruited volunteers, and chased down fuel, food and medical supplies that others thought nonexistent. Though more people were coming in now to direct rescue efforts on the city and state level, Este already had a chain of command in place and was overseeing the mass exodus of over a million people to relative safety in Wisconsin and Ontario.

She'd opened water routes to Michigan's Upper Peninsula as well as loading sites in Manitowoc, Traverse City and Green Bay. She'd directed overland traffic to hubs she'd learned about talking to state troopers as far west as Grand Forks and as far north as Thunder Bay. She did all this with a single radio and a voice of authority; someone who knew what was needed and how to make it happen before the next person down the pike had thought of it.

But even while coordinating disaster response, her primary focus was on attending to the most severely injured of the survivors and getting them evacuated. She had a number of assistants now, including a veterinarian, Justin, who followed her from patient to patient, handing everyone cards they'd pass to the next medical staffer up the water, and the whole thing was running much, much more smoothly than anyone should've expected.

'First off the barge, first in a transport,' she told Justin after evaluating one survivor before moving on to the next. 'Stable. Send on foot to an aid station.'

Even as she moved things along, however, Alice was seldom far from her mind. With each new arrival, she expected to see her friend hurt or shell-shocked, possibly wide-eyed and naked, maybe even with no memory of her, Wilfredo, or anything past the year 2003, having died and been resurrected from her old starting point.

Instead, it was an endless parade of people forcibly coming to terms with the fact that life as they knew it had unalterably changed forever.

'Ma'am?' she said to one elderly woman with no visible signs of trauma beyond some light dehydration. 'We have buses coming. The barges are for those who need emergency treatment. Could you please wait for the buses?'

She hated mentioning the buses. They'd been promised for hours but never materialized. It had become shorthand on *Goddess of Winter* for a needed item (oil for the barge's engine, more topical antibiotics for burn patients) that everyone knew by now would never arrive.

Luckily, she didn't have to lie further. The elderly woman simply drifted away somewhere.

She wondered not for the first time if Ganske might've been right. If this elderly woman could return to the mindset of who she was, say, two years prior and be told about the destruction rather than suffering through it, would her life expectancy increase? Or even if right now they did an extraction and she went dormant only to be revived a hundred years hence in whatever new world emerged after the quakes? Would this result in a better quality of life than just, 'Hey, wait for the buses?'

She was pretty sure she knew the answer to this.

They made another round-trip and the number of people waiting had doubled again. There were still no buses. Out on the bow, Casey barked. There'd been nothing in the way of aftershocks yet, so it made Este's hair stand on end. She felt lulled into complacency.

Until she followed the Alsatian's gaze to the shoreline. Pushing through the crowd was Alice.

'Oh my God!' Este cried, hurrying to the gangplank. 'You're alive!'

She wrapped her friend in her arms but then took a quick step back to check her eyes for recognition. This was *her* Alice, right?

'I'm sorry I left you behind,' Alice whispered. 'I was so scared you'd get hurt.'

'It's OK,' Este said. 'I'm just so happy to see you.'

Alice nodded, her head buried in Este's shoulder. When they finally broke apart, Este looked her friend up and down, finally noticing the fireman's boots Alice wore.

'So, what happened?' she asked.

'They're gone,' Alice said. 'All of them. The ghosts. Gone.'

'How's that possible?' Este asked, incredulous. 'The whole city's on fire.'

'I don't know,' Alice said. 'I spoke to the other fire teams. No one saw Ben or any kind of evacuation of trucks or equipment, just rivers of people. The highways out of the city were destroyed. So were the rail lines. Same with O'Hare and Chicago Midway.'

Este thought about this. 'That leaves the water.'

'You think he took a barge?' Alice asked.

Este frowned. All the barges on Lake Michigan were requisitioned by what was left of the Marine Operations Unit of Chicago PD. Also, given the debris field down around the city, a barge wouldn't have been able to get through.

But then Este got an idea.

'Come with me,' she said, taking Alice's hand.

They hurried to the pilot shack where Big Time had spent the day chasing caffeine pills with Dr Pepper to stay awake. Este eyed the equipment in front of him.

'Is there any way to track container ships on the lake?'

'I can radio,' he offered. 'But if you mean after the quake, I doubt anything got out.'

'I'm not saying it was easy, but we have reason to believe someone did,' Este said. 'Within the first twenty-four hours.'

Big Time cocked an eyebrow and got to work on the radio.

'Where would he have taken them?' Alice asked quietly.

'I don't know,' Este said. 'But his company must've had labs all over the world. One of them has to be intact. He had no shortage of resources. With a container ship, he could get to the Atlantic through the St Lawrence Seaway. If he gets that far, we may never catch up with him.'

Alice fell silent. Este imagined some globe-trotting hunt to free the ghosts as the world crumbled. It would be crazy. No, impossible. They had to stop Ganske now.

'Um, I think I got a hit,' Big Time said, turning back to them. 'Big container ship passed the Thumb about four hours ago. Huron

County station radioed and were told they were heading to Calumet Harbor and were forced to turn around by the fires. But when they traced their IMO number, they had them docked in Chicago going back three months.'

'Where are they now?' Este asked.

Big Time shrugged. 'They can't be going too fast, but they still have a lot of hours on you. You need to radio them? Get them to slow down?'

'We have to go after them.'

'After them?' Big Time asked. 'What for?'

Of all the people Este didn't want to lie to, this man was high on the list. He was a good guy, an indefatigable barge captain who was killing himself to help others. Alice seemed to recognize this and cut in.

'Human trafficking,' Alice said, speaking quietly. 'He's got people on that ship. In containers.'

'You know this for a fact?' Big Time asked, eyes wide.

'Yes,' Alice continued. 'I was one of them until Este here rescued me.'

'Jesus Christ!' Big Time exclaimed. 'Can't we call in the police? The military? Anybody?'

'They're tied up with the recovery efforts,' Este said, which was true. 'All over the country. In the amount of time it'd take to muster a response, heck, to convince folks of its importance, the ship could be in international waters.'

Big Time looked from Alice to Este as if weighing their story.

'*Goddess of Winter* doesn't have the horsepower for a pursuit, but I got a friend with a light tug a couple of miles up who has been asking all day how he can help. I'll give him a call.'

'Thank you,' Este said. 'We really appreciate it.'

'If it was anybody else trying to sell me this story on any other day, Ms Quiñones, I'd show them the door,' Big Time said. 'But I've seen nothing but crazy today and you've been the only person clear-headed enough to navigate through it. Least I can do is make a phone call.'

FORTY-NINE

The tug, called *Yemanja*, was captained by Owen Cagan and crewed by two of his cousins, Brendan and Miles. When it pulled alongside *Goddess of Winter* two hours after Big Time's call, the trio was fired up and ready to give chase.

'Friend working the Port of Detroit said a big auto-driven container came down the water about an hour ago,' Owen said as Este, Alice, Wilfredo and Casey boarded. 'We'll have to gun it to catch up, but containers are slow in the narrows where we can be fast.'

'Can we still catch up?' Este asked.

'Yeah, probably in Lake Erie,' Owen said. 'Something else. Heard they've got official papers from both the US and Canadian governments to bypass Customs. Says they're earthquake aid bound for South America. You said they're human traffickers? That's a good cover. Ship's called the *CRC Triumph*. Should overtake her in about five or six hours.'

'What's auto-driven?' Alice asked.

'Crewless,' Owen said. 'All autopilot. But that's a lot of ships these days. Doesn't mean there's no one aboard.'

Alice asked if there was anywhere she might get some sleep. Owen brought her to a cabin under the tug's tiny bridge and lowered a bunk from the wall. The noise from the engine directly under the cabin was near deafening. If that wasn't bad enough, there was a heavy stench of diesel fuel rising through the cabin's floor.

'I know it's loud!' Owen shouted. 'But it becomes white noise after a while!'

'Nothing could keep me awake at this point!' Alice said.

After Owen left, Alice's head hit the pillow and she was out. She awoke a while later to see Este in the doorway carrying Casey. She put the tired Alsatian on the bed next to Alice and slipped out again. The next time Alice woke up, it was to the sound of people moving around in the cockpit above her.

She emerged and saw Wilfredo upstairs chatting animatedly with Owen, standing at the wheel, and his cousins. She looked around for Este, finding her out on the prow staring into the night through binoculars. Alice joined her and Este pointed out into the night.

'There,' she said.

At first, Alice saw nothing. The only lights were on shore or the reflection of the moon in the waves up ahead. Then she spotted a pair of dim red lights flashing on and off in the distance, too low to be an airplane, too high to be on land.

'That's them?' Alice asked.

'Believe so,' Este said. 'Won't know till we're closer, but there can't be many container ships on the water right now.'

'So, we have to get on board, see if the canisters are even there, and . . . then what?'

'Either secure them ourselves and somehow get them back onto the tug or, well, just find where they are and sound the alarm,' Este said. 'Go public on a wider scale. What we don't want, what we're not equipped for, is any kind of fight. We get on, we search, we get off. Faster the better. But we don't get a second chance here. We end it now or risk Ben getting away for good.'

'Crewless or not, if Ben's on board, he'll notice our approach, right?'

'Owen wasn't so sure,' Este said. 'There's a lot of debris in the water, and if we pull alongside, match speed, and scramble on board, the tug might have time to fall back before anyone comes to investigate.'

'That sounds . . . so incredibly dangerous,' Alice admitted.

'Says the person who marched into fire and descended twenty-something floors in a rickety elevator shaft.'

'Point taken. But still.'

'Yeah, well, it's why we're going it alone,' Este said. 'No Wilfredo, no Casey. If anything happens, it's on us, and only the bad guys get hurt. Make sense?'

Alice wasn't sure but nodded anyway. Thirty minutes later, *Yemanja* caught up to *Triumph*. Owen slowed the engines and let the container ship slowly pull alongside until they were both chugging along at around sixteen knots. The ladder that Owen's cousins provided to Este was too short to reach *Triumph*'s deck, so they tied a set of collapsible dive steps to the bottom.

'This should work,' Brendan said, raising the ladder straight up.

Wilfredo and Casey moved to the bow behind Este. She'd told him they'd be tackling this on their own, but it didn't make it any easier to leave him behind again.

'I need to know you're safe or I can't go,' she'd told Wilfredo minutes before. 'I need to know you'll be here when I get back. If you die up there, or worse, if I end up killing you, there'd be nothing left on this stupid planet for me.'

'Wow, it actually sounded like you meant that one,' he'd replied.

And that's when Este realized she did. Wilfredo agreed to stay behind. They'd kissed. Then kissed a little more. Then it was time to go.

The tires hanging off *Yemanja* bounced gently off *Triumph* as Owen brought the tug in close. Este nodded to Alice to go first as the brothers Cagan hooked the top rungs of the boarding ladder over the container ship's guardrail. Alice stared up to the container ship's deck, easily four stories over them.

'Thought I was done with scary flimsy ladders for the day,' she quipped, grabbing the plastic collapsible steps extending down from the ladder's bottom rung.

Este was about to reply, but *Yemanja* bounced high over the churning wake kicked up by *Triumph*'s hull.

'Can't keep her steady like this,' Miles said. 'Gotta move.'

Alice shot one last look to Este, pulled on her backpack, then started up the ladder. She didn't look down, realizing that if she fell, she'd hit either the deck of the tug and break her neck, fall between the boats and potentially get crushed, or make it all the way to the water only to get sucked into *Triumph*'s propellers.

None of these options felt great.

She ascended the rungs slowly but surely, blocking out the roar of the engines and the wind trying to throw her from the ladder. It wasn't easy, but four stories, even with rungs slicked with lake water, was a shorter climb than her descent into the Kellner Group building had been.

Alice reached *Triumph*'s top deck and stepped over the rail. She hadn't known quite what to expect, having only glimpsed the behemoth in the dark, but was surprised to see just how unlike a ship it was. Instead, it appeared to be more like a great, ocean-going railroad flat car covered in stacks of cargo containers. There were so many. Este had suggested a couple thousand in total, but Alice hadn't been able to conceive of this. Staring at them now, she couldn't imagine where they'd start their hunt.

She'd come up just behind the bridge tower. Owen had figured it would be in the blind spot of anyone watching from the wheelhouse.

She looked around for signs of people. Though lights were visible through the portholes of the tower, she saw no movement.

Este slipped over the guardrail next and stared up at the containers in amazement.

'That's . . . a lot,' Este said.

'Maybe we should've brought Casey,' Alice said. 'He could've sniffed through all of them in seconds.'

Este grinned then unhooked the ladder. They watched as *Yemanja* retreated back, slipping into the darkness.

'Where to?' Alice asked.

Este eyed the top rows. 'If they really did manage to get out of Chicago after the quake, then the ghost canisters would be on top – last-minute loading,' she suggested. 'All these others – probably actual emergency supplies in case they get searched or need to bribe someone – would've already been in place. So, we should start at the top.'

'More climbing?' Alice asked.

'After you.' Este nodded to the nearest stack.

The containers were laid out in nineteen rows stacked twelve high and eighteen across. To get up to the top, they had to first descend a ladder into the hull and approach the container stacks one bay at a time. Unlike the tug, *Triumph* rode easy in the water, too large to be affected by tide or current. Climbing the ladders to the different scaffolding-like brackets that held the containers in place was relatively easy.

'What're we looking for?' Alice asked, reaching one of the cargo containers up top.

'Your guess is as good as mine,' Este said. 'Just start opening them up.'

This wasn't so easy. To get to the doors, they had to swing out from the corner post, grab the locking bar, and lift the latch handle. Then they had to pull the door open, only to try and see around and into the otherwise dark and cramped space.

After a few failed attempts at this, Este came up with a new plan.

'All right, we'll stand on either side of the doors,' she said. 'I'll unlatch, you open, then I'll look inside.'

'Copy that,' Alice replied.

Everything ran a little smoother after this. The first container was filled with bags of buckwheat. The second with corn. The third with red wheat. It was just as the Customs forms suggested

– all emergency aid destined for earthquake-torn countries, their contents stenciled onto the bags in multiple languages.

'Could we be wrong?' Alice asked.

'No, if anything, seeing all this makes sense,' Este said. 'If they were actually inspected, they could open these to the Customs folks and look honest.'

'And anywhere they land, they could use supplies to bribe folks to look the other way,' Alice added.

'True,' Este agreed.

But as they kept going, Alice grew disheartened. Container after container was filled with grains. No canisters. No storage units.

When they reached the eighth row, Alice got a strange feeling as Este unlatched the door to the first container. She didn't know what it was. Maybe something unconscious, something different about the container's markings, but before she even opened it, she knew the ghosts were inside.

'Jackpot,' Este whispered, shining a light inside.

Alice looked around the open door and saw the same thing. Dozens of canister storage units all up and running, all glowing a pale pink from some internal battery. She climbed into the container itself as Este opened the one next to it.

'There are a few hundred in here,' Alice said.

'Same number in the one next to it,' Este replied. 'We found them.'

Alice, happy for Este not to see her in this moment, opened one of the storage units and ran her fingers over the canisters. They were just pressurized metal tubes but, in Alice's mind, there was nothing more human than what lay at her fingertips. This had been her not so long ago, trapped in an endless cycle of violence and pain. But now, what was contained inside could be human once more. Could walk down the street, make choices of their own free will, and confront the uncertain future as human beings, not as someone else's lab rats, puppets.

In the great, grand scheme of things, maybe it was minor or even small compared to what else was happening. But Alice had gone from feeling helpless against the tide of an unforgiving future to taking a stand and righting a wrong. Just her with the help of a couple of new friends.

And if they had managed to do that, what might the world accomplish once everyone stepped forward to do their part?

'My God, is that you, Alice?' a familiar voice called up from below. 'We lost track of you. Glad to know you're alive and thriving.'

Alice's blood ran cold. She stepped to the edge of the container and looked down. One of the older Ben Ganskes stared up at her and Este, flanked by two dozen guards that looked suspiciously like other versions of himself. All wore hazmat suits.

'No need to bring extra workers when you can create an army of true believers,' Este whispered.

Large work lights shone up at the open containers. A few of the guards aimed rifles their way. Este put a hand on one of the incendiary grenades on her waistband, but then two more guards showed up, leading Wilfredo and the three Cagans.

'No funny business, Ms Quiñones,' Ben said. 'We know what you're capable of.'

Este took her hand away from the bomb and looked down at their friends, scanning for injury.

'Are you OK, Wilfredo?' Este yelled.

'Yeah, but they tranq'd Casey and left him on the boat,' he yelled back.

'They better not have hurt him!' Este yelled back.

'We didn't, but we would've been well within our rights,' Ben said. 'You're all trespassing. Those canisters and, more importantly, what they contain are my legal property.'

'They're people!' Alice cried. 'You've enslaved them!'

'If they're people, how come I can't see them?' Ben asked. 'That's what any inspector will ask you. To them, to everyone else, they're just cells. What they can be used for in a laboratory setting is a different story, but that's . . . well, that's something for the courts to decide. Even if it wasn't for the quakes, that's the kind of thing that'd get tied up in litigation for a decade. As it stands now, there's not a single official on the planet who'd stand in the way of someone trying to save people's lives any way they can. Even yours.'

Alice wanted to retort. Wanted to tell Ben how wrong he was. But he was absolutely, horribly correct. As long as he was able to claim they were just cells for medical testing with no right to free will, he would own all of these people, including several versions of herself, in perpetuity.

'I'm not going to wait much longer, Alice,' Ben said. 'Get down here or we'll come up after you. And not only do we outnumber you, killing yourself to release your ghost will kill your friends here, not any of us wearing these suits. If you even get that far. These rifles don't fire bullets, they fire tranquilizer darts laced with the governor serum.'

This gave Alice an idea. She glanced down to her pack, knowing what she hoped to accomplish might never work in a million years. But it was the only way.

'I'll go first,' she told Este.

'You're giving up?' Este asked.

Alice took something from her bag and showed it to her friend. Este's eyes went wide.

'What is that?' Este asked.

Alice told her.

'You're crazy,' Este said.

'But if it works,' Alice whispered back, 'then we may get out of this alive.'

'Yeah, *if*,' Este said, but Alice could tell she had faith in her.

Alice made the long descent down the stacks of containers until she was opposite the older Ben and his comrades.

'Search her,' Ben said, nodding to one of the other Bens.

Alice raised her hands, holding out the pack as she did. The Ben reached over to take it from her, but it slipped from her fingers during the handover.

'Oh, sorry,' Alice said, bending down to grab it at the same time as the guard.

When the guard had bent low enough that his weapon was aimed at the hull, Alice slipped the canister she'd taken from her pack into her hand and stabbed its extractor needle through the man's hazmat suit. As he cried out in pain and surprise, Alice turned back to the container stack.

'Now!' she yelled.

Through the darkness, one of the incendiary grenades arced through the air. The older Ben stepped backward as his guards raised their rifles, only for the grenade to land several feet behind them.

'Down!' Ben cried as the bomb exploded, showering the guards with sparks and a few burning embers but little else.

Once the explosion had all but fizzled out, the older Ben eyed Alice with a blend of amusement and annoyance.

'Next time bring someone who can aim,' he said, scoffing.

Alice smiled. 'I did,' she said.

Ben glanced back to his men. Tiny sparks of flame were burning themselves through a few of his guards' hazmat suits, creating tiny holes. Ben turned back to Alice, face mad with fury.

'What did you do?' he demanded.

She pressed down the plunger on the canister in her hand and tossed it over to the guards with the newly ventilated suits. Ben's eyes went wide as he recognized the canister arcing through the air.

'No!' he cried, though it was far too late.

Less than a second after the canister landed, the guard nearest began to writhe in agony. A second cried out, his torso contorting as if it were being wrung out by two powerful hands. A third fell to his knees.

The guard Alice had stabbed stumbled away from her, only to lose control of his legs and fall to the hull, his suit seeming to deflate even before his body was all the way down.

'What's going on?' one of the other Bens cried out in terror.

Before Alice could respond, a growl echoed out across the hull. Standing only a couple of yards behind Ben was one of the chimeric mountain lions, complete with white tufts on its ears and tail.

'You've killed us all,' the eldest Ben hissed as the lion glanced toward Wilfredo and the Cagans, all of whom stood frozen with fear.

'No, not all of us,' Alice said, the lion turning from her friends back to Ben. 'Just all of you.'

Ben's eyes went wide with terror as the lion leaped at his neck.

As the other Bens rushed in to help their comrade, Alice and Este hurried out of harm's way. The Bens fired several rounds at the lion, but the beast was too quick, the hull too dark, and their fear too great for any of the darts to hit their target. The oldest Ben, however, managed to fire a single dart directly into the lion's right flank. It roared in anger, pawing at the tiny projectile.

Oh, no, Alice thought.

She waited for the tranquilizer to take effect, for her last-ditch plan to be for nothing. But if the drug had any pacifying effect, it was drowned out by the ferocious intensity of the creature's rage. It shook its torso violently, loosening the dart until it fell away. Then it pounced on the nearest guard, sinking its teeth into the man's neck with such rage that it almost decapitated him.

The creation annihilating its creator, over and over.

In the confusion, Wilfredo, Este and the Cagans retrieved the rifles from the fallen guards and fired tranq darts laden with the governor serum at the remaining Bens.

Este was surprised at how easy this task was, one accomplished in a matter of seconds. Then she realized the Bens weren't fighting men at all. Their one advantage was a feeling of invincibility. Once this was removed, they panicked like anyone else might.

The lion's attacks were quick and efficient, delivering one killing blow after another. Alice waited in fear with each death, terrified a ghost would emerge. Had they forgotten that guard? Had the dart just missed or maybe not gone deep enough to inject the governor serum?

But time and again, they fell and didn't rise again. One Ben tried to run for the ladder, only for the lion to gallop after him, almost slamming into Alice.

'Get down!' Este cried, half-tackling her friend to knock her out of the way.

The Ben was five rungs up the ladder when the lion leaped, not high enough to sink its jaws into the guard's neck but enough to stab three claws into the man's back before dragging them all the way down his torso. The guard screamed, fell from the ladder, and looked up in time to see the jaws of the lion closing around his skull.

Alice leveled a rifle at the lion, but Este shook her head.

'Let it finish,' Este said.

Alice thought it just about the coldest thing she'd ever heard anyone say aloud, though she knew Este was right. The lion left the dead guard behind, sniffed the air, and moved through the ship. Alice and Este followed, the latter with incendiary grenades in hand.

'Este!' Wilfredo whispered, trying to hold them back, but Este raised a hand.

'Get off the ship,' she said. 'It's not safe for you here.'

After an exhaustive hunt, it turned out there were only three more Bens on board the ship and they'd all gone to the bridge. Alice and Este followed the lion up the bridge tower's stairs even as one of the remaining Bens fired bullets rather than darts at the animal. The big cat was undeterred and kept coming, shaking off the rounds that struck its right rear flank.

Alice tried to aim her rifle into the bridge to dart the Bens, but they were out of sight.

'I can't get a shot!' she cried.

'Maybe we won't need to,' Este replied, hot on the heels of the lion.

A maelstrom of bullets flew out the open bridge door, ricocheting down the hallway. Alice and Este ducked away. The lion, meanwhile, leapt directly into the line of fire. Este turned in time to see the injured animal slam into the wall just inside the door, roaring in anger though blood poured from its many wounds.

Though it had only been hit by a single dart, Alice didn't doubt the governor serum had struck home. The lion wouldn't regenerate.

'Ha!' one of the Bens cried out from the bridge. 'That all you've got?'

Alice looked to Este. Este pulled the pin on an incendiary grenade, slid up next to the door, and tossed it just behind the dying lion.

'No, no, no!' yelled one of the Bens.

But Este was already pulling the watertight door shut and spinning the screw, sealing the Bens, the dying lion, and the grenade inside. A second later, a small explosion rocked the bridge tower followed by screams of terror. These soon ebbed.

Alice waited to hear voices, any indication that any of the trio of Bens had managed to resurrect. There was no sound but the crackling of flames.

'Let's go,' Este said, taking Alice's hand.

Together, the two made their way out of the bridge tower. Only when they were safely back on deck did Alice look back.

'You think that got them?' she asked.

'I hope so,' Este said.

They went to the bulwark and looked down at *Yemanja*, which was now matching *Triumph*'s speed as it continued through the darkness, presumably on autopilot. At least, Alice hoped it was, given the bridge was now in ruin.

She stared out to the stacks and stacks of cargo containers, imagining all the lives inside, waiting to be renewed in a strange new future. Her gaze traveled past them to the dark waters ahead and laughed at the Universe for laying out such a heavy-handed metaphor.

EPILOGUE

No one much noticed the container ship making its way into the Saint Lawrence Seaway a few days after the St Louis quake and Chicago fire. It crawled out past Toronto, beyond Montreal, and finally sailed past Port-Cartier and into the Atlantic. Its paperwork was in order. It was on a mission of mercy. Though America was dealing with its most devastating quake yet, the rest of the planet had turned its attention to the South Pacific, where the largest magnitude quake recorded in human history had just struck.

The ship made its way down the eastern coast of the US over several days, then on to the Straits of Magellan. The Panama Canal had been disabled in a quake centered in Limón, Costa Rica, three hundred miles to the west. From there, the ship sailed up the west coast of South America, then Mexico, before finally arriving at the ruined port of Long Beach four weeks after leaving Chicago.

It hadn't been easy. The bridge had been completely immolated. Owen Cagan had managed to transfer control to the engine room and had piloted the ship from there with help from his cousins.

The good news for Este and Alice was that they'd found ten vials of the governor serum in one of the Bens' cabins. The two debated what to do with it before Este asked to be injected right away.

'I don't want to put anyone else in harm's way,' she said.

Alice understood and prepared a syringe. Este's short time as an immortal was at an end.

Alice hemmed and hawed about her own immortality, finally deciding to make a ghost copy of herself as she was right then and putting it aside with the other canisters in case she changed her mind. She then administered the governor serum to herself and, in some small way, felt free of a weight she didn't realize she'd been carrying.

Getting the three Cagans to travel with them all the way to the LAQZ had been easier than Este expected. When she'd spoken with Owen, she didn't think he'd want to take them so far from home given all that was happening. But once he learned about the ghosts, he surprised her by saying that he thought maybe it was a calling, God having put something miraculous in his path at a time of worldwide tragedy. Este thanked him by offering him a percentage of the supplies on board. They'd briefly stopped at Kingston, Ontario, as several of Owen's friends arrived and shuttled to and from the container ship on flat boats to collect sacks of grain.

Casey hadn't left Este's side once since her resurrection. They didn't have much in the way of dog food on the ship, but Brendan made it a habit, when the boat slowed, to indulge his love of fishing. It took the Alsatian a few days to adjust to a seafood diet, but he soon preferred cod to hot dogs.

Alice waited for there to be some contact from the world, but none came. No one radioed, barely anyone checked in. She couldn't imagine that Ben didn't have some failsafe out there, a copy or two in case the ship ran into trouble. He had resources. She knew that, at some point, he could make himself known.

During the voyage, Alice and Este discussed resurrecting a few of the ghosts from their containers in order to better crew the ship. But with only nine vials of the governor serum left and the need to replicate it on the horizon, this idea was abandoned, as was keeping any ghosts alive without the serum. One storm, one slip on the deck, and it would all be over.

By the time they reached the LAQZ, rumors from those with radios had reached the 'steaders that a strange ghost ark would be arriving any day. As *Triumph* dropped anchor, more than a hundred people gathered along the semi-shattered breakwater at Long Beach Harbor to watch in disbelief that the outlandish rumor could be true. Once the 'steaders learned that the ship bore rice, grains, powdered milk and even medical supplies, watercraft lashed together in a makeshift pier were extended to the ship. It took three days to manually empty just the first two rows of containers.

When all the supplies were ashore, the bounty was such that the 'steaders allowed themselves a small Thanksgiving-like celebration, inviting everyone in the region. Folks came in from all over the LAQZ but also up from San Diego, bringing wine, game and fresh citrus.

Given the situation across the country, Este thought it might've been the most festive Thanksgiving in the hemisphere that year.

As winter set in and more in the LAQZ came to understand exactly what was being housed aboard *Triumph*, Alice waited for someone to step up and lead the group, coming up with a plan as to how best they could replicate the governor serum, as well as how and when they should potentially resurrect the other ghosts. An entire week went by before she realized everyone was waiting for her to do this.

She gathered Este, Wilfredo, the Cagans, and a couple dozen sympathetic volunteers from the LAQZ homesteads, and outlined a rough idea of how to go forward.

'We need to start going over the LAQZ looking for working lab equipment, particularly anything that can aid us in breaking down the composition of a liquid,' she said. 'We need to keep it secret, though. The last thing we need is some group from the LoP coming in here and trying to steal all this.'

They moved on to how it would work once the serum could be replicated.

'When ghosts are resurrected, I or one of the other ghosts needs to be the first face they see,' she insisted. 'We need to explain what's happened, find out names, dates of birth, any personal information they have. We also need to be ready to put them in touch with surviving family members or make a place for them here.'

'When I was digging through the canisters,' Este began, 'I found a few individuals with multiple ghosts – samples taken at their original death but also after various resurrections. Which do you resurrect?'

'Maybe the one with the latest date but keep the other canisters,' Alice suggested. 'Once they understand the situation, if the resurrected person wants to switch to the earlier strand, they can.'

And so, they began a new life in the LAQZ, setting up a small colony that could eventually meet the needs of thousands.

The canisters were kept on the ship and monitored closely. The ship had been rigged with explosives on the outer hull. If there was an accident, they would be triggered and the ship would be sunk. Alice wasn't sure this would be enough, but it was the best they could do.

Within weeks, lab equipment was recovered from various universities. Though electricity was scarce, they were soon hooked up to gas-fueled generators. A chemist recruited on the sly down from the SFQZ got to work.

He told them it would be only a matter of weeks, if not days, before he'd have a result.

Alice was ecstatic. Este, however, felt the pull of the world. Alice wasn't surprised when Este announced that she'd be leaving the LAQZ soon to head east.

'You're sure?' Alice asked.

'I am,' Este said. 'I know Wilfredo wants to see his parents, and he won't go without me.'

They embraced. 'Love you, Alice,' Este said, realizing in the moment just how much she meant it.

'Love you, too, Este,' Alice said, voice quavering at the knowledge that her one real connection to this strange new world was ready to leave her behind. 'Come back some time.'

'I will,' Este replied, though Alice wasn't sure she meant it.

Este and Wilfredo left the next morning. The decision to leave Casey with Alice wasn't one Este took lightly. She loved the dog, had gone through hell with the dog, but had seen how he had bonded with Alice. Just as Este went where she was needed, she knew Casey was imbued with that instinct as well. And he was needed in the LAQZ. At least for now.

The chemist was wrong. The governor serum took another four months to replicate.

But in the weeks after his success, the population of what would soon be known as Ghost City grew in leaps and bounds.

At first, the outside world had no idea what was going on in the LAQZ. Rumors, some deeply crazy, others surprisingly close to the truth, trickled out about the origins of the rapidly increasing number of people in a colony dubbed Ghost City. But once they began trading up and down the coast with the other QZs, as far north as Juneau, Alaska, and eventually as far south as Lima, Peru, concern for the people dwindled as interest in their wares – generally fish caught in the rich waters between Long Beach and the Channel Islands – took over.

True to her word, Alice was the first person each new ghost encountered. When she laid out what had happened to them, many were terrified, a few exhilarated, a handful reluctant. There were, in those early days, a few assisted suicides. This went against the beliefs of several in the LAQZ at large, but those in Ghost City understood.

The first winter was difficult, but spring brought the first pregnancies to Ghost City, including for Alice. She'd had a fling with a fisherman down from Alaska, a guy named Evgeny, who was part of a larger Northern Pacific fleet. She sent word about the baby but wasn't sure when – or whether – she'd see him again. She didn't mind. It hadn't really been love. And though she had some trepidation about giving birth in the QZ, she was very much looking forward to introducing her child to the new world she was building.

Este and Wilfredo stayed together for all of three weeks after they'd joined his parents in Arizona, two and a half weeks longer than Este had figured they would. She knew using him as an excuse to leave Ghost City was lame, but it had served its purpose.

After leaving Wilfredo, she trekked down to Mexico, staying in Michoacán for a while before continuing on to Acapulco and Salina Cruz. When a major earthquake struck Guayaquil, Ecuador, she traveled there by boat and worked search and rescue. There, she hooked up with a tri-national rescue group out of Argentina, Chile and Paraguay, and trained with them just in time to work the Valparaíso quake.

She thought she could outrun her PTSD this way, but finally, one day, she collapsed on a work site. Two weeks in an Ecuadoran hospital later, a doctor gently told her that she needed to take a break from rescue work.

About a week later, as she traveled back up through Mexico in the general direction of the States, the earthquakes stopped. She hadn't quite known where she was going, but by the time she reached the LAQZ on a sunny day in late May, there hadn't been a major earthquake in eight weeks.

'You're back!' Alice, well into her second trimester, exclaimed when Este arrived at Ghost City.

'You're pregnant!' Este exclaimed right back.

They embraced, only to be tackled by Casey a moment later. Each wasn't initially certain the other's enthusiasm was genuine, but they soon recognized that it was.

'How are you?' Alice asked. 'I tried contacting you half a dozen times, but no one knew where you were.'

Este explained about Wilfredo as Alice led her around Ghost City. It wasn't so different from any other homestead Este had visited, except that this one was maintained by people from seemingly all walks of life, not just those looking to get off the grid.

'How many are you?' Este asked.

'Six thousand five hundred,' Alice said. 'We've had a few deaths and a small number of suicides. About a third opted to either go look for their families or start over somewhere else in the LoP.'

'Do many come back?' Este asked.

'Yeah,' Alice said. 'I mean, you just did, right?'

They moved past Ghost City's farm fields, their warehouse, the residential sections. Alice showed her the kitchen, the mess tents, and the generators they used primarily to create ice that was then sent out with the fishing fleet to preserve the part of the catch that wasn't salted and dried.

'I heard about that part,' Este admitted. 'You're some kind of trading baron?'

Alice laughed. 'Not hardly. But we get by.'

When Alice didn't say anything for a while, Este realized she was holding something back.

'What is it?' she asked.

'I . . . I need to show you something,' Alice admitted. 'It's a little bit of a drive. Are you up for that?'

'I think so,' Este said, unsure.

Alice brought her to a pair of motorcycles, one with a sidecar for Casey. They gassed them up, put doggles on Casey, helmets on themselves, and headed north. As she followed Alice, Este marveled at the well-cut paths now running through the QZ. But she was also stung by the absence of Wilfredo out ahead of her. It felt so strange to ride here without him.

They reached the southwest corner of D-Town and Alice waved to a couple of 'steaders breaking up pavement. Este could see that it was part of a larger project. For a long stretch, streets and sidewalks had been pulled up to expose the long-buried earth to the sun.

'More farmland?' Este asked when they parked the bikes on the edge of what was once the Financial District.

'The ground is too poor to cultivate right now due to all the chemical run-off,' Alice said. 'But we're thinking ahead a couple of decades, hoping to bring it back.'

Este smiled to herself, still marveling at the woman Alice had become. The Alice she'd gotten to know over a relatively short amount of time was puckish, brave, scared, exhilarated, and her friend. This one, shaped by necessity and a population looking to her for direction, was more direct, more serious. A leader. And a formidable one at that.

'In here,' Alice said, indicating the entrance to the abandoned 7th Street/Metro Center rail station as she handed a solar-powered flashlight to Este. 'One of our people found this a few months back. Given our great gaps of knowledge, it's been useful.'

Este had no idea what Alice was referring to. As they descended into the twisted ruins of the station, she saw not just the paintings and mosaics that had been there before the quakes, showing the history of California, but new ones, painted over cracked walls. Scenes of LA-1, -2, and -3. The Benedict Canyon fire that wiped out the hills above East LA and spread to Hollywood formed much of the backdrop. The collapse of the overpasses on the 101 freeway, the fall of the downtown skyscrapers, then the citywide rescue efforts, showing people in orange vests picking over crushed homes, vehicles, apartments and office towers.

Este just stared, trying to delay the inevitable. She'd known since the moment she saw the mural that it was her sister's work. She just couldn't bear to admit it.

'Inés,' Este whispered, spying her sister's elaborate signature at the bottom of one of the panels.

'Apparently, there was some kind of emergency hospice in here after LA-3, where people came for medical care if they couldn't be evacuated,' Alice explained. 'It only lasted a few weeks, but hundreds of people came through. Including, it seems, your sister.'

'How'd you know it was her?' Este asked.

'I didn't. But someone who knew you from the QZ told me the story and led us to this.'

Alice pointed to a nearby alcove. It was filled with colorful snapshot-sized images from top to bottom. Este slowly swept her flashlight over the tiny paintings and immediately recognized scenes from her own life, her sister's life, their mother's. There were also single-frame illustrations of stories told by their grandfather and great-grandmother back in Texas.

'That's from when we drove to San Antonio to see the Alamo but ended up doing the Riverwalk instead,' Este said, pointing at one. 'My mother took a picture of us in front of all that ivy. And that's the grocery store where my great-grandmother worked with her brothers. And that one' – she pointed to a picture of herself and her sister weeping in the arms of their uniformed mother – 'is from when Mom came back from her first deployment and we couldn't stop crying.'

Este stared at the pictures. She remembered the depicted events, but they were from unfamiliar angles, highlighting details that she'd forgotten or never noticed. What was so important and in the foreground in her own memory was often sidelined in her sister's.

She marveled at this. But that's when she saw a list carved into a pillar nearby.

There were first names and last names, though sometimes not both. Birthplaces on occasion, even birthdays. But the death dates were all clustered around May 2024. She didn't seek out Inés's name, already knowing it would be there, but it appeared to her anyway. May 30, 2024, was the only new information.

'How did she die?'

'They didn't have clean water, to say nothing of medicine,' Alice said. 'If she'd been injured when she came here, the risk from infection would've been tremendous.'

Este nodded. 'Thank you for showing me this,' she said. 'I knew something was pulling me back here. Now I know what.'

Este turned to go. Alice shook her head.

'Um, Este,' she began. 'That's not why I brought you here.'

'It's not?'

'Also, not why I was so desperate to find you,' Alice said. 'We found this place when we were working on the governor serum. It wasn't going well. It didn't look like there'd be a solution. Those people, their ghosts, were trapped.'

'So, what'd you do?'

'We were at a dead end until we found your sister's body,' Alice admitted. 'She and the others were preserved down here in peat for burial later, but that had never happened. We were in the process of interring the bodies when we realized Inés was among them. We took a sample and, combining it with the DNA profile from one of the samples we still had of you, well . . . we were able to create and test the governor serum, allowing for the resurrection of the entire captured population.'

Este realized where this was leading and felt dizzy. 'Where . . . where is she?'

'Well, that's just it,' Alice said. 'The reason I needed you to see all this first is because your sister, as you knew her, is gone. She really did die down here. Or, that part of her that you knew died down here.'

'But another part . . .?'

'She returned to us like the other ghosts, physically as she was when she died,' Alice said. 'Mentally, however, she remembered nothing. She hasn't lived. She has no past. She had to be taught everything, almost like a newborn. She had to learn language, how to walk, how to speak. But, we learned so much watching her brain come back into its own. We brought her down here to help explain who she was and where she came from. But, she could really use your help with the rest of it.'

The daylight coming in from above flickered as someone entered the space.

'You wanted me to meet you here?' It was a familiar voice, though one Este hadn't heard for years.

She turned, even though she knew she wasn't ready for what stood behind her. Her hair was different, and her smile more guarded than Este remembered, but it was Inés through and through.

Both young women gasped at the same time.

'It's you!' Inés said. 'From the picture. This . . . sister I have.'

Este was caught off guard but then nodded. 'I am.'

'You recognize me?' Inés said.

'I do.'

'Because, I barely recognize myself.'

Este laughed a little. Inés smiled. Though the smile was familiar, her words were those of a stranger. Still, there was something there Este recognized on a bone-deep level.

'How much do you know about me?' Inés asked.

'Everything, I guess,' Este said. 'Well, everything about the old you. I know nothing about the you standing in front of me now.'

'You know the me of the past, not the me of the present,' Inés said.

'That,' Este agreed, still stunned by what was happening. 'Which, I suppose, gives us a lot to talk about.'

Without a word, Inés threw her arms around Este and pulled her close. Este closed her eyes tightly, even as a rush of tears flooded out of them.

She'd finally found what she'd been looking for.

Neither woman noticed when Alice slipped out, but Alice was OK with that. Casey padded along beside her, glancing up every so often to make sure his partner was OK.

Alice rested one hand on her stomach and another on Casey's head. As she stared out over the broken landscape, she realized she had absolutely no idea what the coming months would bring, much less the coming days.

But, for the first time in recent memory, the thought didn't scare her.

ACKNOWLEDGMENTS

I grew up believing books were the work of a single person, the author whose name was on the cover. Now that I'm a writer I can tell you, for me, this is not true. I have, for a few titles now, relied on the notes, ideas, edits, eye rolls, gentle conversations with, and admonishments from a handful of richly creative individuals who I am lucky enough to call collaborators.

First and foremost, there's my friend, Lisa French. We met ages ago on some nerdy movie message board, bonding over a mutual love of genre films. When I began trying to figure it out as a writer of genre fiction, she mentioned her own history as an editor and we threw in together. She continues to be the first person to read anything I type (and will hopefully continue to be?!). Which she proceeds to shred and send back. I could never thank her enough but here I am again, thanking her anyway.

Next up I must thank Jacque Ben-Zekry, my former editor at Thomas & Mercer who now freelance edits all sorts of great authors (and also me) across all genres. When at Thomas & Mercer, she juggled a massive slate of genre titles. No one has a better handle on the genre than she. She is a secret weapon to many because of the way she's able to dive in a broken Möbius strip of a story and stitch it back together. I sometimes feel I'm delivering her a car crash and she, nicely, sends the pages back all fixed up with solutions in place with no evidence of distress.

I must also thank my longtime agent, Laura Dail. Laura doesn't just edit my books one at a time, she's significantly altered my writing from the beginning, changing not only how I bang out a title but how I approach a story from its inception. She works with a wide variety of authors and it shows. I benefit not only from her approach to my kind of story but her experience pulling finished tales from so many. Even better, the tenacity she uses to tear apart my writing, she also uses in getting my books in front of readers. For this, I am also grateful.

Finally, there's my wife, Lauren Kisilevsky. As with all those above, Lauren works professionally in a creative field, she as a television network executive. Since we met almost twenty years ago on a mostly forgotten horror film, Lauren has . . . what? Not merely edited, not boostered, not talked through, not simply influenced my writing, but done all those things and more. This is done not only in her notes but also in my providing an up-close example to follow as she works on her own creative endeavors. Having a front-row seat to someone working so hard and so effectively in a story-driven industry has a substantial impact on how I approach my own work. I couldn't ask for a better partner.

All that to say, I would not be getting away with writing books if I wasn't surrounded by richly creative people who do this professionally and add so much to my typing.

Adding now to this, I'd like to thank Carl Smith at Severn House for taking a chance on me and this book. This is our first time working together and his notes, ideas, edits, and modifications have done wonders to the draft. I am deeply grateful to him pushing the piece further in a number of directions all to make for a more satisfactory experience for the reader. Also, I need to thank him for taking a chance on this strange book of ghosts and quakes in the first place.

Finally, and at long last, a thank you to my longtime friend, Ken Plume. He knows what he did. And does.